Waltzing with Ghosts

By Pamela Cartlidge

Other novels by Pamela Cartlidge

Bluebells and tin hats
Rhubarb without Sugar
Restless yew Tree Cottage
Text me from your Grave

Soon to be published by Pamela Cartlidge, her first novel in the genre of crime.

The Keeper

Della hadn't planned to abduct three child. Recently widowed, all she wanted was to get away from her old life in Plymouth. Constantly having to avoid the police, her move to Chester with her young daughter was not the new beginning she had hoped for.

**This book is dedicated to my friends
Kath, Janet and Linda**

Acknowledgements

Thank you to my sister Lesley for her support and help in writing this book. She has tirelessly read through several edits. Also thank you to Sarah for reading and providing advice on my earlier draft. Sarah and the rest of Cardiff Writers Circle have provided me with a lot of encouragement which was very much appreciated, especially through those first lockdowns.

I would also like to thank Kath my sister-in-law for her help with my research.

Researching for this book gave me as much pleasure as writing it. Talking to local people and family members has provided me with valuable historical information about Rossett which has been fascinating.

Other valuable sources:-

HistoryPoints.org
Wrexham Leader.

Waltzing with Ghosts

CHAPTER ONE

Summer 2019

The squeal of Deborah's brakes should have reminded her to get her car serviced. Instead her attention focused on the *For Sale* sign nailed to the door of her favourite pub. She had heard rumours that business was poor, but had hoped that unlike other failing pubs in the area, *The Golden Peacock* would survive.

Saddened, she continued on her way to see Jessica, memories of good times at the thirteenth century inn filling her mind.

Her friend was already aware of the sale.

'It's such a shame,' Deborah lamented over a cup of coffee. 'I wish I could buy it.'

'I can't see you running *The Golden Peacock*.' Jessica raised an eyebrow as she bit into an oat and raisin biscuit. 'Anyway, don't take this the wrong way, but don't you think you're a bit old to start managing a pub?' Unable to resist the opportunity to drag up a well-worn joke, she added,

'I suppose you could hold concerts to entertain people on your baby grand piano!' She laughed as she imagined the concept. Turning her head she exchanged a smirk with her sister Kirsty, sitting by the window.

From her armchair, Deborah calmly surveyed two of her oldest and dearest friends over the rim of her coffee cup. She was used to Jessica's 'go for the throat' approach. Kirsty was usually more tactful, but when they got together they played off each other's wits.

'Actually I would live in it if I could raise enough cash.'

'In a big place like that? On your own?' Jessica rolled her eyes as she shared her sister's puzzled expression. Her mouth twitched as she addressed her friend.

'Why would you want to live in a sprawling place like an old coaching inn? I would have thought you were thinking of downsizing not the opposite.'

A smile traced Kirsty's face as she joined in the idle banter. 'You'd have to alter it quite a bit; you'd have to take the old pub sign down, or you'd have people turning up for a pint!'

Deborah shrugged. 'It's just a wild fantasy. I know it won't happen. Like I said, I haven't the capital.'

'You wouldn't catch me living there on my own. It's too isolated. It's at least two miles away from the main road. Beautiful scenery, granted,' Jessica admitted, 'and of course it is a lovely building.'

'People say it's haunted you know, Kirsty said, getting out of her chair. 'I've never witnessed anything though, and I've been there plenty of times.' She put down her coffee cup. 'I have to go.'

'I don't believe those rumours about it being haunted,' Deborah smiled. 'I just think it would be a nice place to live. I have happy memories of being there with Clive before he died.'

'Don't you have happy memories of Clive living where you are now?' Kirsty pulled on her cotton jacket as she spoke, then with a hand pressed on her back, in a vain attempt to massage her aching muscles she hovered near the bay window. Outside, her sister's rambling garden caught her attention. The hedges needed cutting; weeds were well established in the flowerbeds and the camellia was overgrown. Shrivelled petals had lain on the ground underneath it for months, wisps of pink hinting of the shrub's past glory. It reminded Kirsty of her husband. A heart attack had taken him just after he'd planted a similar shrub in their own garden. That was twenty-five years ago and she still remembered the day vividly.

Deborah chose her words carefully, 'Yes I do have good memories of Clive at home, but, four years watching him deteriorate has clouded them for me. Even though its two years since he passed, my house just reminds me of that last, sad period of our life together. Whereas *The Golden Peacock* reminds me of good times. I can't bear the thought of a developer coming along and knocking it down.'

'Isn't it a listed building?' Kirsty turned to face her friend, genuine interest displayed on her face. She pulled a wisp of blonde hair out of one of her eyes and tossed her head back.

'Apparently not. There's some dispute about it according to the local paper,' Jessica advised them. 'I read that just a few weeks ago.'

Deborah finished her coffee and got up stiffly. Her joints always ached after sitting down for more than an hour. 'I must go too.'

Jessica accompanied her two visitors to the door.

'Never mind Debbie, it's a shame that pub is up for sale. It seems to be the trend these days. I dare say it will be bought soon and converted into a care home for old crocks like us.'

Kirsty, who was half way down the garden path turned to agree. 'More than likely. Then in a few years we can all move in together. That's if it hasn't been knocked down to make way for a housing estate!'

Driving home, Kirsty's last words hammered in Deborah's mind. The thought of living in a care home terrified her. On the other hand, she feared being old, frail and alone. She accepted that her two sons wouldn't be able to look after her. Anyway, she didn't want to go to London to live with David and his wife, and living in France with Steve and his wife didn't appeal to her either.

Then an idea came to her. Why not set up home with her friends? They could buy the old inn themselves. They could grow old together.

At home she dumped her bag and coat on the piano stool, then edged around the famed baby grand piano to the small table near the window. It was the most convenient place for her laptop.

The piano dominated the room. It had been supplied by *Randalls Music* in Rossett. A frequent customer at the shop, Deborah had gamely bought a £5 raffle ticket thinking she'd never win anything in the 'Grand Raffle.' No-one was more surprised than she was, to hear she'd won first prize. She'd been ecstatic. Her friends had said that they would have preferred to win a car. The prize had provided them with a lot of amusement for several weeks.

She patted it affectionately then turned her attention to her notepad and the task she'd set herself.

Having made a list of her closest friends, she counted ten, then went through the list again. She crossed off two, thinking that they would not be ideal living companions. Fond of them as she was, the thought of living permanently with their idiosyncrasies did not appeal to her. She supposed that Barbara at a push would be ok, but her pompous 'know it all' husband Derek, would be too much to bear.

As she worked, she became acutely aware that if she did end up in a care home, she would have to share the last years of her life with strangers. She wanted something better than that.

Doubly motivated she searched for the website of the estate agent who was selling the pub. After checking the price and taking advantage of the video that gave her views of the entire building, she made up her mind. She had a healthy bank account, what was the use of it sitting there doing nothing? She was confident that Jessica and Kirsty had disposable capital. Their gardening business had been lucrative. They had sold it only two years earlier, and the new owners seemed to be doing well. Both sisters owned their own homes, and they had confided that neither had mortgages to worry about.

Her friend Joy's husband Terry was a builder, he would be useful around the house. Deborah knew that when Terry retired, they had invested their savings in premium bonds, and on a number of occasions had been lucky to win some substantial sums of money.

Unable to contain her excitement any further, Deborah picked up her mobile and pressed their contact number.

Heavy and laboured breathing accompanied Joy's voice when she answered the call. Instantly Deborah had some misgivings.

'Joy it's me, Deborah. Are you alright? You sound out of breath.'

'Hi, Debbie, yes of course I'm ok. I've just come off my new exercise bike. I've done almost ten miles today without leaving the house.'

'Well done. That's a relief, I thought you were ill. Listen, I've got a proposal for you. It might take your breath away completely.' Deborah laughed at the irony of it. 'Maybe I should call you back later.'

'No, no. Go ahead. I'll be fine.' As she spoke, Joy's breathing steadied and Deborah outlined her plan. Joy listened without interrupting. That's what Deborah liked about her friend. She never interrupted.

'So what do you think?' Deborah asked anxiously.

'Wow, Deborah, where did that idea come from? I must admit, I always liked that old pub. It would be a shame to see it knocked down. But to buy it and live in it with my friends, wow!'

'I know that what I'm suggesting has come out of the blue,' Deborah said. 'But I think it would work. We all get on so well together. I'm trying to prepare for the rest of my life – our lives.'

'Well yes, I can understand that. We all should really,' Joy admitted. 'But this is a big step. I need to think about it. I'm not sure what Terry will think. He's not here at the moment, so I can't ask him. He's playing boules with Roy, a mate of his in Gresford. He'll be home in about an hour. I'll talk it over with him and call you back... But Debbie...'

'Yes?'

10

'I always thought you would go and live with one of your sons, when things got, you know... too much for you.'

'That's not what I want for me or for them. I enjoy my weekend breaks at both their places but to live with them permanently is not the way I want to end my days. So far I'm fit and healthy, despite my aches and pains. I'm hoping to live an active life for at least another twenty years. It would be much better to grow old with friends rather than an old folks home with strangers, don't you think?'

Joy exhaled deeply. 'I must admit it sounds a better alternative to what might happen to all of us in time. Every now and again Terry and I talk about our future but we never come to a decision. As soon as he's home I'll make sure we have a good chat.'

Encouraged by Joy's reaction, Deborah made her next call to Grace and Simon. Grace answered the phone and her reaction was similar to Joy's. After listening to Deborah's reasons for her proposal, she asked a lot of questions.

'How many do you think you need to make it work?'

'I reckon to raise enough for the asking price, then make the modifications to make it a proper home, we would need six, possibly eight investors.'

'Does that include husbands, wives, partners?'

'Yes. At this stage I need to be flexible to see who's interested. I'm thinking a couple would share a room so it would be the same price as widows such as myself. We would have to negotiate on that.'

'So who have you asked?'

'I spoke to Joy first and now you.'

'What did she say?'

'She's thinking about it.'

'So who else are you going to ask?'

Deborah related to Grace the list of their mutual friends.

'Fine. Anybody else?'

'Barbara and Derek? As a last resort.'

'Hmm. I'll talk to Simon and ring you back later.'

Deborah was satisfied. Grace hadn't rejected her idea and it was reasonable that she needed time to think it through. She hadn't consulted Jessica and Kirsty yet, but planned to call to see them individually the next day.

Checking her mobile for the time, she calculated that Shirley would be just getting home from work. She lived just a couple of streets away, so on an impulse, she grabbed her light weight jacket, and walked the short distance to her friend's cottage. She had an hour free before one of her students arrived for a music lesson.

Deborah was an accomplished pianist and had performed at various music festivals across the United Kingdom. In the large outspread village of Rossett, situated half way between the town of Wrexham and the city of Chester, she was a local celebrity.

Shirley had flung on a flamboyant dressing gown to answer the door. She hugged the top part closely to her chest, leaving her smart, dark trousers still visible underneath. Deborah ducked mechanically under the low hanging wind chimes to get into the living room of her friend's cottage.

'I was just getting out of my work garb and into something more my style. Give me a few minutes and I'll be with you. The kettle is full, just make yourself some tea. I'll have a lemon and ginger.'

Five minutes later Shirley emerged in a colourful tie-die loose dress that reminded Deborah of the sixties. Over their mugs of tea she explained the reason for her visit.

Shirley's long winded response was no surprise to Deborah. She asked a lot more questions than Grace, and ended up by saying that she didn't think she had the capital.

'I would have to sell this place and it could take ages. I can't retire for another year, at least, that is if I wait for my state pension. If I retire now I'd get a lump sum from work but a reduced pension. Bloody government moving the retirement age.' She shrugged. 'I'm not saying I'm not interested though Debbie.'

Deborah nodded sympathetically, she'd heard Shirley rant about money so many times. She herself had chosen to work an extra two and a half years before retiring, so that she could claim her state pension as well as her work pension.

'And of course there is Tony to consider,' Shirley added, coyly glancing at Deborah. She fiddled with the coloured beads around her neck.

'Who is Tony?'

Shirley took a deep breath. 'He's my new... lover.' A wide smile curved her lips.

'Oh. Wow. Since when?'

'Since Christmas actually. I've been keeping it quiet, because I didn't know how it would go, but we get on well and um...well...we love each other.' Shirley breathed deeply.

'That's marvellous,' Deborah replied, she could see that Shirley was glad to get the news out in the open. 'I'm so pleased for you. So are you both going to live together?'

Deborah was thinking, that if Shirley and Tony were an item and wanted to start a life together, they wouldn't want to move in to *The Golden Peacock*. Damn, that would mean she would have to fall back on Barbara and the dreaded Derek instead.

Shirley laughed and Deborah rejoiced to hear her friend happy again. Her husband Barry's fatal car accident three years earlier had been a terrible shock.

'Actually, Tony is seven years older than me. We haven't really discussed the future properly, but it's something we'll have to discuss sooner or later. He might like the idea of us all living together in an old pub. But in any case you haven't met him.' Shirley hesitated. 'He's been asking me to introduce him to my friends, so this idea of yours seems like the right time to do it.'

Deborah had mixed feelings. Shirley seemed open to her suggestion, but if she and their other close friends disliked Tony – a complete stranger - would it cause a problem?

As if sensing her friend's thoughts, Shirley offered to invite everyone over to her cottage to get to know him. 'How about Friday night? That gives everyone four days to think about your proposal. I could ring them all now.'

'Good idea, but when you invite Jessica and Kirsty, can you not mention *the pub* thing until I speak to them? I'll go and see them tomorrow.'

'Fine.'

*

Deborah didn't bother knocking on Jessica's front door, the following afternoon. As instructed over the phone earlier that day, she strolled along the driveway to the back garden. Jessica was sitting at the patio table shelling peas. Kirsty was gathering up the empty pea pods for the compost bin.

Even though they'd sold their business, the sisters were still keen horticulturists and spent much of their time in their large gardens. The scene was idyllic and familiar to Deborah. She'd attended many afternoon teas and barbeques in this garden and in Kirsty's. To save Deborah a journey to Kirsty's house, Jessica had invited her sister to join them.

Jessica straightened up and put her arm on her aching back, when she caught sight of Deborah. She waved a greeting with her free arm.

'So, what's the mystery?' She walked around the table, and leaned over a plastic chair to face Deborah who at that point helped herself to one of the other chairs and sat down.

'Let me guess. You've bought *The Golden Peacock*!' Kirsty chipped.

Deborah stared at her incredulously. 'So you know? Who told you? Not Shirley?'

'What? You haven't! Have you?' Kirsty shrieked. She and her sister fixed Deborah with perplexed expressions.

'Shirley invited us round to meet Tony on Friday night. She said nothing about you and *The* Golden *Peacock.*' Jessica frowned. 'What's going on?'

Deborah took a deep breath and plunged in. She finished by telling them the names of those she had contacted.

Jessica looked astonished. 'And no-one has said no?'

Deborah shook her head, fiddling with an empty pea pod. 'Not exactly, but no-one has said yes either.'

Kirsty was quiet for a moment, then surprised them both. 'Well, let me be the first to say yes! Brilliant idea Deborah.'

Jessica stared at her sister and Deborah incredulously. 'Have you both gone crazy?' She looked from one face to the other. 'Kirsty, you were scoffing the idea yesterday, when Debbie came complaining about the place being for sale, and now...'

'Think about it Jess, we're not getting any younger. Look at yourself, holding your back as if the arthritis will miraculously go away. Don't look at me like that. I've got the same pain! In a couple of years it may be so bad you won't be able to keep this garden tidy without a lot of help. It's barely neat now. I'm having difficulty with my own, and don't even mention the housework. These days, when I go to the stables, I have to have a leg up to get on a horse.'

'I'll cross that bridge when I get to it.' Jessica glared at her sister. 'In any case I could hire people to do it for me. Why should I move house?'

Kirsty picked up a stray pea and looked her sister in the eye. 'I may as well tell you this now. I have been thinking about my future for some time. I had intended to sell my house this year. I thought I would buy a bungalow with a little garden. In fact I've been searching the area but there aren't many available in this part of town. Then when they started building those luxury retirement flats next to the lake in Gresford, I wondered if that might be an alternative option. I would have preferred a little garden but the flats have balconies overlooking the lake.' She paused, meeting her sister's astonished glare with a defiant one of her own.

'Deborah's proposal seems a wonderful opportunity. It would mean I would have good company, and from what I can remember of that old pub, it has a substantial vegetable plot and a rose garden. That would suit me and it would you too Jess, if you'd just think about it. Living with friends we trust and where everyone could help each other.' She turned to Deborah, 'I am assuming we would all have our own bedrooms and we would operate as some kind of a co-operative?'

Deborah nodded her agreement risking an anxious glance at Jessica.

'I haven't worked everything out. I'm just trying to see what the interest is. We would need to agree about the accommodation and all the running costs of course. We might consider any alterations to make it suitable for our varying needs as we get older. But I know from the estate agent's video that there are six good sized bedrooms upstairs, though only two bathrooms.'

'Have you made an offer?' Jessica asked. She sat down again, stony faced at the picnic table to face her friend.

'Not yet. Even if I sold my house and put it with my capital I would still be short. I am willing to put up a lot of the money initially until everyone interested has sold their homes. But I would still need some help.' She addressed her words to Kirsty, though she knew Jessica was listening intently.

'So are you serious about this Kirsty?' Jessica asked her sister.

'Absolutely!' Kirsty turned to Deborah. 'I could help with the cash shortfall, until the others sell their houses. That place might be snapped up by developers, we need to act fast. The next thing you know there will be builders on the site demolishing the place.'

Buoyed up by Kirsty's support Deborah turned to Jessica. 'Would you even consider the idea? We can discuss it in more depth on Friday night at Shirley's place.'

'Let's see what the others say.' Jessica took off her gardening gloves and tossed them on to the table. 'I'll go and make some coffee.' She marched off to the kitchen leaving Deborah and Kirsty to discuss the project.

'Don't worry, she'll come round,' Kirsty whispered. 'She knows it makes sense. This house and garden is getting too much for her to handle. She would be better with a smaller plot. It's all very well saying she would hire people, but I know she wouldn't trust them to do things the way she wanted and she'd just get herself stressed. Sooner or later she will have to face up to the fact that she can't manage alone. She could buy a bungalow I suppose, but your suggestion is more fun. Let's hope the rest of our gang will see it our way.'

Kirsty's words of reassurance brought home to Deborah how important the venture was to her and how much her friends mattered.

CHAPTER TWO

On Friday evening at Shirley's cottage, they were introduced to Anthony Grant. He told them that he was a retired chiropodist.

As they chatted, Deborah could see that Anthony or Tony, the name he preferred to be called by, and Shirley were in love. Deborah liked him and after furtively checking the animated expressions of her friends, she was relieved that they seemed to like him too. When the conversation eventually turned to *The Peacock proposal*, as she referred to it, she held her breath.

Joy and Terry were the first to make their decision known. The relaxed ambience in the room shifted to a loaded silence as Terry spoke.

'We like this idea of Deborah's a lot. As it happened we have been thinking of selling up and getting a retirement flat, but this sounds a much better plan...'

'Not the ones being built near the lake in Gresford?' Kirsty interrupted with a smile. Her blue eyes gleamed.

'As it happens yes.' Terry focused on Kirsty's face. 'Have you seen them?'

'Yes. I've already made inquiries.'

Terry laughed. 'We did too, they look great, but we think Deborah's proposal is better. What could be nicer than living and growing old with good friends?' He checked Joy's rapturous face then continued. 'So we are in.'

Joy gestured a thumbs up sign and Deborah felt the weight on her chest lessen slightly.

'Me too!' Kirsty said, sending a defiant glance towards her sister.

'Fantastic. Thanks.' Deborah was delighted. 'That means with four of us, we can go ahead with making an offer on the place, even if the rest of you don't want to invest in *The Golden Peacock*. We still need a few more people though, to help with the costs. Maybe I could ask Barbara and Derek. It will take time to raise the money and to do the alterations but...'

'Hold your horses. Tony and I are eager to do this, but we have a couple of complications. I need to carry on working for another two years, but I can put this place up for sale. I'm not sure how much it will bring, and I still have a mortgage, though not much to pay off now.' Shirley took a breath. 'I don't know how much ready cash you need Deborah, but, Tony would like to contribute too.'

Deborah was overwhelmed. She could see the project materialising before her eyes.

'Of course, of course, I understand Shirley. We need to discuss it all thoroughly.' She sipped her wine, daring to let her eyes sweep the faces of the rest of her friends. Jessica was frowning, whereas Grace and Simon looked uncomfortable.

In the end, Grace spoke. 'We think it's a great idea, but we want to leave our house to our grandson. If we sold it to pay our share in *The Golden Peacock*, we won't be able to leave him anything when we die.'

Kirsty choked on her wine, and it took some effort for Deborah not to do the same.

'Well there is nothing I can say to that,' Deborah said... She felt disappointed, but understood their sentiments. So when Jessica finally spoke, her words came as a surprise.

'You could have something put in the agreement that your grandson inherits your investment share of *The Golden Peacock*. It would have to be a sum agreeable to the rest of the parties. In fact, we would all need to make provision for what happens to our investment after we have died. For example, when I leave this world, my room would belong to my two sons. They could use it for holidays or rent it out, or come to some other arrangement with the rest of the investors. You could probably add a codicil in your will to that effect. We could also add a covenant or an easement in the deeds.'

The silence that fell after Jessica's words, seemed weird to Deborah.

Realization suddenly hit Kirsty. 'We? Did you say we? So does that mean you are in?' She eyed her sister wryly.

Jessica raised her shoulders with a majestic sigh and returned the look. 'Yes.'

Relief crept through Deborah. 'Thanks.' She glanced furtively at Grace who had been wedged on the sofa with her husband on one side and Shirley and Tony on the other. As if reading her thoughts, Grace got up from the sofa with the aid of several helping hands on her backside pushing her forward across the room to join Deborah.

'It's not that we don't like the idea, but you know, like I said, we just want Katie and our grandson to have an inheritance.'

'Will you think over what Jessica suggested? As a matter of fact, Jessica has made a valid point. We will all need to consider what to do with our assets, once we have conked out.'

'Alright. I'll talk it over again with Simon. Give us a couple of days. You have enough interest now to go ahead without us anyway don't you?'

'Yes, but it would make it financially easier, if you and Simon were in too. It would make a great difference to the running costs. We'll also have to pay for some alterations before we move in.'

'I suppose so.'

Another thought entered Deborah's head. 'Had you considered that your Katie would probably have to sell your house to pay for you and Simon to go into a care home? Always supposing that would be necessary. I mean, would you both move in with Katie in Manchester?'

Grace looked shaken. 'No, I suppose I hadn't thought about that.'

'Time you did,' Deborah said gently. 'And another thing for you to consider,' Deborah's lips twitched as she delivered what she thought was her trump card, 'didn't you tell me not long ago that your grandson was a trainee in catering?'

Grace nodded, as a glimmer of a smile returned to her face at the mention of her grandson.

'I was thinking we might want to hire a cook in the future.' She congratulated herself on the suggestion when Grace's smile widened. She knew her friend doted on her only grandchild.

'What a wonderful idea. Dan finishes college later this year.' Then her face fell. But that might be too late?'

Deborah felt like laughing. It sounded like Grace was already changing her mind. 'It will be several months before we get everything sorted. We need to sell our houses for one thing. It's just an idea I had for our future catering needs. Obviously we need to discuss it as a cooperative. But Dan might prefer something more glamourous.'

'I'm not so sure. I think he's at that age where he just wants to earn money. If he gets it using his cooking skills, so much the better.' She took a sip of her lemon and lime with soda. 'I promise I will talk to Simon again. If what Jessica said is feasible, we may be able to take you up on your suggestion. I actually feel quite excited about it. It would be wonderful to live in such a lovely place knowing I am with all my friends.' She turned away to re-join her husband.

Deborah sipped her wine as she watched Grace move across the room. She felt pleased with herself. I should have been a politician,' she muttered quietly.

'What are you looking so smug about?' Jessica gently elbowed her, a smile playing on her lips as she sidled towards Deborah. 'As if I didn't know! I suppose you think you have made a 'fait accompli,' as they say.'

'You helped. How come you changed your mind so dramatically?'

'I rang Richard in London. Wills and conveyancing are his thing. He convinced me that it is a good idea as long as we draw up a proper contract, to protect ourselves and make sure our next of kin don't lose out.'

'I have every intention of doing that. I have my own two sons to worry about too.'

Momentarily side tracked, Jessica asked if she'd actually consulted her offspring.

'Not yet. I will tell them when I'm ready.'

'Do you think they might try to talk you out of it?' Jessica didn't bother to listen for a reply. 'Richard was quite enthusiastic. He said he needn't have to worry about me being alone, especially now I'm almost seventy. Cheeky brat.'

Kirsty joined them, ostensibly to top up their glasses. She laughed at her sister as she wielded the bottle of wine. 'So you saw some sense in the end. I take it you've been talking to my dear nephew Richard? My own son and his partner are delighted.'

Jessica nodded. 'I thought it all over like you told me too. Then I chatted with Richard and Martin. I hadn't realised how much they had both already been discussing my future! I'm not sure to be delighted or outraged.' She took a sip of wine. 'So what do we do next?' They both turned towards Deborah.

'We have enough people committed to it and I'm confident, now that you two plus Tony have offered financial help, that we can raise enough capital to make a cash offer. I'll contact the estate agent tomorrow and make an appointment to see the place. We need to make sure the building is in good shape.'

'I'll come with you if you like. I know a bit about that kind of thing.' Simon had sneaked up behind them.

'Perfect!' Deborah smiled at him. 'I'd forgotten you were a builder Simon. You used to work with Terry at one time didn't you?'

'Yep. I still am, sort of. Working, I mean. I do odd jobs for people. Let me know when and I can pick you up, or we can meet at the property.' He moved off, then turned to say over his shoulder, 'by the way, I've heard that old pub is haunted. It wouldn't bother me, but you ought to know.' He grinned.

'Fine. The more the merrier. I don't believe it for a second.' Deborah's remark was endorsed by the sisters.

Kirsty sniggered. 'Oh and Debbie, before I forget, nice idea about Dan.'

'Yes it is,' Jessica agreed.

'Thanks.'

'Is there a story attached to this so called ghost? I'm intrigued.' Tony had moved from Shirley's side to join the trio near the doorway that led towards the kitchen. 'If I'm going to live with you *and* a ghost I ought to know a bit more about the place. Shirley has told me it was a thirteenth century coaching inn, and I'm looking forward to seeing it.'

His bright brown eyes sparkled expectantly as his gaze flicked from one to the other in the little group. Deborah studied his amiable face. His easy grin had won her over as soon as she'd been introduced to him. He was very tall, and leaned against the wall for support as he lowered his height in order to chat.

Jessica laughed again. 'I don't really know the full story. I doubt anybody does. The tale varies depending on who you talk to. Something about a so called ancestor of the pub owner.'

'Has anyone ever seen it?'

'Not that I've heard.' Jessica raised a quizzical eyebrow towards Kirsty then Deborah. Both shook their heads.

'Just a yarn invented by the previous owner to get people to come and drink in his pub,' Deborah suggested. 'People have a tendency to invent ghosts for old buildings. A load of rubbish!'

'Still it would be interesting if there was one, as long as it's harmless of course,' he added. 'I know Shirley is interested in the paranormal.'

'Yes we noticed that by the type of books she recommends at the book club,' Deborah grinned.

'Shirley told me about the book club. Are you all members?'

'Just the women in this room, although it's not a women only group. We also have Malcolm and Adrian. They seem to be interested in 'sci-fi', - don't they Jess?' Deborah turned towards Jessica who had suddenly become absorbed with studying the dish of olives on the book shelf beside her.

'Yes that's right, Adrian more so,' Kirsty affirmed. Her focus was on her sister's demeanour as she spoke. Deborah sensed some kind of tension between her two friends but said nothing. Tony seemed unruffled and she gave him her full attention.

'I hope it's a friendly kind of ghost, I'm getting too old to chase malevolent phantoms, he said.'

Getting the full attention of the three women again, he assumed they were trying to work out his age so he told them. 'I was seventy last month.'

'Jessica smiled. 'Debbie and I will be seventy next year. The others, the women that is, aren't far behind. The men are a bit ahead by a year or two. I think Shirley is the youngest of our crowd.' Jessica tossed her head as she explained to Tony the relationship between them all.

'We three and Joy over there, were all in school together, though not in the same year. We met Shirley at the book club. Joy organised it in the village.'

'Yes, she told me that Joy is a librarian.'

'How did you and Shirley meet?' Kirsty asked. She grinned. 'Please don't tell me you fell in love when you were cutting her toe nails!'

Tony laughed. 'No, we met at a wine tasting actually. Shirl was in a party of four from work and I had accompanied my next-door neighbour whose wife was unable to go at the last minute. Another two people made up the required number for the event to go ahead. Apparently the organiser prefers groups of eight to make it viable.'

Deborah nodded. 'Yes I remember Shirley telling me about the wine tasting.' She didn't add that she'd never mentioned Tony.

Between sips of his beer, Tony told them that his parents arrived in Britain in nineteen forty-eight from Jamaica. He was born a year later.

'So did you meet Grace at the book club too?' Tony asked.

'No, although as it happens, she's just joined the club. We met her a few years ago through Simon, who is a friend of Terry's. They both worked in the construction industry, though not in the same company. Terry was subcontracted to Simon's firm for a few months and they got friendly. The rest, is history as they say,' Deborah explained.

As they chatted, Deborah saw Joy and Terry get up to leave. They lingered to say goodbye as they headed for the front door. Terry hesitated at the entrance to the narrow porch. 'So we will wait to hear from you Deborah?'

'Yes, hopefully very soon.'

Joy gave her friends the thumbs up sign again, then opened the front door. The jangle of the wind chime as she and Terry left, suggested a done deal.

CHAPTER THREE

Deborah arranged to meet the estate agents at the property two days later. Unexpectedly, Terry joined her with Joy. A few minutes later, Simon arrived and to Deborah's delight, Jessica turned up too. She watched her carefully parking her *Ford Mustang* in what had been the pub's carpark. Immediately, the car, Jessica's prized possession, invited interest from the estate agent. Or maybe it was Jessica's shoulder length blonde hair that was the lure. She'd dressed it with a navy and white spotted bandeau, tied on the top of her head with a bow. Whatever it was, she always managed to draw a crowd. Her sister Kirsty exuded the same magnetism.

Joy, who shared Jessica's enthusiasm for sports cars, had also never been short of fans. She made a bee-line towards Jessica's car, Terry close behind her.

Standing a little distance away, Deborah admired how Jessica confidently entertained the aficionados. Waiting patiently for them to join her, she observed them affectionately. She smiled to note that her old school friends still looked youthful despite the fact they were almost seventy.

'I thought I might as well see what I'm committing myself to,' Jessica declared eventually. Followed by her retinue, she sauntered across the stony car park to Deborah.

'Of course.'

The estate agent conducted the little group around the property. Already familiar with the place as a pub, viewing the building as prospective buyers changed their attitudes. They admired, not for the first time, the timber beams across the ceiling and the stable like wooden partitions between various sitting areas. Moving from one spacious room to another usually meant stepping down or up to various floor levels. The estate agent explained that the building was old, and the floors were uneven. Some were made of slate, others had been levelled off and covered with wooden tiles. Added to that, subsequent owners over the centuries, had extended the building with a hotchpotch of additions.

When they stepped in to the conservatory Jessica gasped. 'I'd forgotten about this.' A huge smile spread across her face as she peered through the grimy windows at the neglected vegetable patch outside.

'Me too.' Joy murmured.

'It was added on only three years ago,' the estate agent informed them. 'It wasn't open to the public. It's very spacious and has a good aspect across the gardens. I understand the sunsets are quite spectacular from here. Probably the reason the family kept it for themselves.'

Upstairs, the six double bedrooms met with approval from the friends.

'You could easily turn them into ensuites,' Simon suggested.

Before anyone could reply, the estate agent agreed. 'Yes, easily, there is adequate space.'

'Just a shower and toilet and basin would do me,' Jessica muttered.

Joy laughed. 'For us too. We don't bother with baths anymore.'

Between the first floor and ground floor a door opened on to a concealed mezzanine. In that space, they were shown a smaller room with its own ensuite.

'Wow! An extra room. I wasn't expecting that. I don't remember reading that on the description.' Deborah frowned trying to remember.

The estate agent shook his head. 'Yes, I'm sorry about that. It was inadvertently omitted from the original details.'

Out of hearing, Jessica whispered to Deborah, 'Handy for guests.' She nodded her agreement.

In the car park later, Deborah asked the estate agent if anyone else was interested in the property.

'We've had no offers, though I know a building company has shown interest in the land. The builder intimated to my colleague that he would knock the building down and build a dozen houses instead.'

Deborah stared at him in horror. 'But this is a thirteenth century coaching inn, surely it will be a listed building?'

The estate agent shook his head. 'That's been a stumbling block for the sale for quite some time. Local residents have tried to oppose it. Maybe you have seen their petitions?'

'No...I..!'

'Yes, I have,' Jessica broke in. 'I drive past this place a lot and have seen a few protesters hanging around. From what I can gather there is no evidence that this place is as old as people claim, so it can't be listed.'

'That's right.'

'Now you mention it, I saw something about it in the *Wrexham Leader*, a while ago.' Joy ventured.

Deborah frowned. 'I must admit I didn't notice it. The only reason I became aware of it a few days ago is because I chose this route to get to your house. I don't normally drive this way.' Deborah addressed Jessica as she spoke. 'If I am visiting you I use the main road not these lanes.'

'Are you interested in making an offer?' the estate agent asked eagerly.

'We'll have to think about it.' Terry stepped in with a wink at Deborah. She inclined her head. 'We'll be in touch,' she added.

They watched the estate agent drive away. Deborah turned over his business card in her hand.

'So what do you think?' She asked anxiously. 'Should we make an offer?' She was relieved when they said yes.

'But not the full asking price,' Joy suggested. 'Let's try to save a few thousand.'

Simon agreed. 'Yes, you'll need to make some alterations before you can move in so if you can save some money so much the better. Structurally though the building seems sound. But, I can understand why a building firm would want to knock it down. There's a good bit of land. You could easily get a dozen three bedroomed semi-detached houses on it.'

'Not if I can help it!' Deborah vowed. She was on edge for two days before she put in an offer. She'd waited that long under the advice of Terry and Simon.

To her delight their offer, twenty thousand pounds lower than the asking price was accepted, and as it was a cash purchase, they were able to exchange contracts at the end of autumn.

Modifications to the interior was supervised by Simon who called in some favours from his building mates. Terry helped by managing the project. Whilst they were waiting for the builders to get started, Grace and Simon finally made up their mind to enter the cooperative with them.

'That's a relief. I don't have to ask Barbara and Derek,' Deborah confided in Grace when she told her the news.

'I must admit, I was the one holding back. Simon was really keen right from the beginning, and when he saw the size of the bedrooms, twice the size of ours, he was even more convinced.'

'So why did you change your mind? Did Simon put pressure on you?'

'Not really. He's been very good about it. I took advice just as Jessica suggested, and now I know that my next of kin will benefit after I'm gone, I feel better.'

Deborah hugged her sympathetically. 'I know you worry about Dan and of course Katie after all she's been through at work. But her husband looks after her well, doesn't he?'

Grace nodded, tears in her eyes.

'And it's not as if she can't visit us every now and again.'

'I know.' She smiled. 'Everything's fine really. I'm just a worrier.'

*

It was during a bitterly cold day at the beginning of March when they all moved. The next day was Deborah's seventieth birthday.

'We can have a double celebration,' Kirsty enthused. 'Growing old together and Deborah's birthday.'

'I think I'd prefer to think of it as 'a new beginning and Deborah's birthday,' Joy said. 'I'm not old, I'm only sixty-nine.'

Terry laughed. 'Well I'm seventy two, and I don't feel old either. Just that my legs don't want to work as well as they used to.'

During the afternoon, Deborah's two sons and their wives arrived bringing her several birthday presents. She apologised that there was only one guest room, though many of the sofas downstairs converted into beds. This was due to some thoughtful planning by the cooperative.

'Mum, it's fine, we weren't expecting to have accommodation, we have reserved a room at *Rossett Hall Hotel*,' David informed her. He peered into the guest room in the mezzanine and was surprised to see a compact yet comfortable room with modern furniture. A double bed placed against a wall, a narrow chest of drawers and matching wardrobe had been fitted next to the existing shower unit and toilet. 'It looks very nice though.'

'You could join us for breakfast, if you haven't already booked?'

'After a swift glance at his wife who nodded with a smile, David agreed. 'Great. Thanks Mum.'

Deborah proudly conducted them around the rest of the house. 'The whole place has got Wi-Fi too. Joy insisted on it. She still likes to do a lot of research. It must be the ex-librarian in her.

'Shirley will be the only one of us to continue working. She is able to work from home occasionally, so she needs good internet connection to be able to use her laptop. In fact, we've all got laptops. I wouldn't be without mine. It's proved invaluable, especially over the last six months, since we took on the project.'

'If it's alright with you we'll have the guest room,' Steve said after they'd returned to Deborah's own room. Steve glanced at his wife and she nodded turning to check something with Deborah. 'Zoe can take one of those sofa beds you suggested if it's alright.'

'Cool.' The girl's face beamed.

'Of course it is Clare. I'm pleased that you and Steve want to stay.' Deborah turned to Zoe. 'You could sleep on the sofa bed here in my room if you prefer.'

'Cool.'

Deborah was thrilled to see her fourteen year old grand-daughter. Zoe had linked her arm through hers as she had led them around the house.

David's wife Lucy hovered in the doorway. She smiled, 'I'm sure when the boys have finished their exams they'll want to come and stay. It's a lovely spot. You've done well. What a marvellous idea.'

Clare agreed with her sister-in-law then hugged Deborah. 'Yes, it really is lovely.'

Zoe sat on the bed whilst the rest of the group squashed themselves together on the sofa, tactfully leaving the reclining armchair for Deborah. They watched her getting cups and saucers from a cupboard ready to make tea.

'I see you've brought some of your old furniture Mum,' Steve remarked. 'I recognise that coffee table and the tea set. The armchair recliner is new though.'

'I brought my favourite items with me, then sold off the rest. I'm lucky it's such a spacious room. I have everything I need.'

'I'm impressed,' Clare said. It's a bit like a super luxury bedsit and you still have all the trappings of a proper home down stairs. Your friends seem nice too.'

'I noticed you didn't leave the baby grand piano behind,' David teased. 'It looks great in that large sitting room. Will you be playing it later?'

'Yes, I thought I'd play a few songs before we go out for our meal. Where are we going?'

David and Steve exchanged looks. 'We thought we'd try *The Alyn*. It's recently been renovated and has good reviews. It's a bit cold to sit out by the river but we've asked for a river-view table. The table is booked for six o'clock. Is that alright?"

'Sounds good. I haven't been there since it re-opened.'

'Granny, are you worried about that horrible virus that's spreading from Italy?' Zoe asked.

'Not really. As long as it stays there we are not worrying.' Deborah sipped her tea. 'We're taking hygiene very seriously and have all the cleaning equipment we need, and hope that we will be alright.'

'Have you got plenty of toilet paper Mum?' Steve asked.

'What do you mean?' Deborah frowned at her son.

Zoe laughed, 'people have been panic buying and stocking up on toilet paper and food. Didn't you know Granny?'

Deborah shook her head. 'I've been too busy these last few days to listen to the news. I think I have enough for the next week though.' An anxious frown passed over her face as she realised that apart from a few rolls in her own ensuite, there were just two in the guest room. Would things get worse? She'd better go shopping and warn her friends to do the same.

'We brought a few extra with us from France,' Clare said.

Lucy nodded. 'We brought a pack of six for you too, and a food hamper, just to be on the safe side.'

Deborah's eyes watered. 'So thoughtful of you all.'

'You don't think there'll be a problem with you getting back to Brittany?' David asked his brother.

Steve shared an anxious glance with Clare then shrugged. 'At the moment we think we'll be fine, but there are rumours of restrictions on travel, that's why we decided to only stay two nights. We're getting the overnight ferry back from Plymouth, so we will have to leave early on Monday morning. Sorry Mother, short and sweet.'

Deborah smiled. 'It was good of you to come.'

'A special day like today, we had to come,' Clare smiled affectionately.

'I can't believe you're seventy Granny,' Zoe chimed in.

'Neither can I,' Deborah replied.

'We'll have to go back tomorrow,' David hugged his mother as he told her. 'But we'll come again soon, hopefully when it's a bit warmer. I'm looking forward to rowing a boat on the River Dee again.'

Seated at the piano an hour later, Deborah played a few cheerful sixties pop songs and finished to applause from her friends.

'Entertainment without having to leave home. Brilliant,' Terry said. 'I didn't know you could play pop music, Debbie, I thought you only played classical stuff.'

'I can stretch to more than Beethoven and Bach you know!'

'That's a relief!'

Joy opened a bottle of Champagne. 'Happy birthday!'

'Thank you and here's to us all on this new adventure together.' Deborah sipped her drink happily.

'Taxi's here,' David informed the family as he heard the familiar beep on his mobile.

Grace checked Deborah's hair, she'd cut it into a youthful bob earlier that day. She'd persuaded her to let her colour the greys beginning to show through the dark brown. Both had been pleased with the end result.

After they'd left, Jessica and Kirsty found themselves alone in the piano room.

'It's been a funny day. Let's finish it off with another bottle of Champagne,' Jessica suggested.

'Great, I'll fetch some clean glasses.'

At ten minutes to eight, both women foraged in the kitchen for some left over party food from the birthday lunch. A few minutes later, Deborah and her younger son and his family returned. David and Lucy had gone to check into their hotel.

Whilst Zoe ran upstairs to Deborah's room, the others chatted in the kitchen for a while. So at eight o'clock not one of them saw the empty Champagne bottle coast across the table, float through the empty hallway and then settle on the windowsill in the conservatory.

CHAPTER FOUR

To dedicate the conservatory as the dining room had been a unanimous decision. The tables and chairs, brought from the previous homes of the housemates had been strategically placed. They were of varying styles and sizes but the overall effect satisfied everyone. A sun trap for most of the day, the room provided a pleasant place to eat whilst overlooking the garden. A selection of plants supplied by Kirsty and Jessica completed the space.

The door from the conservatory opened on to a long and wide hallway leading to the staircase. Three side doors from the hallway gave access to the rest of the communal rooms.

The morning after Deborah's birthday, everyone appeared to be in high spirits; conversation over breakfast energetic. Having guests after just two days of moving in, then a major birthday celebration contributed to the sparkling chatter.

Jessica, Kirsty, Grace and Simon sat at a table near a window. It was only when Kirsty looked up from eating her poached eggs on toast that she noticed the empty Champagne bottle set on the window ledge.

'I don't remember leaving that bottle over here. I thought I'd left it on a little table in the piano room.' She imparted a questioning look to her sister. 'Did you move it?'

'No, I thought you did. I must admit, I thought it was a funny place to put it. Maybe one of the others put it there.' Unperturbed, Jessica buttered a piece of toast then poured another mug of tea.

Grace twisted her head around to look. 'I'm sure I didn't. Did you Simon?'

Simon shook his head. 'No, not me. Does it matter?'

'No of course not. I was just curious why it had moved from the piano lounge.' Kirsty glanced across to the table where Deborah was obviously enjoying the company of her family.

'Perhaps, it was the ghost,' Grace whispered theatrically. A grin etched her face.

'Oh don't you start about ghosts!' Jessica returned. 'No such things.'

Simon got up. 'I'm going into the television lounge to watch the morning news.'

Grace laughed. 'Television lounge seems a bit old folksy. I thought we'd agreed we would call it the library.'

'Well, at the moment there aren't any books in that room so it can hardly be a library. At least there's a piano in the piano lounge.'

'I think Joy was going to start unpacking all our boxes of books today,' Grace informed him as she trailed behind him out of the conservatory.

'Do you think we should help her with the books?' Kirsty asked half-heartedly, as she stared out of the window. 'It seems a bit unfair to let her do it all by herself.'

Jessica sipped her tea. 'I wouldn't worry about it. She'll be in her element. We haven't brought such a huge amount of books that will overwhelm an ex-librarian like Joy.'

Kirsty wasn't listening. Her attention had drifted to the garden. Jessica followed her gaze.

'I think we should get those tomato seeds going,' Kirsty suggested. 'We could put a few pots around the windowsills in here. It's too cold yet to put them in one of our greenhouses.'

'Good idea. There's plenty of space.' Jessica got up to retrieve the Champagne bottle and laughed as she waved it in the air. 'There will be no space on the shelf for this kind of thing. That will scupper any ghost!'

At the mention of a ghost, Deborah's grand-daughter turned to face Jessica. 'Ghost! Did you say ghost?' The girl looked excited and Jessica bit her tongue for talking too loudly.

'No, there isn't any ghost here Zoe. There's nothing to be afraid of.' Deborah tried to reassure the young girl, but she'd misunderstood Zoe's interest.

'I was wondering if the place was haunted. It's such an old building and I'm sure I thought I saw something weird last night. It was like a shimmering shape on the stairs, just after we'd got back from the restaurant.'

The girl turned back to face the sceptical expressions on her parents' faces, as well as that of her grandmother's.

Poltergeist, Jessica silently mouthed mischievously to Kirsty.

'Probably the moonlight catching the colours of that Tiffany lampshade,' David offered an explanation to his niece. 'It was quite bright last night. The moon I mean.' He got up checking his watch. 'We need to go.' He glanced at his wife. Lucy nodded. 'I'll clear our dishes away first, if you get the bags from upstairs. Mine is ready.'

Everyone except Tony and Shirley left the conservatory. Deborah lingered in the hallway waiting

40

for her son and his wife to return. She overheard a conversation between Tony and Shirley.

'Do you think there really is something supernatural here?' Tony asked. He spread lime marmalade on to his toast. It was his favourite flavour.

Shirley shook her head. 'There's always been rumours about ghosts here when it used to be a pub. I think ghost stories tend to go hand in hand with old buildings. Some people just love the idea of them. Does it bother you?'

Tony smiled. 'Hardly, just intrigued. Are you?'

Shirley shrugged. 'If there is, why worry? After all, what harm could it do? We've spent a lot of time working here over the last few weeks and no-one has seen a ghost, or at least they haven't said so. I'm sure they would have mentioned it. Actually I wouldn't mind if there was. I've always been fascinated by such things.'

'Are you sure it wouldn't scare you?'

'Probably.' Shirley laughed as she got up and wiped her mouth with a serviette. 'I'll take these plates out to the kitchen. Do you want some more coffee?'

Deborah's guests reappeared in the hall and Shirley threaded her way through bags and rucksacks to get to the kitchen. When she returned to the conservatory with a fresh pot of coffee, Deborah and her family were standing on the driveway to wave goodbye to David and Lucy. It was a cold March morning, and as they shivered in their winter coats, Steve helped David to scrape ice off his windscreen.

'Mum, Clare wants to go and see an old aunt of hers who lives in Llangollen. Would you like to come with us? We could have Sunday lunch somewhere,' Steve suggested.

Deborah shook her head. 'No thanks. I'm sure Clare and her aunt have a lot to talk about. She hasn't seen her for a long time.' She smiled. 'You go and enjoy yourselves. I'll see you all later.'

After they had gone, Terry and Simon ambled outside to look at the overgrown ground. They were hoping to create a boules pitch. Putting on her coat again Deborah walked to the back of the house to see what she could do to help.

Within a few minutes, Jessica appeared, followed closely by her sister. As the three women strolled together along the stone path, a ramshackle old building at the end of the garden attracted their attention. It was mostly covered in ivy, several bricks were missing and those that remained were cracked and brittle. One of the walls looked as if it were about to collapse. Simon and Terry were already surveying it.

'If we make this habitable, it could be a kind of a club house for the boules,' Terry enthused.

'We are looking for a place to store our garden tools,' Jessica said. 'At the moment we've put everything in Kirsty's greenhouse. We bought a new shed between us, but it's still in a flat box waiting to be constructed."

'I'm sure we could find space for everything,' Simon assured her. 'We could put it alongside the large shed we bought to store our building tools.'

'It would be nice to have a drink in our own club house whilst waiting to throw the boules,' Terry remarked. He pulled a piece of ivy off the old brickwork. 'But don't worry we'll help you get that shed up.'

Jessica and Kirsty satisfied, moved away to inspect other sections of the large rambling garden. Some areas were more overgrown than others.

Deborah left the experts to make an analysis on what work needed to be done. When they were ready for her help she would give it.

In the hallway was a comfortable armchair. Sitting in that she was content to gaze outside watching the workers in the garden. To her left, the sounds of pop music was just audible over the clatter of breakfast dishes being cleared away in the conservatory. Grace had switched on the radio as she chatted and helped Tony and Shirley. As they cleaned, they realised that the news bulletins were dominated by updates on the coronavirus.

'I hope it doesn't spread here,' Tony said. 'We're all at that vulnerable age.'

Deborah followed them into the kitchen. 'It's worrying how it's spreading across the world,' she said.

Grace nodded as she watched Deborah open a packet of coffee beans. 'I'm trying not to think about it. But it's hard when we get so many regular reminders on the television and radio.'

Later that morning Simon and Terry announced that they had found a grave stone in the outbuilding.

'What?' Whose is it?' Grace frowned as they sat in the kitchen drinking their coffee.

'It says James Tyler born 1917 died 1944.' Simon said. 'No mention of a wife or family like you sometimes get on headstones.'

Grace poured her husband a mug of coffee from one of the three cafetieres that she'd lined up on the kitchen table. 'Perhaps he's the so called ghost that people talk about?' she said idly.

'So is there a grave as well?' Jessica asked rolling her eyes at Grace's comment who reciprocated with a shrug. 'I sincerely hope there isn't,' Jessica added. She cupped her cold hands around her mug of coffee.

Simon shook his head. 'It looks like it's been taken off a grave and dumped in that old shack. Whoever put it there has forgotten about it.'

'The name doesn't mean anything to me,' Terry said. 'When we signed the contract to buy this place, the names of the vendor was Gibson. So who was James Tyler? Does it ring a bell Deborah?'

'No, I'm afraid it doesn't. I've never heard of him. I'm as baffled as the rest of you.'

The sound of his mobile phone distracted Terry and he fumbled in his jacket pocket to reach it. He walked out in to the hallway to talk, almost bumping into Kirsty. She rubbed her hands to get warm, then helped herself to coffee, turning to face Grace.

'Thanks for making the coffee. It's really cold out there.'

'You're welcome. Thanks for sorting out the garden, I'll help soon. I still have things to arrange in our bedroom first. That will keep me busy for a couple of days.'

Terry finished his call and poured a mug of coffee for Joy when he saw her walking to the kitchen to join them. She rubbed dust off her knees. She'd been kneeling on the floor unpacking boxes in the adjoining room.

'I've nearly finished sorting the books. I'm still putting them in alphabetical order. It might take another day or two to get it done.' She picked up her coffee and returned to her task.

'And then we will have a library and television lounge.' Terry smiled and blew his wife a kiss through the open door on his way back to the garden. Simon followed him out.

*

When Deborah's son and his family returned from Llangollen they commented on the social distancing that was taking place in the cafés and shops.

'There are rumours of closing schools and encouraging people to work at home,' Steve said.

'It's worrying what's happening in Italy and Spain. 'I hope we won't have problems with the ferry tomorrow. We can't afford to be stranded here indefinitely.'

Whilst Steve and his family went upstairs to pack their things, Deborah searched the kitchen for some biscuits to serve her guests with some tea.

'Covid19 and a gravestone, what next?' Grace sighed heavily. 'A ghost?' She laughed.

'You aren't talking about ghosts again, are you?' Deborah lowered her voice. She looked around her furtively to check that Zoe was out of earshot.

Please don't mention the gravestone to Zoe. She's already suggested we go hunting for ghosts.'

After supper, most of the housemates sat watching the television. Joy and Terry occupied a corner of the same room with a jigsaw.

Tony and Shirley were in the piano lounge sharing a bottle of Prosecco, whilst discussing plans for a holiday later in the year.

At eight o' clock, both of them stared open-mouthed as the bottle of Prosecco lifted itself into the air and floated across the table. Tony made a grab for it and replaced it. It stayed put for five seconds and then it moved again. When Tony tried to grasp it for a second time, it flew out of his reach and floated towards the hall. There it hovered for a second and then propelled itself into the conservatory.

Between gasps they both got to their feet in disbelief. Exchanging bewildered glances, they stepped silently into the conservatory. Mesmerised, they watched the bottle suspend itself over the exact spot where the empty bottle of Champagne had been placed the night before. It tilted in the air for a few seconds then tapped at the window, before it settled on the shelf and became still.

'We'd better not say anything about this until tomorrow,' Tony whispered. Shirley agreed, her eyes wide, still fixed on the empty bottle. Her hand trembled as she reached out towards it, but Tony pulled her back. 'Let's leave it for now. We might disturb something sinister.'

Tony's words seemed to startle Shirley and she drew her arm back quickly. 'You could be right,' she murmured, her voice barely audible.

Neither of them had seen Zoe in the doorway of the library. She had been looking for a book and had witnessed something neither Shirley nor Tony had seen. Unperturbed, the girl made her way up to Deborah's room. Her grandmother and the rest of her family were chatting in the kitchen. Zoe opened her book and forgot about the incident.

CHAPTER FIVE

Early on Monday morning, Deborah stood outside to wave goodbye to Steve, Clare and Zoe.   Two hours later, Shirley drove to work. She and Tony had agreed to wait until the evening to tell their friends about their supernatural experience the night before.

Whilst everyone in the house, busied themselves with various chores, Tony sneaked stealthily into the conservatory. Throughout breakfast, he and Shirley had waited for someone to comment on the Prosecco bottle, but no-one had mentioned it. Tentatively he reached out his hand and grabbed the bottle, half expecting it to resist his touch. He nearly dropped it when a voice startled him.

'Ah ha! I was wondering who left that bottle there!'

'Joy! You gave me a fright.'

'I can see that. Are you alright?'   You look as if you've seen a ghost.'

When Joy peered kindly into Tony's face, her ready smile turned into a concerned frown. 'Here sit down Tony. Let me take that bottle off you before you drop it.'

Tony sat down and released the bottle. Joy put it on the table waiting for her companion to say something. After several seconds of silence had passed, Joy eyed Tony impatiently. He looked secretive.

'Is it something to do with the bottle of Champagne that was in the same place yesterday?'

'I promised not to say anything until Shirley gets home.'

Not to be put off, Joy wanted to know what was making Tony's behaviour so odd. She acknowledged that she hadn't known Tony a long time, but nevertheless she could see that something was definitely troubling the man. Joy was curious by nature and very inquisitive. She was determined to prise an explanation from Tony.

'It's several hours before Shirley gets home. Why don't you tell me what's bothering you? I promise I won't say anything to the others. You'll probably feel better if you get it off your chest, even if it is just to me.'

Tony easily fell victim to Joy's coaxing. All night he had tried to think of an explanation about what he'd seen. He'd never experienced anything so disturbing. Shirley had been frightened too, despite her bravado to him days before, when they'd talked about it. She was fascinated by the paranormal and had watched a lot of programmes on television about strange phenomena. Yet he knew she'd been shaken. He was glad to confide in Joy.

They were alone in the conservatory, so were unaware that a bouquet of flowers had just been delivered to the kitchen door. David and Lucy had sent the flowers as a "*Good luck in your new home*" gesture to everyone in the house. The delivery had sent several of the friends searching their rooms for vases. Meanwhile, Simon and Terry had gone to a local building merchant to look for suitable materials for the boules court and to renovate the old shack.

'It's about the ghost,' Tony began and then changed his mind. He felt as if he was betraying Shirley.

'Ah ha,' Joy said. 'I had a feeling you would say that. Are you saying that, you and Shirley didn't move that Prosecco bottle and it ended up this morning in the same place the Champagne bottle was yesterday?'

Tony nodded, relieved that he didn't have to say anything.

'Go on,' Joy encouraged. She was very persuasive. He convinced himself Shirley wouldn't mind. After all she was in work, whereas he had the burden of keeping secret their experience of the previous night.

'And you think a ghost moved it?' Joy asked. She tried to wheedle more information.

'We saw it!' Tony said.

Joy's smile froze. 'A ghost?'

'No. The bottle! I mean it floated from the piano lounge to the conservatory.'

'Are you sure you weren't both drunk?' Joy suggested. She knew very well that neither of them could have been drunk on just one bottle of Prosecco shared between them. Knowing Shirley as she did, she knew it would take more than half or even a full bottle of fizz to get her so drunk she would hallucinate.

'You don't believe me, I know. But when Shirley comes home tonight, she will confirm what I'm saying.' Tony reached out a hand and touched Joy on the arm. 'Please don't tell the others. Let's wait for Shirley.'

Joy nodded. 'Tony I believe you, but it's hard to accept. I have to say I'm sceptical about the whole thing. Not that I'm saying I don't believe in the supernatural. And I'm not saying that I do. I like to keep an open mind. For me seeing is believing, but... still...'

Tony exhaled deeply, glad to share his burden. 'I know. I feel the same way, that's why I'm still shook up.'

'Do you think it's a sign?' Joy asked. She couldn't help but be fascinated by what Tony had told her.

'What of?'

'I don't know. Just a thought. All the ghost stories on television have some kind of spectre that's trying to warn the living about something.' Joy frowned trying to come up with an explanation.

'Do you think it could be malevolent?'

'I really don't know. I hope not. I know Shirley is worried that it might cause mischief. She hardly slept last night.' Tony got up. 'Anyway let's discuss it later with the others. I'm going upstairs to read for a little while and I might take a nap. I need to rest anyway. I'll see you at lunch time.'

'Right. I'm going to finish unpacking the books. I might drive into town after lunch and look in the reference library for something on the supernatural.'

*

Whilst Joy was in Wrexham Central Library, Kirsty and Jessica planted a variety of tomato, pepper and chilli seeds then placed the small plant pots on every windowsill in the conservatory. Pleased with themselves they went upstairs to shower and change clothes.

Meanwhile, Grace sat with Deborah watching the Government's latest bulletin on the television about COVID19. Jessica joined them with a towel wrapped around her wet hair.

'The situation in Italy and Spain is very worrying,' Grace said, sipping her tea.

Jessica nodded, reading the messages being run at the bottom of the television screen. 'Look, it just said that Spain is considering a lockdown. What does that mean? Everything closes down I suppose.' She answered her own question.

'We are advised that we must be extra careful with our hygiene and keep washing our hands,' Deborah announced. She'd just finished giving a music lesson to one of her students. She'd assured him and his mother that she'd cleansed the piano keys and that her hands were clean. She'd also provided sanitiser for her student.

'Let's hope the situation doesn't get any worse.' She leaned over the coffee table to sniff a vase of flowers. It was one of four that had been divided from the main bouquet. The other three had been strategically placed around the house.

'There isn't any perfume on these flowers.'

'That's the trouble when they're forced. It's the wrong time of year for roses and carnations,' Jessica advised her. Unconsciously she leaned over to sniff the scent free blooms. 'Still, it was a nice gesture from your son to send these.'

Deborah smiled. 'Yes, it's been a good start to our new way of living and we're only starting our second week. Another week and it will be the first day of spring.'

'Yes, but we'll have to wait until next year for snowdrops and daffodils, unless there are some already here in that wilderness of a garden. No doubt our two gardening goddesses will sort that out,' Grace chuckled. She turned her head towards the door when she heard a knock and then a youthful voice say, 'Gran, I'm here.'

Before Grace could get out of her chair, a leather jacketed young man had put his arms around her and had kissed her cheek. Beaming at her grandson, Grace introduced him to Jessica and Deborah. 'Do you remember Dan?'

'Of course, though it's a few years since we last met. You were just starting your catering course I believe,' Deborah said.

Dan grinned. 'Yep, and tonight I'm making you all supper.'

Grace glanced at her watch. 'You're early. It's only quarter past four.'

'Yeah, I know. I finished work at lunch time and I've got tomorrow off. I wanted to familiarise myself with the kitchen and things. See what kind of utensils you've got and all that. I've brought my own knives and a few other things. I need to prepare the food too. Can you show me where everything is Gran?'

Grace got up and ushered her grandson to the kitchen. Jessica and Deborah heard her reminding him that there were two vegetarians to consider. She assured him that there was a wide range of implements at his disposal, as everyone had brought some items from their own kitchens.

'She absolutely adores him!' Jessica smiled.

'Yes, she's pleased to have him living so near, seeing as his parents have moved away.'

'I suppose Katie wanted a new start. I'm glad she has such a supportive husband after everything that happened to her.'

Deborah nodded. 'Yes she had a bad time in that last job of hers. At least she won her case.'

'It must have been tough standing up in court to give evidence,' Jessica said.

At six-thirty, Dan proudly served up their evening meal in the conservatory. After he'd served the sweet, Dan got up to retrieve his ruck sack from where he'd dumped it near the stairs. Before stepping into the hall he called over his shoulder, 'by the way, there's plenty of cheesecake left in the fridge if you want more. I'm going for a shower.' He then headed for the guest room.

'He's going out, to meet his friends,' Grace whispered.

Deborah went to the kitchen to fetch the strawberry cheesecake. After she'd dished out generous portions with extra cream, Shirley decided it was a good time to enlighten her friends on the previous night's occurrence.

Always sceptical about anything connected with the supernatural, Deborah stared at both Shirley and Tony in disbelief. 'Is this a joke?'

Kirsty and Jessica laughed. Neither sister had time for ghost stories. The rest of the company wore expressions varying from incredulity to amusement. Terry hinted that they may have been drunk, though he admitted that it was unusual even for drunkards to see floating wine bottles. Despite his grin, he conceded that not even a bottle of Prosecco would have induced such an effect on Shirley. He didn't know Tony very well so couldn't comment. Simon grunted that it was odd. Grace agreed.

'You make me sound like a bloody alcoholic!' Shirley protested. She wound her beaded necklace around her finger as she spoke.

'We definitely saw that bottle glide from the piano lounge to the conservatory!' Tony spoke firmly.

Joy added her opinion and to the surprise of the group, said she believed that there truly was a ghost in the house.

'I've been experiencing some strange occurrences in our bedroom,' Joy started to say. She held Terry's eyes defiantly. He stared at Joy in astonishment, 'You didn't say anything to me.'

Joy inclined her head slightly. 'I wasn't sure at first. It was just little things, I thought it might have been my memory slipping.'

'What do you mean?' Terry asked. He wanted to laugh but catching her unwavering sombre expression, thought better of it. He realised his down to earth, no nonsense wife was serious. The rest of the group held the same opinion regarding Joy. She was the methodical and efficient one, who always took time to analyse things before doing something. They waited intently for her to elucidate.

'For example, my ear-rings. I always take them out in front of the mirror on my dressing table, which is what I did the day we moved in. Yet the next day when I drew back the curtains they were on the window sill. I was annoyed with myself for doing something like that, but thought no more about it. Then the day after that I found a bottle of perfume and my gold chain necklace also on the window sill, which began to worry me.

'Each morning since we've lived here, I've found a piece of jewellery where it shouldn't be. Fears of dementia ran through my mind, and this morning, when I found my pot of night cream on the windowsill as well as some of my best jewellery, I was convinced my memory was failing me, until...' Joy paused, allowing her eyes to sweep the faces of her companions.

'Until, that is, after my little chat with Tony. That's when it became clear to me. We have a ghost.' She took a breath, and would have continued, however this small piece of information was already being dissected in various forms of disbelief, bewilderment and scorn. Shirley and Tony repeated what they'd seen. Joy poured herself another glass of red wine and waited for the hubbub to quieten down. When she'd got their attention again she added to her theory.

'As you know, the windows and that little balcony in our bedroom,' she flashed a reassuring smile at Terry, 'overlook this conservatory. I think the ghost likes this aspect of the house. It would explain why things end up on the windowsill down here in the conservatory.' Her rapt audience was drawn to the windowsill following Joy's theatrical wave of her arm. They then refocused on her as she continued with her conjecture.

'It is as if the ghost is gathering things near the window so that it can escape with certain belongings. I think it's a re-enactment of something that happened before.' She caught Terry's perplexed expression which was mirrored on the faces of most of her companions.

'Are you suggesting our ghost was a burglar?' Shirley turned to address Joy. 'I must say it would make sense I suppose. Perhaps years ago it got caught by the window and couldn't escape. So the ghost's spirit has come back to replay the theft.'

'But surely you don't really believe there are such things as ghosts?' Deborah turned over in her mind what Joy and Shirley had said, meanwhile checking the facial reactions of the rest of her friends for clues about their thoughts. Shirley's known interest in the paranormal fed Deborah's scepticism. As for Joy, she was aware that she had a lot of gold and silver jewellery. Maybe she had been careless and had left some on the windowsill.

'Joy I'm not saying you have dementia of course, but I frequently forget where I put things. It's normal and nothing to worry about.'

'Me too, Jessica confessed. 'I'm always forgetting where I put my glasses or my wretched mobile.'

'I'm serious Debbie, I really think that this place is haunted,' Joy insisted.

'It's the only explanation,' Shirley agreed. She let go of her necklace to examine her red painted fingernails as she spoke. Deborah cast an admiring glance at them, absently thinking what colour they might be the next day.

'When I first met Simon, and he mentioned that the place might be haunted, I was intrigued,' Tony admitted. 'But, I have to say when I saw that bottle floating around, it really spooked me.'

For a moment no-one spoke.

'Perhaps it's that James. You know, the name on that gravestone we found in the old shed,' Simon offered. He was grinning, trying to offer a solution and at the same time diffuse the tense atmosphere.

'What gravestone?' Joy asked.

'The one Terry and I found in the shed yesterday. Jessica and Kirsty have seen it too.'

'You didn't tell me! Where is it now?' Joy frowned.

'You were working in our library. Anyway I didn't think it was that important, I just thought it was odd to find it in the shed, that's all. It must have slipped my mind to tell you.'

Joy sent her husband a reproachful look. Terry shrugged.

'We left it in the shed. We can go and have a look at it now if you want. Let's see if it's moved,' Simon grinned, but no-one laughed.

'Now?' Deborah asked wrinkling her brow, 'let's wait until morning.'

'No time like the present,' Joy said. 'I'd like to see it.'

'Well, I'm going out anyway for a fag,' Simon said getting up. 'I'll get some torches. You'd better put your coats on, it's a bit nippy out there.'

'I'm not going out in the cold and the dark, I've seen it anyway. I'm going upstairs to read,' Jessica muttered impatiently.

'I've seen it too. I'd rather look for my mobile, I can't find it. You're not the only one who misplaces mobiles Jess.' Kirsty got up and wandered into the piano room with a glass of wine in her hand. The rest of the party in a mumbling cluster of theories about ghosts, got coats and torches from the hallway cupboard and followed Joy and Terry outside to the shed.

Whilst they were examining the gravestone, Dan came down the stairs into the hallway. After adjusting his spiky hair style, courtesy of his indulgent grandmother in the mirror, he sat on a chair to put on his trainers. The chair, was one of two antiques that had been placed in the hall particularly for the purpose of easing aged feet into footwear. He finished tying the laces just as the grandfather clock, gifted to the house by Jessica as well as the mirror and chairs, struck eight o'clock. Dan got up to open the door to the kitchen to get his leather jacket where he'd left it. His carefree expression turned to one of astonishment when he saw a bottle half full of wine emerge from out of the piano lounge into the hall. He stood bewildered, as he witnessed the bottle float into the conservatory, where it tapped the window before settling on the windowsill. The image was accompanied by a shimmering swirl of bluish grey. To Dan the shape resembled a sketchy outline of a person though he was so shocked he wasn't sure. A small pot of compost crashed to the floor, as the bottle took its place. Still with his hand on the kitchen door handle, he remained frozen, unable to believe his eyes. Helplessly he watched as another pot of composted seeds fell to the floor, jolting him out of his statuesque stance. The hazy silhouette had vanished.

'Christ! What the hell was that? Gran! Grandad! Where are you?' He turned away and took a few steps down the hall towards the open door that led to the piano lounge.

Before he reached the portal, Kirsty emerged, looking unusually tense. Wide-eyed she focused on Dan's equally incredulous face.

Behind the young chef, the door from the hall to the garden flew open as the small group of companions re-entered the house.

CHAPTER SIX

Grace was still outside with Simon. They were finishing off their cigarettes, pottering around in the garden as they smoked. Though they weren't far from the house, they didn't hear their grandson call out.

In the hallway, a dazed Kirsty and an excited Dan, related what they had seen.

'Are you sure?' Deborah asked. She closed the outside door shivering as she took off her coat and hung it up. She turned to stare from one shocked face to the other. After seeing the gravestone and then hearing of this new incident, her confidence was faltering. She didn't want to believe in the supernatural, yet Shirley and Joy, not forgetting Tony had been adamant and now this latest development...

Kirsty nodded vigorously. 'I'm absolutely sure. It happened twice. Look at the mess on the floor. Those pots of seeds were secure, there was no reason for them to suddenly drop from the windowsill.' She drained her glass, and looked longingly at the wine bottle positioned amongst the remaining plant pots.

Joy was triumphant. 'Told you.'

'What do ya mean by that Joy?' Dan asked. 'Have ya seen this happen too?'

Shirley didn't give Joy chance to answer. 'I have seen it happen, and so has Tony. They didn't believe us, but now I'm hoping that they will.'

'Cool. This place is haunted then!' Dan grinned. 'That's a relief I thought I was seeing things. I was absolutely gobsmacked!'

'It can't be haunted,' Deborah assured him. 'There must be another explanation.'

Dan laughed. 'I definitely saw something pass through the door and then vanish.'

'I didn't see a shape Dan. Are you sure?' Kirsty spoke sharply. She ran her fingers through her hair.

'Yep. I couldn't make out properly what it was, a strange body outline like a blob with a wine bottle.'

'I only saw the floating wine bottle knock the plant pots down,' Kirsty's voice was weak.

'That's right. Shirley said. 'You both have witnessed the same thing that Tony and I saw! But I didn't see a blobby shape. Did you Tony?'

Tony shook his head.

As Shirley spoke, Jessica came downstairs and joined them in the crowded hallway. 'Well, have you lot come to any conclusions about the gravestone?' She threaded her way through them to get to the conservatory. 'I take it there is still some wine left in here? I thought I'd have a glass whilst reading my book.'

'Yes,' Kirsty whispered.

Jessica ignored the intake of breath from her friends as she grabbed the bottle from the windowsill. She frowned as she turned to address her sister.

'Why is there compost on the floor and who knocked over the plant pots?' She poured herself a drink amid gasps from her companions then placed the half full bottle down on one of the tables. Mistaking their gasps as a rebuke for not tidying up the compost, she sat down to face them.

60

'I'll clear this up later don't worry.'

'Jessica, your sister has had a nasty shock,' Joy said. Before she could elaborate, Grace and Simon returned from outside.

'So what's up?' Simon frowned.

Joy explained.

Jessica turned to stare at her sister, 'you're joking!'

Dan got up looking at his watch. 'I have to go, I'm going to be late.' He turned towards his grandparents, reluctantly walking towards the kitchen door. 'Wait 'til I tell them at *The White Hart*. I always thought it was *The Trevor Arms* that was haunted not this place.'

'Do you think all this is related to James? The name on the gravestone.' Shirley suggested.

"The name James Tyler is a mystery to me,' Deborah said.

Joy had been expecting the bottle of wine that Jessica had retrieved, to move again. Nothing happened and so she helped herself to a glass, and sat down next to Jessica. She turned to face the rest of the company, anxiously huddled around the conservatory doorway. Dan still lingered at the end of the hall, gripping the kitchen door handle.

'Actually, after I chatted to Tony earlier, I did some research this afternoon at the library in Wrexham. Apparently this house was owned by a man called James Tyler in seventeen eighty-nine. He was a miller by trade and was a distant relative in some way or other with the man who owned Rossett water mill.'

'The date of death of James Tyler on the gravestone is nineteen forty-four. Deborah commented. 'Could he be a descendant?

'Possibly,' Joy said. 'Funny, I didn't even know about the gravestone this afternoon! She looked accusingly at Terry.

'I always thought this house might have belonged to one of the early Gresford colliery owners,' Simon said.

'It hasn't always been a pub or inn,' Deborah informed him, but it was when they first sank shafts in Gresford. 'Before the *Peacock* became an inn, I believe it was once a large manor house. One old house I know, that belonged to a colliery owner is on the Chester Road near *The White Hart* pub. It's the one set back a bit. Clive and I used to go there a lot, the pub I mean. We used to like going to old fashioned pubs with a bit of history attached to them.'

'Wow, that's where I'm going tonight. They sell *Wrexham Lager* there! Dan chipped. The conversation had enticed him back to listen, though he knew he would be late to meet his friends.

'As I was saying,' Joy interrupted. 'That date relating to our James Tyler may be significant. Simon you just mentioned Gresford pit. Do you know the precise year of that tragic explosion?'

Simon pressed a finger into his forehead to think.

'Umm. Nineteen thirties I think.' His eyes widened as he realised what Joy was hinting at. 'Are you saying our ghost died during the explosion?'

'I thought it might be a possibility.'

'It's here. I've just googled it on my mobile,' Kirsty informed them. 'The disaster occurred on the twenty-second September nineteen thirty-four. It's not the same date on the gravestone. That date is nineteen forty-four. Ten years later.'

'But why is James Tyler's headstone here, and not in the church yard?' Deborah frowned.

'And more to the point why is he haunting us?' Tony commented quietly. 'Always assuming of course that it's James Tyler's ghost troubling us and not a phantom burglar.'

No-one was able to offer an explanation.

'I could try to do a bit more research on the Tyler family. I was actually looking for something on the supernatural, but as usual got side tracked, when I saw a book display about local mills. There's a section on local history, I will have a look at that. Though I must admit I would like to do some research on Gresford pit,' Joy added. 'I'd like to find out a bit more about that disaster.

'Actually, I've got a feeling someone in our book group is doing research on Wrexham collieries.' Joy's eyebrows furrowed in thought, then straightened as she focused on Jessica. 'Yes, I remember now, its Malcolm!'

Jessica suddenly got up. 'Thanks Joy for your work. I'm going to watch the nine o' clock news, ghost or no ghost!'

'Good idea. Let's find out what's happening with this dammed virus,' Simon commented. He grabbed the bottle of wine. If anyone wants another drink, I'll go and get some more from the kitchen.'

'Don't worry, I'll get it.' Terry got to his feet. 'You lot go and find out what's happening. Sod the bloody ghost for now. We need to keep up to date with this coronavirus thing, I've got a feeling it could get worse!'

Deborah sat down heavily on one of the arm chairs in the television room. Despite their agreement to call the room the library, somehow after less than two weeks, it had been dubbed the tele room. She didn't mind that, it made it feel homely. The plan to live together was working and she had no regrets. The discovery of a ghost had not been part of the deal, and even now she hoped there would be a perfect explanation. Yet she couldn't help feeling uneasy that Kirsty, usually so down to earth, had contributed to the belief that the house was haunted.

Joy brought a large sharing bowl of crisps from the kitchen. Terry carried two bottles of red wine and a tray with clean glasses.

'Anyone for another?'

Deborah accepted a glass then settled down to watch the broadcast.

'God, that's not good news. France is going into lockdown in two days' time. Have you heard from your son, Debbie?' Kirsty sent her friend a concerned look, mirrored on the faces of the rest of the group.

'Not yet. I expect he doesn't want to worry me. I'll text him tomorrow. Actually, I'm a bit worried about Barbara and Derek. They were in Spain on holiday when they went into lockdown. I hope they managed to get back home.'

'If they did, they'll be in quarantine for fourteen days,' Grace informed her. 'So we can't invite them round for coffee yet; if they're back that is.'

'I'll text her tomorrow to see what's what.' Sighing, Deborah sipped her wine, 'what with ghosts and pandemics, what next?'

'I'll go back to the library tomorrow. If I'm not mistaken we'll be in lockdown soon and I won't be able to do any more research. And another thing, I heard the supermarkets are running out of food. We'd better sort out our supplies.' Joy drained the rest of her wine glass and got up as she spoke. 'I'm going to bed to read. Goodnight all.'

Terry caught her glance. 'I'll be up shortly. Just want to find out about the football.'

In actual fact Terry was still downstairs at eleven o' clock when he and his companions heard a taxi outside. A few minutes later Dan returned from his drinking session with his friends at '*The White Hart.*' He slumped on to the sofa next to Grace. She smiled at her grandson, 'Did you have a good time?'

Dan grinned as he watched the football match on the television come to a close. Terry turned towards him, 'Did you watch the match at the pub?'

'No, not really. It was on in the other room.'
Simon laughed, 'You're not so keen on it are you?'

'Nah. But I've found out something about your ghost though,' he slurred.

Deborah, who had been half asleep in her arm chair blinked at Dan. Shirley and Tony gave him their full attention.

'What do you mean?' Grace asked.

'Well, when I told Jason and Darren about what I'd seen, Jason said that his dad had told him, a while back, that there was a ghost here. Jason's dad builds conservatories, and Mr Gibson the pub manager employed him to construct the one here. They were working late one night, and his dad said he'd seen a ghost.'

Dan giggled drunkenly.

Grace frowned. 'I wish you didn't drink so much.'

'Leave the lad alone. It's his day off tomorrow. Come on Dan, tell us about the ghost. What did he look like?' Simon gently shook his grandson by the shoulder. His head had lopped to one side and his eyes were closed.

'It wasn't a man, it was a woman,' Dan mumbled, then fell asleep.

CHAPTER SEVEN

The possibility that their spectre was female was the topic of conversation during breakfast. Dan was still in bed, so they had to wait until much later, to ask more questions.

'That changes things a bit,' Joy commented as she buttered her toast. 'I like the idea of the ghost being a woman jewellery thief! I'd better get to the library and see what else I can discover. I'll get going as soon as I've drunk my tea.' She poured herself another cup. 'I'm not wasting this though.'

Deborah finished her own tea. 'If you like,' she offered, 'I'll give you a lift. I thought I'd nip into Sainsbury's and get a few things. Talking of tea, I think we should stock up on that and coffee too. If anybody wants me to get something let me know.'

This offer started a flurry of concern over food supplies. A frantic survey of the kitchen cupboards produced a long shopping list for Deborah.

Jessica and Tony decided to accompany her to the supermarket.

'Perhaps when you've finished shopping, we can meet up at the library and have lunch in their café,' Joy suggested as she got in to Deborah's Honda Jazz.

'Good idea. I've brought an ice box for the frozen food. I knew that cumbersome thing would come in handy one day. I nearly chucked it out. Fortunately, I'd put the icepacks in the freezer.'

'Do you think the UK will go into lockdown?' Jessica asked as they drove into town.

'The news reporters seem to think it's likely,' Deborah answered gloomily. 'They've been putting pressure on the government to follow the example of Spain and France.' She flashed a momentary glance at her passengers in the driver's mirror. They both seemed worried. Sitting at the side of her, Joy looked thoughtful. Deborah dropped Joy at the library then drove to the supermarket, a mile away on the opposite side of town.

'God the place is packed!' Jessica exclaimed. 'Look at the shelves, they've been ransacked.'
Deborah clutched the trolley with determination.

'This is just what Steve said was happening in France. That's why they brought me some extra toilet rolls. Come to think of it, so did David. This must have been going on in London too, unless they guessed that this would happen.'

'This is ridiculous. Let's not go mad,' Tony said. 'We'll just get what we need, and perhaps just a little bit extra. If we do go into lockdown, I'm sure it won't last long.'

Over lunch at the library café Joy said she'd learned a bit more about the history of Wrexham in the nineteen forties, but nothing more about the death of James Tyler. However she said she'd learned that the owners of *The Golden Peacock* had kept peacocks.

Deborah laughed. 'Well I don't think a ghostly peacock is going to pick up bottles of wine!'

'Ghosts apart, it's weird that a gravestone is in that old shed though, you've got to admit,' Tony insisted. 'Debbie, have you managed to speak to the Gibsons to ask about the gravestone?'

'No, I'm afraid not. You aren't going to believe this, but he's in Spain. Apparently he owns a villa there and the place where he is staying has weak internet connections. At least that's what the estate agent told me. He's sent him a text on my behalf, so hopefully, one of them will get back to us soon.' Deborah shrugged cradling her cup of tea.

'You know, I've been thinking. James Tyler may have been killed in 1944 during the Second World War. It's likely, that his body was never found and that his family erected the stone as a memorial.' Jessica stroked her chin as she put her theory to her companions.

'That would explain a lot,' Joy agreed.

'And hardly likely to haunt us if his poor body is somewhere in Arnhem or elsewhere overseas!'

Outside in the carpark, Tony remembered to pick up a prescription for his blood pressure. He walked across the road to the chemist.

'I wonder if Dan is up,' Deborah said as they waited for Tony to return.

Back in Rossett, Grace came out on to the gravel drive to help them unpack the shopping. 'Dan's got a hangover. He's lying down in his room. I told him it's his own fault.'

The others smiled. 'I remember those days. My stolen youth.' Jessica looked up towards the sky with a reminiscent expression on her face.

'Don't we all?' Joy chuckled.

'You speak for yourself. I've never got myself in such a state,' Grace admonished. 'It's not as if he's got money to burn. They don't pay well where he works.'

'Where does he work?' Tony asked.

'*The Crispin Hotel*. It isn't a big place.'

'So we'll have to wait a bit longer for Dan to give us more information about our phantom or phantoms,

'Joy said cheerfully. She carried some shopping bags into the kitchen, the others, laden with other goods followed her.

Deborah filled the kettle, then checked her mobile while she waited for it to boil.

'Any messages?' Joy asked hopefully.

'Nope. Not even from France or London. She poured the water on to the teapot, then set a tray with five mugs.

'I made a jam sponge cake whilst you were out,' Grace informed them. 'Let's have our tea with it in the piano lounge.'

An hour later, a dishevelled Kirsty joined them. She was excited about something.

'We've cleared the old ramshackle shed and got rid of all that ivy and bits of timber hanging around, and guess what?' Kirsty remained standing in the doorway and continued speaking before anyone could hazard a guess.   'We've found some steps leading down to a wine cellar,' she blurted out triumphantly.

Jessica grinned. 'A wine cellar. Marvellous. Any wine in it?'

'You know what this means don't you?' Kirsty said.

Before anyone could speculate on what Kirsty meant, they were joined by Simon who brandished a dusty wine bottle in each hand. His face was smudged with dirt.

'It means we have a supply of vintage wine!'

'Wow. Have you tasted it?' Tony asked.

'I didn't mean that!' Kirsty expostulated. 'I meant that it could be connected to the ghost! You know – the bottles flying around!'

'Who wants to try some?' Simon didn't want to talk about ghosts. He was thrilled with their discovery.

Deborah checked her watch. It was almost four o'
clock. 'Not for me. I've got a music lesson soon.
Maybe in a couple of hours. You go ahead and taste
it.'

Simon was already on his way to the kitchen to get a
corkscrew. Over his shoulder, he called out to them.
'I'll clean up these bottles, then open them to let the
wine breathe. It looks like they've been down in that
cellar a long time. We can all enjoy a drink at six o'
clock before dinner, if that suits everybody?'

'Where's Terry?' Joy asked.

'He's still in the cellar, taking stock! He'll be here in a
minute. I'm going up to get changed, then I'll give Dan
a shake.'

'Good idea. I'll take him a cup of tea.' Grace got up
to take the tray of crockery to the kitchen and to make
a fresh pot for her grandson.

'Taking stock? How many bottles are down there?'
Joy turned to Kirsty.

'Quite a lot. But never mind that. Surely the floating
Prosecco and Champagne bottles must have a
connection with the wine cellar!'

Joy looked at her friend's earnest face and tried to
take in what she was suggesting. Their companions
were more interested in the discovery of the wine.

'So are you saying that the ghost lives in the cellar
and then at night time it picks up a bottle to take to the
conservatory? Then it goes upstairs to get Joy's
jewellery?' Jessica frowned. 'That's a bit far-fetched.'

Kirsty shrugged. 'Have you got any better
suggestions?'

Jessica sighed and admitted she didn't have any
theory and added that she didn't believe in ghosts.

71

'You didn't see what we saw. Don't forget Tony and Shirley saw it, and Dan. I'm just trying to make sense of it.'

Tony backed Kirsty up, but had no theory of his own either, though he conceded that what they'd both seen may have a connection with the wine cellar. Joy was unsure what to think.

Deborah swept her hand through her hair. 'None of it makes sense to me!'

Terry arrived in the piano lounge. Cobwebs clung to his greying hair that protruded from under his baseball cap. Through the dirt that smudged his overalls, and his face, his eyes glistened as he brandished two more bottles of dust covered wine.

'I just hope it hasn't perished and tastes nasty. I'll take them to the kitchen and then I'll go for a shower.'

'Actually there's a nasty smell coming off you, so a shower is a good idea.' Joy wrinkled her nose at him then leaned towards Kirsty's grubby clothes. 'Yuk and you. What is it?'

'Yes, I need to clean myself up too. It's mouldy and filthy in that cellar.'

Kirsty knew she looked like a scarecrow, but she didn't follow Terry out of the room. Mindful of her bedraggled appearance she avoided sitting on the furniture. Instead she lingered in the spacious lounge. She anxiously waited for her companions to come up with a theory about phantoms. After Dan's outburst, she had started to wonder that there could be two. Possibly a man and a woman. She had been thoroughly frightened the night before and wanted an explanation.

For a few minutes, she stood listening to the conversation, hoping for someone to come up with some theories about the ghost. When   no-one

72

offered any plausible theory, Kirsty sighed and left the room to get changed.

Though reluctant to accept that the place was haunted, Deborah was willing to listen to what Kirsty, Tony and Joy had to say. But she was more concerned about why there was a headstone of a deceased man in their cellar. She finished her tea then went to freshen up.

Whilst she washed her hands thoroughly she thought about the advice that was frequently repeated on the television about hand-washing. It made no difference to her, she always washed them regularly. It was something she reminded her students to do when they came for piano lessons. One was due at half past five. Downstairs she cleansed the keyboard and the metronome whilst she waited for eight year old Arthur to be dropped off by his mother.

Five minutes past six, Terry put his head around the piano lounge door to check Deborah was alone. The room was empty so he returned to the kitchen to get the bottles of wine. He assumed she was outside saying goodbye to her student.

Dan stepped barefooted into the kitchen.

Terry laughed, 'You look a lot better mate.'

Dan groaned. 'Sorry about last night.'

'Don't worry. We've all been there. Except your Gran of course.' Terry winked.

Another groan. 'Gran doesn't drink much. I suppose she's annoyed.'

Terry shook his head. 'Nah, she idolises you. She's just a worrier. Do you want to try this wine? We found a cellar.'

'I didn't know there was one.'

'Long story. Come into the piano lounge, everybody is going to sample some. Even Grace. You might like it.'

'I'd rather have a beer. Hair of the dog and all that. Have you got any *Wrexham Lager*?'

Terry searched in one of the fridges. 'There's a couple of bottles here. We're getting low on this. I'd better get some in, just in case we're locked in without booze! Still there's a good stock of wine. That's if it's any good. Can you pick up that tray of glasses and bring them into the other room?'

When both men arrived in the piano lounge, Shirley had returned from work and offered to put some pizzas in the oven.

'It won't take me long. Pour me a glass and I'll be back in a few minutes. Don't wait for me.'

Tony followed her into the kitchen. 'I'll make a start on the salad to save some time.'

Terry poured a small amount in each glass. He swirled his around before sniffing it. He saw the look of surprise on Jessica's face and explained.

'Joy and I went to a vineyard once, in Spain. We had a guided tour and they showed us how much wine to put in a glass to taste it.' He held the glass up to the light. 'That film along the top shows you the alcohol content, unfortunately I couldn't tell you whether that is high low or medium. It might taste bad. It's pretty old.'

'Do you think we should decant it?' Deborah asked. She recalled a tour of a vineyard during her holiday with Clive in Italy. The year before he'd been diagnosed with cancer.

Terry shrugged. 'We could do, but it's a bit late now. Anyway have we got one?'

'I've got several, they're antique actually.' Jessica passed the tray of drinks around as she spoke. She had been to many wine tasting sessions. On one occasion she had accompanied Shirley who was very fond of the stuff. She offered the tray to Shirley and Tony when they returned to the room. Shirley eagerly held hers to the light before sipping.

'Looking good! Here goes.'

Dan drank from his bottle of lager and studied the reactions on their faces. He still hadn't been told all the details about the wine discovery. Grace was observing him and when he caught her glance, she smiled reassuringly before turning to Shirley for her opinion.

'What do you think?'

'This is very good. I'm really surprised.' She whirled her glass around again before taking another sip. She caught Jessica's eye who also considered herself knowledgeable about wine. Jessica didn't hold back to announce her approval of the drink.

'Mmmm. This is a cracker! Which bottle is this one?' Jessica snatched the bottle from the coffee table. 'Damn I can't see, I haven't got my glasses. Anybody seen them? I put them down somewhere.'

Shirley took the bottle from her and read the label. 'This is the Italian one. Chianti nineteen ninety-six.'

'I can't understand why such a good wine was left down there. Why didn't the Gibsons take it when they moved?' Kirsty asked. She held her glass out to be topped up. The others having agreed that the wine was in good condition did the same. Terry dived back to the kitchen for the other bottle of Chianti. 'This Italian wine will go well with the pizza. We can try the Rioja later if you like.'

'I take it they haven't contacted you yet?' Shirley asked Deborah. 'The Gibsons I mean.'

Deborah shook her head and absently contemplated Joy. She was sitting cross legged on the rug next to the fireplace. Practising yoga every day kept her supple in spite of her sixty-nine years. Riding her exercise bicycle and playing bowls regularly, also helped her to stay in good shape. Terry also was a spritely seventy two year old. Both of them were members of *Lavister Bowling Club*. Deborah envied her flexibility. Joy had often invited her to play bowls, but she had never taken her up on the invitation. She'd kept putting it off. She turned again to Shirley as she answered her question.

'No, but as soon as he does I will ask him about the gravestone and try to find out if he knows anything about the history of the place. Should I ask about the wine? Is it his we're drinking? Are we technically stealing?'

'Judging by the state of that shed and the cellar, he's probably forgotten about it,' Simon commented. 'Besides, legally I think it's ours. We own the building and all the property. So the few bottles of wine we found is ours too.'

'There's more than a few!' Kirsty chuckled. 'And for the record, I believe it's ours. I reckon Simon is right. The Gibsons have forgotten about it. Chances are they didn't even know it was there. It might have been put there by the owner before them. No-one's been down those steps for years.'

'That doesn't make sense,' Deborah replied. She frowned, thinking hard. 'When this house was a pub it used to sell wine as well as all the usual stuff, so if they didn't use that particular cellar, where did they store their stock?'

'I can answer that. There's a cupboard within a cupboard under the stairs,' Tony said. 'Funny, I discovered it the other day when I hung up my raincoat in that cupboard where we keep our coats. I often wondered why that strange shaped piece of wood set on the wall in the corner was fixed at an odd angle. It's slightly apart from the rest of the hooks, tucked away and awkward to hang anything on it.

'Anyway, I jigged it a bit and then a panel opened up into a narrow passageway, where I saw racks and racks stacked against a wall obviously used for storing bottles.'

Tony stopped to catch his breath. 'Sorry, I forgot to mention it.' He reached for his drink, just as they heard the oven pinging in the kitchen. Grace got up to check on the pizzas.

'That cupboard you mentioned must travel under the mezzanine where Dan's bedroom is.' Deborah's eyebrows furrowed as she tried to visualise it.

'Yes. I believe so.'

'Was there any wine in that cupboard?' Shirley's eyes gleamed.

Tony smiled at her and shook his head. 'Afraid not.'

'Well that settles it. The hoard is ours.' Joy got up off the floor, after making her announcement. 'Shall we have the pizza in here?' Without waiting for an answer she followed Grace into the kitchen, Tony and Shirley behind her.

CHAPTER EIGHT

When they'd helped themselves to some food, Simon asked his grandson to pick up where he left off the night before, when he made the astonishing statement that the spectre was a female.

'It's only what I was told in the pub. It kind of makes sense. That flying bottle and the weird, blobby shape, that I saw, might have been a woman's dress, same as what Jason's dad saw. The whole thing was scary and it happened so fast.' He stared at his pizza.

'I don't really have much more to say. You'd have to ask Jasie's dad. He's the one who told him about it. Mind you, that David who works behind the bar at *The White Hart*, said that he'd seen some funny goings on here.'

He took a bite of his pizza and chewed on it unaware of the speculative glances flung in his direction.

'I'm not following.' Grace interrupted him. 'You said last night your friend Jason's dad and workmate saw a ghost that was female.'

Dan nodded still munching his food.

'So what's David behind the bar at *The White Hart* got to do with it?'

'He'd overheard me and the others talking last night. When I went to the bar to get another round in, he said that he used to work here, when it was the pub. He said that once a customer complained about a bottle of wine moving on the table.'

'Did it fly in the air, just as we saw it here?' Shirley asked.

Dan shook his head. 'No, I don't think so. I tried to get more details, but David just said the bottle moved on the table, and when it did, the person grabbed it and held on to it. I didn't tell him what we'd seen.'

'So what was the explanation?' Deborah asked. She still hung on to the possibility of a scientific reason.

Dan swallowed his food and reached for his bottle of lager before answering. 'Mr Gilson shrugged and said, "Old James at his tricks again." Apparently he always said that if something strange happened. He tried to make it into a joke. At least that's what David told me.'

'So why James? That's a man's name,' Deborah persisted. 'We're back to James again!'
She would have asked more questions but Jessica broke in with some of her own.

'How long did this David work here? And why did they all blame this James fellow being up to his tricks?'

'I don't know, but the reason might be because some people claimed they'd seen a ghost. David said there used to be a gravestone with the name James Tyler on it? He...'

'James Tyler! The man on the gravestone we found in the old shed!' Kirsty exclaimed.

It was Dan's turn to look shocked. 'I'd forgotten about that. Is his name James Tyler?'

Simon nodded. 'You were getting ready to go out last night when we discussed it. Perhaps you didn't hear us talk about it.'

'Wow. Sick! So that's what David meant.'

'What?' Grace asked anxiously. She was amazed how calmly her grandson was taking the news. Considering he claimed to have seen the same phenomena that Kirsty, Shirley and Tony insisted they'd seen, he seemed to be enjoying the excitement. Whereas she was feeling uneasy.

'That must be the gravestone Dave was on about. He said it used to be at the back of the old fireplace that was in this room.'

'I don't recall seeing it, and I used to come here a lot,' Deborah put in.' She glanced at the fireplace trying to think what it looked like before they moved in. It had been sensitively restored.

Dan shook his head. 'You probably wouldn't have noticed it. The landlady, Mrs. Gibson used to put a large brass vase on the hearth in front of it and it was always filled with artificial flowers. They didn't use it because the chimney hadn't been swept for years.'

'That's what the chimney sweep told us when he came to do it for us,' Simon chuckled. 'Anyway, sorry Dan, go on.'

'Not much more to tell. David and the rest of the staff had to take it in turns to dust the hearth and the flowers.'

'Yuk,' Jessica wrinkled her nose. 'Artificial flowers!'

'Actually, I do remember the flowers! And now you mention it I can recall something else that was behind the brass vase. It looked like a piece of granite blocking the grate!' Deborah turned to her friend, 'and Jessica, the flowers were quite attractive. They weren't like those old fashioned plastic ones we used to get in the nineteen sixties. These were tasteful ferns and papier mâché poppies. Quite stylish.'

Jessica shrugged.

'I remember them now,' Kirsty admitted.

'You don't think he was buried behind that fireplace do you?' Dan asked.

Several pairs of eyes whizzed around to stare at the grate.

'Why would he be?' Terry asked. 'My guess is he was buried in the grounds somewhere, and when the last owners bought the property, decided to use the grave stone as a feature. He's probably in the vegetable patch, or the shrubbery.'

'Bad taste. In my opinion.' Grace sniffed.

'I'll just have to do some more digging in the library. I can go tomorrow,' Joy offered. 'All this sounds fascinating. But we still have no idea of the significance of the woman spectre though.'

Dan laughed. 'I thought you were going to say let's dig in the garden Joy. You never know his bones might be in there somewhere.' That remark earned him a withering look from those sitting around him.

'We could go and ask Jason's dad for more details,' Kirsty offered. 'I don't mind going.'

'That's not a bad idea to go and see him. Actually, I think I met him and his ex-wife when Dan was younger. He's been friends with Jason a long time.' Grace turned to her grandson who confirmed her statement with a nod.

Terry stretched his arms then got up. 'I agree it's a good idea, but, let's leave it for a few days. We have a few leads to follow up. We can all do some detective work. In any case, tomorrow, I might go for a walk down to the River Alyn if the weather improves like the weather forecast said. He checked his watch as he spoke. It was a few minutes before eight o' clock.

'Meanwhile, I'm going to watch television. A good film is about to start.'

'Not a war film, I hope,' Joy said following him out of the room.

'No, not really. One I think we'll all enjoy, even young Dan here.'

After drinking so much wine and sharing ideas about the supernatural, everyone seemed in the mood to settle down to watch a film together. No sooner had they each found somewhere comfortable to sit, than Deborah realised she'd left her glasses behind. She went down the hall to the piano lounge to retrieve them. She picked them up from the coffee table just as the two empty wine bottles floated upwards in front of her.

Bewildered, Deborah's eyes traced the trail of the bottles as they soared towards the hall and through the open door into the conservatory. Without thinking, she followed quietly as if hypnotised. There she helplessly watched, as the bottles savagely tossed three re-composted seedling pots off the shelf. That done, they appeared to tap at the window before setting themselves, as if defeated, on the vacant spaces.

Unable to believe what she'd seen Deborah raised her head to look for some kind of invisible thread that may be attached to the bottles. She wouldn't put it past Terry or Simon to rig up some kind of trick to frighten them all. Yet even as this thought ran through her head, she reasoned that even they might not risk Jessica's wrath for disturbing the seedlings again.

She looked down at the mess in front of her. It was worse than the last time. Almost as if the phantom - there - she'd acknowledged that there could be one, had become angry and had deliberately forced the pots off the shelf. She noticed one was cracked, so that couldn't be re-used.

Ignoring an impulse to tidy up the mess, Deborah attempted to make contact. She felt a bit foolish when she called out, 'Who's there?' Her voice croaked. Moving closer to the window, she called out again authoritatively.

'Who's there? Show yourself!'

A hand fell on her shoulder and Deborah jumped.

'Are you alright?' Jessica asked, then she stared in dismay at the upturned plant pots lying on the floor. 'Not again. There must be a draught coming from somewhere.'

Deborah shook her head. 'No, there's no draught. Look, the two empty wine bottles we left in the piano room are now on the shelf where the tomato seedlings should be. Something weird is going on.'

'Oh not you as well. I thought you had more sense to believe that yarn about ghosts. Somebody must have put the bottles there and accidently nudged the plant pots, so they tumbled down a bit later.'

'I'm telling you I saw the bottles float through that door, cross the hallway and enter the conservatory. Jessica I don't want to believe it any more than you, but I think this place is haunted!'

'Have it your own way, but I'm not convinced. Have you seen my mobile phone? I keep losing it.'

Deborah heaved a sigh. 'No, but now I have found my glasses, I will help you look for it.'

They both scanned the room for obvious places. A light was flashing on the mantelpiece.

'Ah, here it is, and it looks like I've got a text message.' Jessica flicked the mobile. 'It's from

Richard. He wants to know how things are going.' She laughed. 'Shall I tell him we have a poltergeist? My poor son will think I've lost my marbles.'

Deborah sat down on one of the sofas. 'You may laugh, but I'm not making up what I saw. We can't all be seeing things. Tony, Shirley, Dan and even Kirsty have witnessed some kind of a spectacle.'

Jessica eyed her friend kindly. 'Have it your way if you will. I'm sure there is some perfect explanation. All I can say is, that if there is a ghost, it's a damn nuisance. I'll have to find another shelf for the tomato seedlings.'

'Is that all you can say?'

'What do you expect me to say? I'm not going to have hysterics.'

'Do you think I should tell the others?' Deborah contemplated her friend.

'I'd wait until breakfast. They're all hooked on watching *Doctor Zhivago*, it goes on for ages. I think I'll go up to my room and read. I might give Richard a ring, see if he's got time to chat to his mother.'

Alone in the lounge, Deborah was tempted to ring her own two sons. She thought over Jessica's words. Would they think she was losing her marbles? She got up and walked back to the hallway, glancing warily at the conservatory where everything seemed still. Outside, a ribbon of gold stretched from the moon across the dark sky. Within seconds a few grey clouds smudged the spectacle. She suddenly became aware of her own vulnerability.

Deborah had watched the film several times before, but now more than ever, she wanted to feel the security of having her friends around her. She crept back into the television lounge and snuggled into an armchair. Her news could wait until morning.

CHAPTER NINE

Dan was getting ready to return to his bedsit in the *Crispin Hotel* the following morning. After Deborah had told everyone about her experience the night before, he lingered in the hallway, enjoying the drama.

'So that's five of us now that's seen it,' he grinned. 'Pity I've got to go to work, I would have volunteered to stay up tonight to watch for it.'

'That's not a bad idea, to stay up all night,' Joy remarked. 'I can't understand why I haven't seen anything. My jewellery still keeps going missing and then reappearing in different parts of the bedroom. I know I'm not going doolally tap. I have a particular place for my rings and necklaces and they are never where I have left them.'

'I'd forgotten about that!' Deborah said. She raised her eye-brows. 'What about your moisture cream? You told us before, that a tub of cream was out of place too. Does that keep happening?'

Joy nodded and poured herself another cup of tea. At an indication from Jessica, she refilled her cup too.

'Didn't you say there was a woman ghost?' Grace turned to her grandson who finally turned to leave.

Dan nodded. 'Yeah, maybe it's her helping herself whilst you are sleeping. Perhaps your bedroom used to be hers.'

Joy turned her head towards the young man and smiled. 'Well as long as she returns them, I don't mind her borrowing them.' She bit into her toast.

'Cool. So long. See ya. Happy ghost hunting. See ya next week.' He hugged Grace and tapped Simon on the shoulder. 'See ya Grandad.'

Dan put down his rucksack again as a thought struck him. 'Is there anything special you want me to cook next week?'

'Grace told me you make a lovely Pavlova. I wouldn't mind trying that,' Jessica suggested. Her request met with enthusiastic approval from the rest of the group.

'OK. Anything else?'

'Whatever, but something seasonal,' Jessica replied.

'Right see ya.' This time he didn't linger, but picked up his luggage and left. Simon and Grace followed him outside to his car.

'It's not a bad morning. The weather forecast was right. Spring is on its way,' Terry observed. I'm going for a walk if anybody would like to come with me. Joy?'

'Yes. I think I will. I'll just change my shoes.'

'I think the spring equinox will be next week. But did you see how brightly the moon shone last night?' Deborah commented.

'Yes I saw it, 'Tony yawned. 'I was up most of the night. I couldn't sleep. In fact I think I will go back to bed for an hour. I haven't the energy for walking.

'I often lie in bed unable to sleep in the small hours,' Jessica said sympathetically. 'Thankfully I've had no problems since we moved in here. I'm going out in the garden.'

Deborah hadn't slept well either. She'd been turning over in her mind the events of the previous evening. Jessica maintained disbelief. The others were keeping an open mind. She got up to help Grace clear away the breakfast dishes. Later that morning alone at the piano, she played her favourite pieces. Music helped her relax.

'Sorry to disturb you Deborah, I'm just going to put the shepherd's pie in the oven for lunch. Grace made it earlier before she went out with Simon. I've set the timer, so if you hear it can you turn the oven off please? I'm going out in the garden for a smoke.' Shirley was putting on her coat as she spoke. She'd arranged to work from home that day. Deborah closed the piano lid to turn to her friend.'

'I think I'll come with you, just for ten minutes or so, to stretch my legs. The pie will need at least thirty-five minutes.'

Outside they cast furtive glances towards the tumbledown shack that concealed the wine and the gravestone. They were both startled when Jessica appeared from behind the building holding half a dozen daffodils.

'These were growing in the hedge half concealed by bits of rotten timber that's fallen off the shack. Shame to leave them there, nobody can enjoy them in that place. They will brighten up the piano room, now that your birthday bouquet is past its best, Deborah.'

Automatically, Deborah took the flowers from Jessica's outstretched hand.

'What are you two up to? Are you ghost hunting?' Jessica laughed. 'Maybe he's lurking around here watching us. You might even be standing on his grave.'

'You may laugh, but what I saw was real,' Shirley retorted. Nevertheless she looked down at her feet as if she were half expecting the ground to open up.

Deborah was pleased to talk to Shirley about her experience. 'I can't think of any other explanation for bottles of wine flying around. It's worrying. What I saw was rather menacing. Honestly the way those pots of compost were viciously knocked to the floor, it made me think that something bad is in store for us.'

'The phenomena, or whatever you want to call it, didn't seem violent when I saw it,' Shirley revealed. 'Nevertheless it still gave me a fright.' She patted her friend on the shoulder clearly pleased to have another ally.

Jessica snorted. 'If you ask me we should be more worried about this pandemic that's sweeping the country. The world actually. Have you had flu jabs?'

'Tony has had his, I'm not eligible yet,' Shirley said.'

Deborah nodded, 'Yes, I had mine last October. I know Joy and Terry have had theirs, I'm not sure about the others. But that doesn't mean to say we won't get coronavirus, nor flu for that matter.'

'Keep washing your hands, is the advice. Fat lot of good that is, if one of us gets it. What then?' Jessica stood with her arms on her hips and shrugged.

'Self-isolate and wear a mask?' Shirley suggested. 'We'll just have to be extra careful with our hygiene. If you get it, we will lock you out of the house and you can sleep in the greenhouse!'

Deborah tittered, looking affectionately at her friends.

'Ha ha very funny! Jessica contemplated her soiled gardening gloves. 'These offer some protection, but I still need to scrub my hands after a session in the garden.'

'Where's Kirsty?' Deborah scanned the vast garden.

'I don't know. She might be sewing. She told me yesterday, she was going to make some cushion covers for that chaise lounge she's got in her room. Maybe she went riding. I can't remember now. I didn't see her this morning. Did she have an early breakfast?'

Shirley shook her head. 'I don't know.'

'I haven't seen her this morning either,' Deborah said. 'She's not in her room, because I checked earlier.' She peered over Jessica's shoulder. 'So what else have you found besides daffodils underneath all that decaying wood and crumbling stone?'

'Actually, I think all this bit of rotting mess is covering what might have been some stables. It makes sense really considering this place used to be a coaching inn. I think the building went into disrepair and then they collapsed. Probably because of the dragging weight of these Ash saplings and Hazel trees. Both self-seed rapidly. There's still a lot of old timber, stone and brambles to clear away to be certain, not to mention the ivy, but what else could be here?'

Shirley forced a smile. 'A grave?'

Jessica rolled her eyes then relented. 'I suppose that gravestone had to come from somewhere!'

Deborah laughed. She felt her anxiety lessen as she listened to Shirley and Jessica banter. 'Where the gravestone came from is still a mystery,' she said. 'I think you are right about stables. Kirsty would be pleased to hear that, knowing how fond she is of horses.'

Over lunch, Joy informed them that during their walk they had chatted to an elderly neighbour, who confirmed that years ago there used to be peafowl kept in the garden.

'Beautiful creatures, but they make a hell of a noise when they start cackling,' Kirsty said. 'I stayed in a hotel once where there were peacocks strutting up and down the place shrieking their heads off. It sounded like someone was being murdered.'

'Oh well, it was a long time ago. The ones that were here, are probably dead and buried now.' Joy's remark was met with an uneasy silence.

'What's up? What've I said?'

'Nothing really,' Deborah replied. 'Just something Jessica mentioned earlier about graves in the garden.'

'Have you found a grave?' Terry asked. 'Don't tell me, it's in the cellar.' He laughed. 'Old James will be annoyed if we're drinking his wine.'

'No, we haven't found a grave, but it might be in the garden,' Deborah answered quickly. 'Though I don't think we should rule out that he was buried in the cellar.'

'It seems likely,' Kirsty agreed.

Shirley frowned. 'Why do you say that?'

'Well, it adds up, doesn't it? We have a gravestone, we find hidden steps to a wine hoard. The floor underneath could easily have been a grave. Though why bury someone down there? That bit doesn't make sense, I admit.'

'Unless there was a murder,' Shirley said under her breath.

'Murder! That's all we need. A dead person seeking revenge!' Terry groaned.

'We have to consider all possibilities.' Shirley insisted.

'Let's change the subject. I'm going to get the apple crumble.' Jessica got up to go to the kitchen.

'What's the life span of a peafowl?' Joy asked, returning to the topic she had introduced earlier. She was fascinated by peacocks, and was disappointed that her friends seemed disinterested. She didn't want

91

to consider the possibility of a murdered body in their cellar, even if it might have occurred almost eighty years previously.

Jessica put the apple crumble on the table in front of Terry, and he wasted no time in serving it up.

To Joy's surprise, Tony supplied her with more information.

'They can live up to about twenty-five years. Some friends of mine in Cornwall used to run a caravan site and they had several peafowl running around. The male is a peacock and the female is a peahen. I used to go and stay with them. Not the birds, my friends.' He laughed. 'Kirsty is right, they do create a terrible noise. It's like a screeching maniacal scream especially when they are looking for a mate. My friends used to pen them back in a separate field away from the caravans during the peak holiday season. I think it was trendy at one time to have them at pubs. You don't see them so much now though.'

'Don't they fly away?' Deborah asked.
Tony shook his head. 'Not really. I think they try, but they scarcely get off the ground.'

'If we come across any feathers in the garden, we'll let you know,' Jessica offered with a wry smile. 'We're more likely to come across horseshoes.'

That afternoon they were dismayed to hear on the news that the government was considering extreme measures to combat COVID19.

'It's distressing to hear of so many infections rising in the country.' Deborah sat curled on her favourite armchair with a mug of tea, reading the news headlines on the television screen.

'I think we should be alright here in the countryside. It seems to be worse in the cities, especially in

England,' Kirsty commented. 'When we go out though, it's advisable to distance ourselves from people we talk to. In other words don't breath on them or spit on them.'

'I don't spit on people, thank you very much,' Deborah retorted. 'Though I know what you mean. Someone I used to work with, used to stand too close when he was talking to me. That was bad enough, but sometimes bits of saliva would be sprayed on me. Every time I stepped back, he would step forward. Yuk. It makes me feel sick to remember it.' She forced a laugh.

'Sounds horrible.' Kirsty agreed.

Deborah yawned. She made herself more comfortable as they listened to the BBC news update. Warm, well fed and relaxed with her friends she felt content, despite the worry of ghosts and COVID19. Lack of sleep from the night before was beginning to tell on her and she dozed off.

It was Grace who gently shook Deborah awake at seven o' clock.

'We've made a pile of sandwiches and there's sponge cake,' she said. 'We're going to eat in here.'

Deborah blinked to see everyone gathered around the television. Pots of tea were being poured and she took a mug gratefully from Kirsty. At half past eight, the food had been eaten and after helping with clearing away, Deborah headed for her bedroom hoping she would be able to sleep.

That night no-one noticed two wraithlike figures emerge from the piano room then enter the conservatory carrying with them a one-stemmed bud vase. Deborah had put a solitary daffodil in the narrow bud vase earlier that day. There had been no room for it with the others in the slightly wider vase on the mantelpiece. Grace moved it the following morning when she was cleaning and put it with the others on the mantelpiece in the piano lounge. She thought either Jessica or Kirsty had left it there by mistake. Jessica an early riser and keen to see if her seedlings hadn't been disturbed did the same thing on Friday morning. She was pleased to find there was no compost to clean up and no-one had reported seeing flying wine bottles. Equally relieved, Kirsty did the same on Saturday morning and so did Tony when he vacuum cleaned on Sunday morning. Each of them unthinkingly moved the bud vase and replaced it with the others on the mantelpiece in the piano lounge.

CHAPTER TEN

On Monday morning, Deborah was helping Grace clear away the breakfast dishes when her mobile's buzz informed her of a text.

'It's from Mr. Gibson! She remarked, wiping her hands on a towel. Grace looked over her shoulder to read the short message.

'That's not much help!' Grace commented. She sat down on a kitchen chair. 'So if he only owned this place for ten years, and he can't remember the name of the owner before him, what do we do now? How are we going to find out more about James Tyler? Gibson acknowledges the gravestone in his text but nothing else.'

'I suppose I could ring the solicitor who dealt with our purchase. She could look at the deeds and tell us the names of previous owners. I have her details in my room. I'll go up in a minute and get them.'

'In the meantime, could you text this Gibson chap and ask him why he used to put the gravestone in the fireplace? It seems a bizarre thing to do.'

'Yes, you're right. I wish I'd known about that before I last spoke to the estate agent. I'd asked him to ask Gibson about James Tyler and if he knew who the owners of the *Golden Peacock Grove* were during the nineteen forties. During that conversation we'd only just found the blasted thing in the cellar. I was more concerned about finding out who the poor chap was. I didn't want to mention ghosts. We know a bit more now.'

Grace smirked. 'You don't really believe it do you?'

'No... Yes.' Deborah shook her head, 'I believe I saw something weird. But I don't want to believe in ghosts. And yet... I have to say those who claimed to have seen flying bottles are adamant that this house is haunted. And your grandson says he saw some kind of a shape! I accept that they believe they are telling the truth. I just want there to be a scientific explanation.'

'I know, but Dan's young, maybe he got carried away. It all seems far-fetched to me.'

'But I saw the same thing as the others.' Deborah pressed her lips together. She recalled the surprised faces when she'd finally told her friends about her own experience.

'Whatever.' Grace sighed and got up from her chair just as Kirsty sauntered past them. She popped her head around the door.

'I heard what you said, but I'm certain there is a ghost. Believe what you like, Grace, but there are no invisible threads or mirrors to deceive us. Anyway I'll see you later. I'm going to the riding stables.'

Grace shrugged and went outside to have a smoke.

Upstairs ten minutes later, Deborah found the number of the solicitors, *Gittins, Worth and Smith.* She asked to speak to Mrs. Eileen Worth who dealt with the conveyancing of *The Golden Peacock.*

'That's an unusual request Mrs. Moore. Are you doing some research on the history of the place? Not that it's any of my business of course.'

Deborah laughed. 'Something like that. I just want to know the names of the owners over the last hundred years or so.'

'I'll get someone to look it up for you and call you back as soon as we can. I can't promise it will be today, we are very busy at the moment.'

'Thank you Mrs. Worth.'

After her phone call, Deborah walked to the window of her room and looked out into the garden. Jessica was pressure washing her greenhouse. She'd set it up next to Kirsty's at the top end of the garden.

At the opposite corner of the grounds, she could see Simon and Terry measuring a space for the boules pitch. Tony sat on an old wooden bench writing down the measurements as they called them out. He skilfully balanced a notebook in his hand with a cigarette wedged between his fingers. A knack he had evidently acquired over many years, Deborah guessed.

The overall scene of activity lifted Deborah's spirits. Despite the so called phantom and the threat of a deadly virus lurking in the atmosphere, she felt content. She had saved *The Golden Peacock* and she was never going to be lonely again. She went downstairs again to join Grace in the kitchen who seemed always to be pottering about in there. The kitchen was three times the size of Grace's old one and she plainly enjoyed working in it.

'I've just made two fresh pots of coffee,' she greeted her. 'I'll take it to the conservatory then call the others in.'

When everyone had made themselves comfortable Deborah updated them with her recent communications.

'So we're not much further forward,' Simon scratched his head through the wool thickness of his knitted bobble hat.

'I'm sorry. I suppose I didn't really ask the right questions. Things have moved on since I sent the original text. But I've sent another one. I just hope Mr. Gibson gets it. He may have had to move to a different location to make contact. I don't know which part of Spain he is living in.'

'Maybe he's avoiding the subject,' Jessica said.

Deborah sighed. 'I really don't know what to say.'

'Don't worry. Maybe Joy will find something interesting in Wrexham Library,' Terry said. 'She is convinced that something is going on in our bedroom.' He rolled his eyes at the sniggers. 'Ha ha. Very funny. You know what I mean.'

Grace got up to get some scones from the oven, just as Kirsty returned from her morning ride. 'Mmmm, lovely. I could smell these baking from outside,' she said. 'Any coffee left? She shrugged as her eyes fell on the empty cafetieres.

'I'll make some more, and you can have it with a buttered scone.' Grace disappeared to the kitchen, and Kirsty took her place at one of the tables. The exertions of her horse riding still flushed her face and it seemed to Deborah that as her friend peeled off her riding jacket she admitted the fresh country air into the warm conservatory.

Grace brought two fresh pots of coffee and returned to the kitchen. Deborah updated Kirsty on her text messages and her conversation with the solicitor.

'I've got some information that you might find interesting, though I'm not sure it will throw any light on our James Tyler.' Kirsty poured herself a hot drink and smiled appreciatively at Grace who had proudly produced a plate of warm scones, butter oozing down their golden crusts.

'It seems Jeff and Tina at the stables know a bit of history about this place.'

'Who are Jeff and Tina?' Tony interrupted.

'Sorry Tony, I forgot you don't know them. They are the owners of *Woodville Riding School and Stables* at Marford. I've been going there for years. 'Anyway their place is an old building just like this one. They said that centuries ago both their building and this one provided hospitality for travellers. In fact at one time it was called *The Travellers Rest*. Apparently, more recently, there was some kind of rivalry between the owners which wasn't helped when secret trysts occurred between the daughter of the *Travellers Rest* and a male relative of the owners at *The Peacock Grove*.' She bit into her scone and wiped the melting butter from her lips with the back of her hand, 'Mmmm Grace.'

'Yes they are, lovely. Thanks,' the others enthused in varying degrees.

'Sounds like a Shakespearean tragedy,' Jessica muttered. 'Why did you say '*Peacock Grove* and not *Golden Peacock?*'

'I don't know. It's what Tina calls it.'

'So do you think there is a connection between those lovers and our ghost?' Tony asked.

Kirsty licked butter from her fingers then brushed crumbs from her lips, 'It might be. It depends who our ghost is. I really don't know. I just thought I would throw this bit of info into the mix. Apparently the love affair happened during the nineteen twenties. It was something Tina's grandmother told her. She's dead now unfortunately. So who knows? The story might in some way be related to our James Tyler, though not directly about him. Bearing in mind he died in 1944 at

99

the age of twenty-seven he wouldn't have been old enough to have a secret lover in the nineteen twenties.'

'Unless there was an older brother?' Deborah suggested 'Or a cousin.'

Kirsty shrugged. 'This is all conjecture. Anyway, apart from that romantic titbit, Jeff said that he'd heard rumours of bottles of wine moving on the tables.' Kirsty took a breath and examined the thoughtful expressions on her audience before continuing.

'But, that started only about three years ago. Apparently, according to Jeff, when it happened, there was usually a group of drinkers standing around and one of them was always able to reach out and grab the bottle. Some people thought it was just a stunt and laughed it off. Others just assumed the bottle had slipped out of a person's hands.'

'And so it wouldn't get as far as the conservatory,' Tony said.

'Yes.' Kirsty nodded her head. 'Exactly. She sipped her coffee.

'It seems no-one actually saw it lift and sail through the air into another room!'

'And yet when Shirley and I tried to grab it, we couldn't.'

Kirsty fixed Tony with a worried expression. 'Perhaps the power of the ghost is stronger now which is why you couldn't stop it? I didn't even try.'

'When you were at the stables, did you ask Jeff and Tina to give you the names of the lovers?' Deborah asked.

'They can't remember, but they think the name of the male was James.'

'Another James,' Simon said. 'The name was quite common. Mind you so is Tyler.'

'I can't help thinking that the story Tina told me isn't anything to do with James Tyler,' Kirsty said. 'Romantic though it sounds, the story dates back almost a hundred years. Our James died quite young in nineteen forty-four. I just thought you might be interested in a bit of history. Kirsty drained her coffee and got up. 'I'm going to get changed.'

'Perhaps Joy will find something out,' Terry repeated. He reached for another scone. 'These really are lovely Grace.'

'Thank you.'

'Cooking must run in the family. Dan probably takes after you,' Jessica said kindly.

Kirsty lingered by the doorway just inside the hall, then turned around again to face everyone.

'I've just realised something. The conservatory wasn't here when James Tyler died.'

'Does that rule him out as our phantom?' Deborah sighed. 'We still haven't a clue about the female spectre either.'

'Unless there was another building there before the conservatory?' Tony suggested.

'Possibly,' Simon shrugged half-heartedly. 'Though I'm beginning to think we are barking up the wrong tree. That gravestone might be a hoax. Just a gimmick.'

'We need more information. It's pointless speculating until we get more information from our man Gibson. Let's wait until Deborah hears from him or the solicitor. We've got plenty of other things to do.'

'Are you making much progress with the boules pitch?' Deborah asked.

'Yes we've marked it out,' Simon replied. 'The three of us are going to try to get some sand from that builder's yard in Gresford. We'll go this afternoon after lunch. We've just got a bit more preparation to do first.'

'And I've got both greenhouses ready for use too. I need to get some more compost though. I'll get Kirsty to come with me to the garden centre this afternoon to stock up. In the meantime we can start making our own compost. I've set up a section at the back of the garden to take all our veggie waste. So next year we won't have to buy ready-made stuff.'

That afternoon Deborah and Grace sat in the kitchen sipping tea as they watched the news on the television fixed to the wall. It was a large LED screen installed by the mutual agreement of all the friends. Deborah and Grace had been hesitant at having such a thing in the kitchen, but capitulated when it had been pointed out to them that the kitchen was large, and the TV would be useful especially if one of them wanted to follow a recipe with the TV chefs. Grace in particular had found it especially useful.

The ticker notes running across the bottom of the screen alarmed them when they read that the government were considering a lockdown for the UK very soon.

'Surely they can't expect every business to close down?' Grace frowned. She sipped her tea slowly, consternation edging her face. 'It's very disturbing.'

Deborah agreed, and didn't feel any better when Joy arrived home half an hour later and told them that the libraries would have to close too.

'I don't know how all this is going to work, if everything comes to a standstill.' Joy put her hands around the teapot to test the temperature. Deciding the luke-warm tea was not appetising she opened the fridge to get some orange juice.

'I've been trying to do some research, but as usual got side tracked. I've only got bits and pieces and I can't make much sense of it. I'll talk it over properly with you lot tonight. I haven't got time now, as I have to get to the bowling club. I have a match at half past three.' She carried her drink upstairs with her, to get ready for her sport event. Ten minutes later she popped her head around the door to say goodbye. 'See you later.'

Shirley arrived home from work in an agitated state. Arrangements had been made for her to work from home as from the following week. She slumped into an armchair in front of the television where most of her friends had gathered to watch the evening news. Tony handed her a cup of tea.

'It seems I have to set up my lap top here and somehow communicate with my civil service colleagues starting from Monday,' Shirley informed her friends between sips of her hot drink. 'It's going to be a challenge.'

'We can re-arrange the furniture a bit in our room, there's plenty of space,' Tony re-assured her. She cast him a grateful smile.

'From what I can gather from Joy, the library is going to be closed too, so you won't be able to work from there either,' Deborah sympathised.

Shirley groaned. 'It seems the only places that will be open are supermarkets and places that sell food. Not even the pubs will be open.' She took another sip of tea and looked around the room. 'Where's Joy and Terry?'

'Joy is playing bowls. Terry has gone to watch. He said they would stay in the club for a drink after the match with the rest of the team.'

Shirley finished her tea and got up. 'I'm going to dump my stuff upstairs and get changed. See you later.' Tony followed her out.

'If the pubs are going to close as from Friday, maybe we ought to go out this week and make the most of it whilst we can,' Kirsty suggested. 'In any case I was thinking of making some inquiries at *The White Hart*.' She caught her sister's scornful expression. 'You know, I'd like to follow up what Dan told us after his chat with the barman about mysterious goings on.'

Jessica laughed, 'How do you know he won't try to wind you up with invented ghost stories?'

'You can laugh all you like, but I mean to get to the bottom of this mystery. And it seems I have less than a week to investigate.'

'I'll come with you if you like,' Deborah offered. 'I'm still not convinced about this so called ghost, but I would like to learn more history about the local area. I wish I'd taken more of an interest years ago.'

'Well I'm all for a night out at *The White Hart*,' Jessica ventured, 'especially if we're going to be confined to the house for a few weeks. Come to think of it, how long do you think this lockdown will last?'

'It's a bit vague at the moment,' Simon advised her. It seems the Prime Minister will issue instructions tomorrow afternoon.'

'If the supermarkets are going to stay open, then we won't have to worry about food at least,' Grace said. 'Talking of which, I think we ought to start getting our evening meal ready.' She eyed Kirsty expectantly and, taking the hint Kirsty got up to do her stint in the kitchen. "Did Joy and Terry say they would be back for supper?' she called over her shoulder.

'I think they said they would eat at the club house and would be back around eight o clock. Joy was going to tell us what bits of new information she'd picked up from the library about the ghost,' Deborah called.

Jessica sighed, 'Not the wretched ghost again! I've told you there's no such thing.'

At eight o' clock that evening, Jessica changed her mind.

CHAPTER ELEVEN

Unable to keep out of the kitchen, Grace helped Kirsty to prepare their evening meal. Unlike her friend, Kirsty wasn't an accomplished cook. Nevertheless there were certain dishes she was able to produce to a reasonable standard. She didn't resent Grace helping her. Kirsty was more than happy to accept her help.

Over their meal, Kirsty suggested they made their visit to *The White Hart* the following evening. 'We could have a bar snack. May as well make the most of it.'

'I'm going to Gail's tomorrow night, you know, my friend from work. She's having a cheese and wine party. Her snap decision today because of lockdown! Tony's coming too. Sorry.' Shirley glanced at him. He nodded with a smile.

'I suppose those kind of gatherings will be banned as well after Friday,' sighed Deborah.

'Yep, I'm afraid so,' Shirley said, turning to Kirsty. 'You probably won't be able to go riding next Sunday either.'

'What? Are you joking? I'll be out in the fresh air, surely that's allowed?' Kirsty was crestfallen.

Seeing Kirsty's disappointment made Simon frown. He shook his head slowly, trying to remember what he'd heard earlier. 'It said on the news that the government will encourage people to take exercise every day, so maybe you will be able to have your ride.'

'It's not just my exercise, it's the horses too. Plus they need feeding and mucking out and all the rest of it. I usually help with all that.'

'You'll just have to check with Tina, the horses' welfare have to be considered,' Jessica soothed her sister.

'I suppose I'll have to make arrangements with my music students. I only have three but it'll be a shame to interrupt their progress. Maybe I could prepare some extra lessons for them to practise at home.' Deborah got up to go in to the piano lounge. A few minutes later calming sounds of '*Air on a G string*' wafted through to the conservatory.

'She always plays Bach when she's thinking. I love it,' Jessica picked up her glass and sauntered to the piano room to listen more closely to the music. She made herself comfortable on one of the sofas and placed her wine glass on a coffee table. Above the music she could hear the dishes being cleared away behind her. She reminded herself that it would be her turn the next night. Meanwhile she was going to close her eyes and enjoy Deborah's recital.

As the sounds of the communal bustle of domestic chores receded, only the notes from the piano keys filled the air.

Just before eight o'clock, Joy and Terry arrived back at the house. They drifted into the piano lounge to listen to Deborah's playing. She'd barely started *Johann Strauss' Blue Danube.*

Jessica's eyes jolted open as Joy plonked an unopened bottle of wine on the table in front of her.

'Look what I've won!' Joy whispered. 'Our team won the match and we all got a bottle of wine each! I chose the Chablis.' She pulled off her baseball cap and held it in her hands as she sank on to a chair.

'Well done. Congratulations.'

Deborah stopped playing, just as they heard the clock in the hallway chime eight o'clock. Jessica leaned forward to pick up the bottle to examine the label. Before she could touch it, the wine moved from her grasp. Jessica reached for the wine again. At the same time Deborah turned glazed eyes towards her friends. 'What's happening?' She felt dizzy and clutched the piano for support.

Every attempt Jessica made to grasp Joy's prize, was foiled as it moved out of reach. Joy and Terry sat forward in their seats opposite Jessica, their bodies frozen as if captured in time. The Chablis soared high above them and made its way towards the hallway. The door was shut. Joy had closed it. Almost as if frustrated the wine bottle pushed against the door then swung back as if to bang itself against the blocked way out.

'Quick open the door,' Deborah called. She rubbed her eyes and shook herself as if emerging from a deep sleep. 'It wants to go to the conservatory, I know it does.'

Terry, wearing a confused expression, the image replicated in his wife's face, lunged towards the door just as the bottle flung itself at the open space. Motivated by a force, none of the four friends could later explain, they crowded in the doorway to watch the floating bottle. As if suspended by a concealed thread, the Chablis glided across the hall and into the conservatory. The mesmerised group, witnessed two pots of re-seeded compost fall to the floor, as Joy's bottle of wine tapped against the window before taking up their space on the window ledge.

'Oh my God,' Jessica's voice was a strangled whisper. She turned to face Deborah whose shocked expression mirrored her own. Terry looked bewildered. His wife in contrast was triumphant.

'There, I knew it! We have a ghost!'

Without saying a word, they moved in an awed huddle into the conservatory. They stepped carefully over the strewn compost and fixed their eyes on the wine. Joy cautiously reached out her hand and made to grab it. Terry put a restraining hand on her arm. 'Don't! You might upset it.'

But Joy wriggled free determined to get her prize. 'Let's see what happens.' Again she put out her hand, less feebly the second time and as her fingers tightened around the vessel, she heard a sob from the window sill. She whirled around with the Chablis in her hands. 'What was that? Was it you?' She accused first Deborah and then Jessica.

'What are you talking about?' Deborah responded crossly.

'A sob. Did you pretend to cry?'

Jessica and Deborah shook their heads, bewilderment evident in their eyes.

'Of course not!' Jessica turned to Terry. 'Is this one of your jokes?'

'What do you take me for? Do you think I could orchestrate that? I'm as shocked as you.'

'You mean you didn't hear that sob?' Joy ignored Jessica's accusation. She looked from one baffled face to the other.

'No,' they answered in unison.

'What sob?' Jessica asked. She stared at her friend, a frown deepening on her forehead.

'When I reached out to grab the bottle, I heard a cry. A deep wail, as if someone was heartbroken.' Joy turned around again to examine the gap on the windowsill where the two composted pots had each left marked rings. Superimposed over those was a bigger ring where the Chablis had rested for just a few seconds. She put her ear to the window but could hear nothing. She turned to face her husband and two friends again. 'I can't hear anything now.'

'Come on let's go back to the piano lounge and see if it happens again,' Terry suggested. He led the way and the three women followed him in. Joy placed the Chablis in the centre of the table. On the floor was Jessica's upturned empty wineglass. Though unbroken, the red stains on the carpet lay testament to its spilled contents. They sat and waited for the bottle to move again, but nothing happened.

Jessica breathed deeply, 'I need a drink. And I mean something strong. I've got a good malt upstairs. I'll go and get it.'

'We ought to tell the others,' Joy said, when Jessica returned with her whisky. 'I've found out a bit more about this house today at the library. Not much, but it might help if we put our heads together to consider what we know so far.'

'Fine, let's just calm ourselves first,' Terry said. 'That was a bit of a shock.' He checked his watch. 'It's twenty past eight. Shall we wait until after the nine o 'clock news?'

Deborah shook her head. 'No, let's do it before. It's not as if it will be a shock for Kirsty, Shirley and Tony. It will be just confirmation for them. I think Grace and

Simon are more than half way believing it anyway, because of what Dan told them yesterday.'

'It's strange we haven't seen any compost on the floor for a few days,' Jessica remarked.

Fifteen minutes later they decided to make a move.

'I'm not leaving this whisky behind.' Jessica looked over her shoulder as if expecting a ghost to take it from her. She managed a giggle. Deborah patted her shoulder. 'Come on let's get this over with.'

Grace and Simon were watching a soap, so the others slipped noiselessly into arm chairs and waited for the programme to end before they related their encounter. As soon as it finished, Grace got up. 'I'm going to make some tea. Anybody want some?'

Jessica held up her bottle of whisky. 'I think you might want something stronger when you hear what we've got to say.'

'What's happened? Not more ghostly happenings?' Simon joked.

''Actually yes,' Deborah spoke for them all. 'The four of us have just seen the same thing that Shirley, Tony, and I saw.'

'And Kirsty and Dan don't forget,' Joy reminded her.

Grace slipped back on to the sofa, 'Oh no! So that means just the two of us haven't experienced it.'

Simon shrugged, 'So what do you want to do about it? It isn't as if it's causing any harm. Spooky I grant you, but you could get used to it.'

'It's a damn nuisance knocking my plant pots off the window sill!' Jessica commented, 'And how do we know it won't get worse? Smashed doors, windows, bottles?'

'Good point Jess. Do you suppose that's why the previous owners sold it?' Joy raised a quizzical eyebrow.

'Shall we call the others down to discuss it? Joy has a bit more info to tell us, we might as well hear it together,' Deborah suggested. She was on her way out of the room to call Kirsty, Shirley and Tony without waiting for a response.

There was no reply from Kirsty's room, Deborah quietly opened the door, wondering if she was in her ensuite. 'Kirsty?'

Realising her friend must have gone out, she roused Shirley and Tony who followed her downstairs.

When they were settled some ten minutes later, Deborah told them what had occurred in the piano room.

'I'm wondering if it happens only at a certain time during the evening,' Shirley observed. 'I'm in work all day so wouldn't know, but have any of you noticed anything during the day time?'

'I'm in the piano room most of the time and I haven't seen anything unusual. Mind you, I get so absorbed in my music I wouldn't notice anyway.'

'The giveaway sign is the compost on the floor!' Jessica reminded them. 'It usually happens in the evening. Or at least we don't notice it until morning.' She glanced at Simon. 'I suppose if we had to live with it, like you suggest, we could just make room on the windowsill. In any case we wouldn't normally use the conservatory for our seedlings, it was just a temporary measure until we got the greenhouses sorted.'

'But, like you said, if it can smash up pots of compost, who knows what it might smash up next?' Terry pointed out.

112

'Why don't we make a note of the time and see if it happens again tomorrow?' Grace suggested. What time do you think it happened tonight?'

Joy flashed a glance at Terry who was deep in thought. 'I think we got back here just before eight o' clock. We'd barely sat down when my bottle of wine; my prize for winning by the way; took off into the air and floated to the conservatory.' She cast a glance at first Deborah and then Jessica for confirmation. Both of them nodded.

'That's a good idea,' Terry agreed cradling his glass of whisky. 'Why don't we all sit in the piano room tomorrow night at seven thirty with a bottle of wine and wait to see what happens. In the meantime let's hear what snippet Joy has got to tell us.'

Before Joy could speak, Kirsty swept into the room bringing a tang of farm-yard aromas.

'Just in time,' Joy greeted her.

'Are we having a conference?' Kirsty slipped off her coat then turned to retreat to the hall. 'Give me a minute, I need to take my boots off.'

'Right.' Joy tasted her whisky and remarked how good it was. Jessica nodded with a smile.

'Kirsty avoided her sister's inquiring stare as she sat down. 'This must be important if we're drinking a good single malt whisky.'

Deborah updated Kirsty who responded upon hearing the news with a grin.

'You see, I told you I'd seen something, but you wouldn't believe me. And yes please I wouldn't mind a drink.' She grasped the bottle from Jessica and poured herself a generous amount before passing it back.

113

'Anyway to continue with what I have discovered,' Joy began. 'It seems that our James Tyler was a casualty of World War Two. He died, as we know, on the twenty second of September nineteen forty-four. He was in Arnhem. Jessica was right, she guessed something like that had happened.

'That's awful,' Simon said. He was only twenty-seven? So young. Was he married?'

'I couldn't find that bit out. But that date resonates with me. It is actually ten years after the Gresford coal mine tragedy. It makes you wonder if he, or people like him had survived that pit explosion, only to be killed in the war. Joy's face was sad. 'It doesn't bear thinking about.' She took another sip of her whisky.'

'If James Tyler was the son of the owners of *The Golden Peacock*, and we're still not sure that he was, I doubt he would have been a coal miner. He would have helped with running the estate and the stables,' Kirsty advised. 'At least this knowledge of his death, explains why his gravestone has been lying around here for so long. The family would have put it up as a memorial to him.'

'So it's unlikely that he's haunting us,' Jessica muttered. 'And I must say, I'm still coming to terms with the fact that this place *is* haunted.'

'I have to say that though I'd heard all kinds of rumours over the years, I don't recall anyone ever mentioning to me that they'd actually seen a ghost here,' Deborah said.

'Don't forget Dan's friend Jason's dad,' Shirley reminded her. 'He was convinced he saw a ghost and that it was a woman.'

'True,' Deborah admitted. 'But we've only recently found out about that. This is all news to us. And what about this strange phenomena we're experiencing? I hadn't heard anything about that before we moved in.'

'It's one of those things that doesn't get reported in the press,' Shirley said. 'Just because we haven't heard of it, doesn't mean it didn't happen. The regulars would just keep coming or they would stay away, depending on their experience and their attitude!

'If, as Grace suggests it only occurs at a given time, the phenomena would, more often or not, go un-noticed. It would depend on how many people were in the pub. The show lasts barely a couple of minutes. Some people wouldn't bother to mention it. That's my theory for what it's worth.' Shirley scanned the puzzled expressions on her companions' faces.

'I think you have a point, Shirley,' Jessica said. 'Judging from what you guys have witnessed previously and what I have seen tonight, it seems to happen only in one corner of the piano room. Just a small amount of customers would witness it.'

'Perhaps, if there wasn't a bottle of wine on the table, other things started moving around, like coasters or glasses? If that happened, people would just think it was clumsiness or someone messing about. I probably would,' Jessica added.

Grace put her hand to her mouth. 'Oh.'

'What?' Simon was startled at Grace's exclamation.

'The other day, I noticed that glass bud vase on the windowsill next to the seedlings. I moved it back to the fireplace thinking Jess or Kirsty had forgotten they'd put it there.'

'It was in the conservatory the next day, and I put it back on the mantelpiece,' Jessica said, her eyes wide.

To tell you the truth I was more concerned about making sure the seedlings were safe.'

'I noticed it too on Saturday morning,' Kirsty said.

'And I did yesterday,' Tony admitted. '

'I moved it this morning before I went to work. I remember thinking how it fitted neatly between the two composted seedlings,' Shirley added. 'The daffodil had wilted so I chucked it away and washed the vase.' She glanced at the mantelpiece to see where she had left it.

'So each time it must have happened the night before when we were in the other room, or somewhere else in the house.' Deborah acknowledged.

'How do we explain the movement of some of Joy's jewellery? Is it still happening?' Kirsty asked wrinkling her brow trying to come up with a theory of her own.

'Yep.'

'Was there anything else you discovered at the library?' Deborah asked.

'Just a bit of general information that might help us. 'It concerns that old pub where Dan went.'

'*The White Hart*'. Grace supplied.

'Yes. It appears that it was one of many of the old coaching inns that were in Rossett at one time or another. Just like this house was and the old house at the stables that Kirsty told us about. *The White Hart* and *The Golden Peacock* were business rivals.'

'Like Romeo and Juliet?' Deborah asked. She loved the thought of a romance, and in any case she loved the history of old houses.

'Not quite as bad as that. Well at least I don't think so. They were actually friendly rivals looking for trade.

Apparently when each inn was full, they would direct travellers for hospitality to the other and vice versa.'

'Hmm so you are suggesting that there might be a faint connection with the two inns and our ghost who may be a woman?' Deborah asked. She was getting pulled into the fantasy despite herself. She noted her friends were also becoming absorbed with Joy's tale.

'Yes. That's why I think some of us could go there tomorrow for lunch and talk to the landlord instead of tomorrow night as planned. That way we could get back here in time for our appointment with the phantom.'

Kirsty laughed. Good idea. Let's see if the landlord of *The White Hart* can give us some information that might help us.'

Simon sighed. 'I'd like to know more, but Terry and I hoped to start on constructing the boules pitch tomorrow. We also need to get more materials. We may not be able to get them next week after the lockdown, so the sooner we make a start the better.'

'I'll be in work,' Shirley said gloomily, 'and now Tony has made arrangements to catch up with some old colleagues for lunch, too. Before lockdown!' She finished that last part of her statement with a sigh and a swift glance at Tony who agreed with a slight inclination of his head. He added that he was going to *The Golden Lion*. 'Actually that's not far from *The White Hart*, but I don't think I'll be able to join you. By the way, from what I can gather from my mates, *The Golden Lion* is also several centuries old. I'll see if I can find out anything about its history.'

'Great! So that's five us for lunch at *The White Hart* tomorrow then,' Deborah said. 'Sorry Shirley you can't come with us.'

Shirley shrugged. 'No worries.'

'Should I book a table do you think?' Deborah asked.

'Make it four,' Grace said suddenly. 'I think I'll stay here. It doesn't seem fair to leave Simon and Terry without food when they will be out in the cold working.'

'Don't be daft Love. We can manage with a few sandwiches, and we're not completely helpless. Terry can make tea and coffee,' Simon grinned.

'Of course he can,' Joy protested. 'In fact Terry is pretty good in the kitchen, so don't worry about them Grace.' She turned to her friend. 'It may be your last opportunity to get out and see the world.'

'You make it sound as if we're going to be locked up indefinitely.'

'Who knows what the lockdown will be like?' Joy muttered, 'Anyway suit yourself. I'm off to bed.' She raised herself easily off the floor. This seemed to be the signal for everyone else to get up too. Deborah went to the kitchen to make herself some camomile tea offering to make some for the others. Only Kirsty followed her. The others went to bed.

As they waited for the kettle to boil, Kirsty surprised Deborah when she said that she felt as if she was living out a part in a children's story book.

'Honestly, although it's disconcerting to have a ghost or maybe two,' she giggled, 'it's also exciting. Just imagine, if we hadn't decided to live in this little co-operative of ours, we'd all be in our individual houses bored to death and lonely. And with the lockdown almost on us, we would be lonelier and more bored than ever. So here's to you Debbie. Thanks for the wonderful idea.'

Deborah poured the hot water on to the teabags in each mug and smiled. 'Thanks for saying that. I'm glad you feel that way, and I have an inkling the others feel the same. No-one has actually said so, but no-one has grumbled or mentioned regrets.'

'I'm sure you are right. We all know each other so well, you'd know if anyone was unhappy. We're thriving!

'But what about Grace?' Deborah asked. 'Why won't she come out with us tomorrow?'

'That's simple. Don't worry about our Grace. She loves this place. She's in her element pretending to be Lady of the Manor. Haven't you noticed how she's always dusting, polishing and tidying up after us, as if she owns the place?'

'I suppose I have, now you mention it. She even polishes my metronome and straightens my music for me when I leave it on the piano.'

'Exactly.' Kirsty's eyes twinkled. 'And have you noticed how she follows any one of us into the kitchen to help, even when it isn't her turn to make dinner? Not that I mind, she's a good cook, and as far as I'm concerned if she wants to share the load, she can.'

Deborah smiled, 'I think you've got a point there.'

'Believe me, Grace will be in her element tomorrow when we're all out. She'll have the place to herself for several hours.'

CHAPTER TWELVE

The next morning, Deborah rang *The White Hart* and reserved a table for twelve thirty. She doubted that Wednesday's would be busy at the pub, it being mid-week, but with lockdown looming she thought it would be wise to book ahead. As expected, no amount of coaxing could persuade Grace to accompany them.

'I'll drive,' Deborah offered. 'I've got a student coming for a music lesson at four-thirty, so I won't drink. I don't want to breathe alcohol fumes over him.'

'Suits me,' Joy said. She followed Deborah outside to the car and waited for Kirsty and Jessica to join them.

'Grace couldn't wait for us to go,' grinned Kirsty.

'As long as she's happy,' Deborah said. The others nodded their agreement.

Deborah felt cheerful that day as she drove the few miles to the old inn. It was located off the Chester Road in the centre of Rossett village. The village itself sprawled in all directions in ad hoc clusters of houses; each in various shapes and sizes. Many were built of stone with a timber façade suggesting their construction was centuries old. Rossett appeared to have developed without any formal building plan. The picturesque village was unique in there being no large housing estates save for two small knots of tastefully constructed council houses; each group, unobtrusively occupied separate pieces of land.

At *The White Hart*, they ordered their drinks and were taken to their reserved table overlooking the garden. Jessica went to the bar to get a couple of menus. 'Let's order our food first and then make a plan of action.'

Joy laughed. 'You make it sound like a military coup.'

'We can't just start asking about ghosts. They'll think we're tapped,' Jessica retorted. 'Before you know it the whole village will know, the press will be outside our place and there will be calls for the church to come and purge the evil spirits out of our home.'

Deborah and Kirsty choked on their drinks at Jessica's outburst.

Joy stared at Jessica, then realised she was dramatizing. She put her hand over her chest in mock relief. 'You had me worried for a minute. But you're right, we don't want to attract attention.' She sipped her white wine. 'So what do you suggest, Jess?'

'Like I said, we'll eat our food and then one of us should go to the bar and try to engage whoever is serving, with simple conversation about the history of this place. Depending on the response, try to guide the conversation into whether there was a connection between *The White Hart* and *The Golden Peacock*. Maybe start by asking about the peacocks, try to find out what happened to them.'

'Right. Good plan. All agreed?' Joy raised her glass and the rest chinked theirs with hers.

They decided that as Joy had done the initial research, that she should start the conversation with the bar man. Deborah went with her to carry the drinks. Luckily it was the landlord himself who served them.

121

He seemed keen to tell the story of his pub and didn't need much prompting.

'This place goes back to the fourteenth century,' he said proudly. 'Some people say that Oliver Cromwell stayed here during the civil war when they tried to capture Charles Stuart.'

'That's interesting,' Deborah said. 'It's plausible when you think Chester isn't too far away and it's said that the battlefields could be seen from the city walls.' The landlord nodded, pleased to get an audience.

'Do you think there's any connection with your pub and the old inn that was *The Golden Peacock?*' Joy ventured, risking a wink at Deborah.

'More than likely, there were all sorts of connections with the landowners and inn keepers. I know there was something of an alliance or whatever you call it, with one of the daughters of the Hayes who owned Rossett Mill and the son of this pub *The White Hart*. I don't know what happened to them. Around about that time, I think it was during the eighteen hundreds, the mill house became a hotel. It's a pub now, called *The Miller.*' The landlord paused and eyed them curiously. Satisfied he had attentive listeners, he carried on with his story. 'It was a very important hotel, the old mill house, I'll have you know. That and *The White Hart* were often used as court houses.' The landlord straightened his back, evidently proud of the fact.

Joy and Deborah listened intently. Deborah, feeling as if the landlord's eyes rested heavily upon her looked down at the wooden counter. She turned her head to see Jessica and Kirsty eagerly watching.

The landlord switched his attention to Joy. 'But I think there was some scandal with one of the other

122

daughters at the mill. I'm not sure which one but that scandal was connected in some kind of way with the Slaters who owned *The Golden Peacock*. I read something about all this a while back, I can't remember exactly. To tell you the truth, I heard something about it from an interesting regular of mine. He's pushing ninety and comes here every Saturday for a pint. He can relate all kinds of tales he'd been told as a lad by his grandad. It's amazing what you learn from the locals...'

'Slater? Joy frowned, 'You don't mean Tyler?'

'Definitely Slater. I don't know anything about a Tyler.'

'So you don't know what exactly the connection was with those two families? Perhaps there was some rivalry?' Joy persisted. 'Perhaps business or romance?'

'You could be right about both. I can't honestly say. This happened a long time ago. There was a lot of rivalry in those days and not just for business. If you listen to local folklore and add bits of information you get from reading the deeds, you can piece together what may have happened. 'Course not everybody is interested.' His eyes fell on Deborah again, this time she held his gaze, though she felt uncomfortable under such close scrutiny.

'We are very interested,' she said hurriedly and was pleased that the landlord continued his story. He was obviously enjoying relating it, she could tell.

'The owners of *The Miller* are new to the area. They didn't inherit. Same here with me, I didn't inherit this place. Bought it at auction.' He paused allowing himself the opportunity to study the two women in front of him.

'Seeing as they would have had to get through a lot of red tape to make the renovations to the mill house, they may have done some research. When they opened, I went to have a look and they have done a good job on incorporating some of what was left of the decaying building into '*The Miller.*' They seem to be doing alright with it as a pub. Are you doing some research on the area?' He examined their faces curiously.

'Yes actually,' Deborah admitted. 'We're both interested in the history of Rossett. We've moved in to what was once *The Golden Peacock* and we'd like to know a bit more about the pub and the village.'

'Are you not from around here then?'

'Oh yes, we're more or less local. We're from the surrounding villages, and we're familiar with Rossett. It's just that we've never bothered to find out much about the past,' Deborah explained. She hoped that imparting this information would meet with Jessica's instructions. 'As a matter of fact I lived in Farndon and recently sold my house.'

'So you must be the ones who saved *The Golden Peacock* from demolition? I'd heard that several people had moved in.'

'Yes,' Joy said. There are nine of us all together. I used to live just up the road in Lavister.'

'So that's why you're asking all these questions. So how are you settling in? I've heard the place is haunted. Is it true?' The landlord grinned.

'Why? What makes you say that?' Joy put on an innocent expression. Deborah stared the landlord out, determined to appear casual.

'Only rumours, about things going missing and turning up in odd places.'

'How do..?' Joy began.

Just then a customer caught the landlord's attention and he excused himself. Joy and Deborah collected the drinks and returned to their table.

'Anything to report?' Kirsty asked in a low voice.

'Not much yet, but he seems well informed.' Joy put Jessica's fresh drink in front of her and moved her dead glass out of the way. 'Just as it got interesting, he had to serve a customer. Let's try to catch his eye on our way out.' Joy checked her watch, then covertly surveyed the room, noting the amount of customers sitting at the tables. 'Most people will have gone in an hour. Everyone seems to be eating. I think this place does well for serving lunch time meals.'

At two thirty the four women deliberately loitered at the door, waiting to catch the attention of the landlord. He saw them and smiled, 'I take it the four of you are the new people at the old *Peacock*?'

'Pleased to meet you, Jessica Rogers and this is my sister, Kirsty Wright.'

'Of course we're not new to Rossett exactly,' Kirsty said. 'We all used to socialise in the various pubs here from time to time. And this isn't my first visit here either, though it's been a while.'

'I've only been landlord here myself six years. Rossett is a fascinating place isn't it?'

'You mentioned to my friends something about a ghost. What did you mean?' Jessica asked. She scrutinised the landlord shrewdly. Her startling blue eyes met his perceptive brown ones.

'You've seen it haven't you?'

To give him credit, he lowered his voice as he spoke. Jessica checked the reactions of her companions, and satisfied she had their silent consent, turned to face the landlord's suspicious expression.

'Not exactly, but we suspect something.'

'I knew it. There was a young lad here the other night asking questions about the place. So, is he related to you?'

'Kind of,' Jessica replied unwilling to go into details.

'We wondered if there was a connection with our place and yours,' Kirsty added. 'We know nothing about the history, even though we all lived around these parts off and on over the last sixty odd years.'

'So you haven't seen any floating objects? Apparently it got worse after the conservatory was built. That's why the previous owner sold up. Didn't he tell you?'

The four women shook their heads, refusing to be drawn.

'Wily old git that Gibson! But I don't blame him. Not that he was losing business. I reckon his wife got tired of the mess that she had to clean up every day. And I don't mean the usual pub rubbish either.'

The landlord didn't miss the exchanged look between the friends, though Deborah had been convinced they were being discreet.

'How come you know all this?' She asked.

'We belong to the Victuallers Association,' he said smugly, satisfied that this announcement resulted in the little group clustering eagerly together to hear more. 'Actually we don't call it that any more, but I like the old title. It's basically a club for licensees. We get together and discuss local drinking trends and the like.'

'I see. So at one of your meetings Mr. Gibson told you he had problems at his pub?' Deborah tilted her

126

head slightly to meet the landlord's eye. Immediately she wished she hadn't. She felt awkward under his penetrating gaze. She coloured slightly.

'Yep. He was getting tired of the pub and of course he wanted to live somewhere warmer; which is why he sold up and went to Spain. Can't blame 'im. He's managed to avoid the lockdown on Friday. God knows what's going to happen to my trade. Though I hear there's a lockdown in Spain. But he hasn't got a pub to run now.'

Deborah was sympathetic about the lockdown effect on *The White Hart*, but she wanted to find out more about the unwanted guests in her new home. Reluctantly she had acknowledged that there may be more than one ghost. 'Did he give you exact details – about the mess?'

The landlord shook his head, just a mess every morning in the conservatory and his missus' jewellery going missing. I got interested because I know this place is just as old, if not older. I wanted to get some ideas about what I could do about my own pub. So like I said I asked the locals about the names of the people on the deeds, and that's how I found out about the sisters at the old mill.' He scratched his head. 'I've just had a thought. There might be a clue at *The Trevalyn Inn*. Now there's an old place steeped in history, I bet. Have you made inquiries there yet?'

'Not yet, but now you mention it we will. I haven't been there for a long time,' Jessica checked with her friends who nodded.

'With regard to '*The Miller*, I don't think it was all that old,' Joy offered. The mill itself is centuries old, but the house that was next to it was eighteenth century. I used to live in Allington before I moved to Lavister, and

I remember reading somewhere that the mill house converted to a hotel after the railway station was set up in Rosset. It's a shame that it was closed again. The station I mean. I think because of that damned Beeching report that advised the government to close thousands of railway stations. Rossett being one of them. I still get upset about it.'

'Anyway, you mentioned deeds,' Deborah steered the conversation away from the railway. 'I don't suppose you can remember the names of previous owners or anything about them or anything else about *The Peacock*?'

'I'm afraid I've forgotten a lot, but I will be delighted to dig out some stuff for you if you want to come back in a couple of days. Obviously before this flaming' lockdown on Friday?' He sighed.

Deborah didn't want to be dragged into a fruitless discussion about the lockdown. She hurried on. 'Thanks. I'll give you my mobile number, perhaps you can text me?'

'It will be my pleasure.'

As Deborah scrabbled in her bag for a notebook and pen, Kirsty sidled up closer to the bar beaming at the landlord, 'And would you happen to have a map showing the land when it was built?'

'I think there is a map with the title deeds. I'll have a look. He smiled at Kirsty, 'is there anything else ladies? Can I get you another drink?'

'We have to go now. Thanks for your help. But please let us know if you have found anything? Here's my contact details, I've included my email address,' Deborah said.

The landlord waved his hand as the four moved towards the door. 'The name's Dennis by the way.'

'Well I think that was worth the effort,' Kirsty said as they walked across the car park. 'I enjoyed my meal too.'

'Perhaps we should have lunch in *The Miller* tomorrow, and perhaps try *The Trevalyn* on Friday,' suggested Jessica. 'Who knows what we could discover. I haven't been there for such a long time. It will be a treat before... lockdown!' They all said the word with a groan.

'*The Miller* may not be as old as the other pubs, but it's still over a century and a half in age. We don't know how old our ghost is, or where it came from, so I don't think we should write it off yet,' Deborah mused as they got into her car.

'I can't make lunch tomorrow. I've got a bowls match at Gresford. Terry is on the team too.'

'Does that mean you might win another bottle of Chablis?' Kirsty smiled.

'No, it's a friendly. No prizes this time.'

'I can't make it either. I promised I would help out at the stables. Tina and Jeff have offered to do lunch.'

'Whilst you are there maybe you could find out a bit more about the secret lovers you told us about,' her sister said with a meaningful grin. Meanwhile Deborah and I can do some detective work at *The Miller*. Perhaps Grace or some of the others will want to come.'

At supper time, Shirley told them that her friend Gail had cancelled the cheese and wine party because everyone had said they didn't want to risk catching the virus.

'It looks like a lot of my other social events have been cancelled too,' she complained. 'Tony and I had tickets for a concert in Chester next week.'

Joy's face fell. 'I hope our concert tickets in Liverpool next month haven't been cancelled.'

Shirley twiddled with her beads. 'You might be lucky. At least we'll get a refund.'

At half past seven, everyone gathered in the piano room. A coal and wood fire burned in the grate, re-stoked several times since Deborah lit it a few hours earlier, for the benefit of her student. The warmth and the reassuring glow of the flames provided a comforting mantle that covered the erratic emotions running around the room.

On the coffee table in front of Deborah, Shirley, Tony and Kirsty, were two opened bottles of wine. Terry picked up one and topped up his and Joy's glasses. He offered to do the same for his companions.

'Not for me,' Grace assured him from her arm chair by the fire. She had a good view of the coffee table. Her husband sat in an armchair opposite her. He had re-arranged both chairs so they could watch for anything untoward. He was aware that he and Grace were the only occupants of the house who had not witnessed any strange occurrences. Both of them were more uneasy than they cared to admit to each other.

'I'll have a drop more mate.' Simon got up to take the bottle from Terry, topped up his glass then offered it to Jessica who was sharing a sofa with Joy and Terry.

'We may as well start this one,' Kirsty said. 'Why don't you keep that bottle over there with you, save getting up all the time?'

Terry put the bottle on the small table in front of him. It was one of a nest of three that Joy had brought to the house.

'There's plenty more wine in the kitchen. Tony and I have stocked up with as much as we could carry.'

'Are we expecting to see the spectre move two bottles of wine from two tables?' Shirley asked. 'And if we do see something what should we do? I mean do we get up and follow it, or do we make a grab for it?'

'I think we should talk to it!' Joy said.

'Talk to it?' Joy met Shirley's inquiring gaze.

'Yes, why not. So far, those of us who have witnessed flying wine bottles,' she stopped to grin at the notion, 'have been so shocked that we didn't bother to speak. So, I think we should say something like, 'Hey what are you doing?'

Terry at the side of her laughed, 'and what will you do if it answers you?'

Undeterred, Joy turned to her husband and fixed him a scornful look, 'I'll be pleased.'

'Will you?'

'I've always been fascinated by ghosts.'

'Since when? I didn't know that. Have you been holding out on me with some extra sensory powers?' He prodded her in the ribs. 'You are real aren't you?'

Joy wriggled away from him causing her to spill a drop of her wine on to her hand. 'Terry stop it!'

'Oops sorry. Don't waste the good wine. Anyway, I'm not sure I want to talk to a ghost.'

'I don't to want to either, but actually I did try,' Deborah admitted. 'The other night, I said "show yourself!" but nothing happened.'

Deborah peered over her wine glass studying Joy wiping her hand clean with a tissue. Jessica caught her eye, 'so that's what you were doing. I heard you.' Despite acknowledging Deborah's admission, with nods and docile glances, no-one else made a comment. Deborah felt an air of expectancy in the room. She suspected that her friends were secretly enjoying the notion of having a phantom in the house.

Breaking the silence, the clock in the hall struck eight o' clock. As anticipated, the wine bottle on the larger of the coffee tables veered from side to side. Shirley automatically put her hand out to anchor it. For a few seconds it remained motionless. Then on its release it began to rise again more swiftly. Before she could grab it, the bottle raised itself above their heads and glided towards the closed door to the hallway.

Mesmerised, they watched as the bottle retraced its route then soared again, as if gathering up momentum for another attempt to leave the room. For a few seconds, it hovered high over the table then rose higher into the air with an astonishing speed. Shirley's effort to reach it, knocked the coffee table over, taking with it two full glasses of wine. Fortunately both Deborah and Kirsty were still holding their own drinks.

'It's heading for the conservatory again, Joy cried. 'Quick somebody open the door to the hallway.'

Kirsty who was closest, leapt up from her chair and seized the door handle just as the wine bottle swung over her head and into the hallway. Kirsty followed it and watched it make its way to the conservatory, where fortuitously the door was sufficiently ajar for the wine bottle to slip through.

'What do you want?' Joy called. She had crept up behind Kirsty as quickly as she could get out of her hemmed position between Terry and Jessica on the sofa. The others crowded behind her.

Disappointed not to get any kind of response, Joy pushed past Kirsty and repeated her question, the door was open wide now and the rest of the companions gathered into the portico of the conservatory.

'Don't knock over my plants!' Jessica called gamely to the astonishment of Deborah, who gripped her arm for moral support.

When they heard the crash of two plant pots falling to the ground, they knew that Jessica's command had not been heeded. On the windowsill the wine bottle settled itself, as before on previous nights.

'Why did you do that?' Joy spoke to the bottle then snatched it from its post. Expecting some resistance she held it tightly, yet it remained motionless in her hands. She turned to her friends. 'It feels really cold, and yet it's been in the piano room for several hours where we know it's warm.

'I don't think you should be talking to the bottle of wine,' Shirley observed. 'I think that whatever moved it is in here. Why don't we turn off the light?'

Fear riddled with excitement fell heavily on the group at Shirley's words. Obligingly Simon who was nearest to the light switch did as she suggested. Behind him Terry stepped back to turn off the hall light.

As their eyes became accustomed to the dark, each person strained to find something on which to focus. Deborah still clutched Jessica's arm, whilst everyone else except Joy remained huddled together.

'Who are you?' They heard Joy call. No response broke the weighted silence.

'We don't wish you any harm. Just tell us what you want.' Joy was determined not to give up. She edged her way towards the windowsill and repeated her questions. Then as she put out a hand on the window pane she saw a shape outside the glass. She shrieked.

At the sound of Joy's distress, Simon turned the light on again. Joy's hands were pressed against the window pane.

Terry pushed his way through the huddled group to get to her.

'What's up? Did you see something?' He prised her hands from the window pane and led her towards the door. The knot of friends moved backwards in one orchestrated movement into the hall, allowing Terry to guide his wife back to the piano room. The rest followed in a medley of whispers.

Joy's face was pinched. She sank onto the sofa gripping her husband's hand.

'Did you see something Love? You look terrible.' He tried to lighten the mood with a grin, but she wasn't in the mood for humour.

'It was something outside, or rather inside and outside. It's like I saw a kind of shape slip through the glass and join another shape on the outside. It became one large mass that faded into the night.'

Grace breathed slowly. 'Does this mean we've really got two ghosts?'

Joy nodded. Her bright eyes trailed the room noting the array of astonished expressions of her companions.

'Did you hear anything?' Kirsty asked. She moved to sit next to Joy, where she grasped one of her cold hands.

'No, I didn't hear anything at all but I felt some kind of energy pulse through the room and then just as suddenly leave. It was at the same time as I grabbed the bottle of wine. I think as soon as the bottle steadied itself on the windowsill, the force, or whatever you call it, slipped through the glass pane. When I picked up the bottle I felt nothing.'

'That's peculiar,' Shirley remarked. 'When I tried to grasp it, just now, I felt a kind of aura in the room, yet the other day, when I lifted the bottle off the windowsill that sense of energy had gone.'

'I had the same experience,' Jessica said.

'Anybody else?' Deborah asked tentatively. 'Kirsty you saw it the same time as Dan?'

'Yes, but I didn't try to remove it. We left it until the next day, I think. Oh no. I remember now. Jessica came down and she lifted it.'

'Yes, that's right. I didn't notice anything.'

'So what do you think it means?' Grace asked.

Deborah took a deep breath, 'After our discussions today and what with the bits of information we have all picked up, I think we have two phantoms, perhaps lovers, I don't know, who meet every night around this time. The significance of the wine bottle I can't explain.'

'I think that's plausible, but despite taking into consideration what the landlord of *The White Hart* told us, we really don't know who they are and whether they are of this century or the last,' Jessica added. 'They could even be several centuries old.'

'But either way, the phantoms could have connections to *The Peacock* and maybe another pub?' Tony suggested.

'Something like that,' Deborah acknowledged. 'But it is all conjecture. We are not even sure of the age of this building. If you consider the other inns in the area of similar construction, our house could be several hundred years old. *The White Hart* is fourteenth century, and the house at the stables, that Tina and

Jeff own is thirteenth century. *The Trevalyn* is more or less the same age, whereas *The Miller* is mid nineteenth century.'

'And I shouldn't wonder that they all have their own ghosts?' Tony frowned. 'I tried to find out some history regarding *The Golden Lion*. There must be ghosts there too. Apparently, it was also used for hearing court cases, just like *The White Hart.*' Offenders were sentenced to death for a variety of crimes. If you ask me, Rossett's pubs are full of ghosts. It's just unfortunate for us we have one swinging bottles of wine around.'

Deborah managed a weak smile as did the rest of her companions. 'I can't dispute that, but what I'm getting at is, that the landlord of *The White Hart* told us of a scandal of some sort between someone from this house and a person or persons from one of the other inns. He said he thought it might have been *The Miller*. I think we need to try to find out the names and to pinpoint a date. He mentioned the Slaters and it was during the eighteen hundreds.'

Simon got up, went out to the conservatory and returned with the half bottle of wine. 'We may as well finish this. I could do with another drink after that little episode. I don't mind telling you I'm gobsmacked.'

'Good idea, I'll fetch another one from the kitchen,' Terry said. He returned five minutes later with two bottles and a bowl of potato crisps. The temporary bustling that followed with replenishing glasses and passing around snacks helped to lighten the atmosphere. The conversation turned to how to discover more information.

'Did you mention the gravestone to the landlord?' Terry asked.

'We didn't get round to that,' Deborah answered. 'In fact we were careful to not mention the ghost either, but Dennis guessed we were being haunted.' Deborah caught Jessica's eye as she imparted that snippet.

Jessica inclined her head slightly with agreement and took up the tale.

'Dennis seems as genuinely interested about *The Golden Peacock* as we are. He suggested we go to *The Miller* for some research, but I think that going there may not give us the answers we're looking for Debbie. I think we'd better go to *The Trevalyn Inn* tomorrow for our lunch. I have a notion something is lurking there waiting for us to find out.'

Attention swivelled towards Jessica at this suggestion.

'Why do you say that?' Deborah asked.

'It's just a feeling I have. I remember talking to someone who drinks at *The Trevalyn* regularly. He told me some tales about that place, some of it unpleasant. Unfortunately, I didn't take much notice at the time, so I can't really recall anything, sorry. In any case, I would like to go there again, the history of the place intrigues me.'

'Fine by me, Deborah said. 'I'm interested in the history too. Anybody else fancy lunch tomorrow at *The Trevalyn?*'

CHAPTER THIRTEEN

Thursday lunch times at *The Trevalyn Inn* offered a "Two for One" lunch deal. This proved popular with the locals, and so tables got booked up very quickly.

The harassed bar attendant informed Deborah that they would have to wait at least twenty minutes for a table. Social distancing had made it more difficult to accommodate all their customers.

'Quick, let's stand in that corner by the window,' Jessica said carrying their drinks as she spoke. Deborah followed, pulling her shoulder bag to her chest to avoid pushing into anyone.

'They seem to be doing well for trade, I wonder if the lockdown tomorrow has got anything to do with it, beside the food deal.'

'Could be. It's just as well there's only two of us, we'd have to wait a lot longer if the others had decided to come with us.' Jessica took a long drink of her lime and soda. 'That's better. I was thirsty.' Examining her companion's face she saw that Deborah's attention was focused on something that was on the wall above Jessica's head. She turned around to look at it too.

'An old painting of *Trevalyn Hall*,' Deborah commented leaning closer to read the inscription underneath. Dated Sixteen forty-nine. Probably a copy.'

'I think the hall was built during the fifteen hundreds. This must have been painted much later. That's the year Cromwell signed the death warrant of Charles the first.'

'Is it? Since when did you become an expert on the civil war?' Deborah smiled.

'I'm not. Just one of those things I remembered from a quiz show I watched. It just stuck in my head.'

'The signature on the painting is *S. F. Milton.*' Deborah propped herself on the window ledge to check the fine lettering. 'I've never heard of him or her. Perhaps it was a local painter.'

Jessica drained her glass and caught the eye of the bar attendant who waved them through to the adjoining room. A table had been laid for them.

'Can I get you some more drinks?' The bar attendant managed a smile as she took their order for food. She appeared less stressed now that some of the customers were leaving.

'Just a bottle of mineral water for me please,' Jessica replied. Debbie?

'Lemonade and lime please.'

Jessica surveyed the wood panelled room and timber beams across the ceiling. 'It's similar to the way *The Golden Peacock* used to be and how *The White Hart is now,*' she commented approvingly.

'They have a lot of pictures on the walls. I wouldn't mind looking at them later, after we've had our food.' Deborah glanced at the grandfather clock which had just chimed the half hour.

'That clock looks like the one you brought to our house. I wonder if it's as old as yours?' She liked the sound of saying 'our house.'

Jessica got up to appraise the clock, though made no comment. She claimed to have some expertise in antiques. Deborah watched her fondly but didn't bother to join her. She was more interested in their quest for knowledge about the paranormal. From her seat, she

139

surveyed the room looking for clues. Meanwhile her friend sat down then checked her mobile for messages. Presently they were served with their food.

Jessica pierced a chip with her fork, holding it in mid-air, 'We need to ask some questions about the history of this place, and try to guide the conversation into ghosts and what have you.' She stared into Deborah's face and laughed.

'Less than a week ago, I didn't believe in ghosts, neither did you! Now here we are, not only accepting our lovely home is haunted, but we're discussing the possibility of having two phantoms! Honestly, I really don't know what to say. I suppose if you believe in one ghost, you might as well believe there are more.'

Deborah chuckled. 'You're right. And it seems the rest of the gang have accepted that we're haunted. From that point of view I'm relieved.'

'What that we're haunted?' Jessica grinned mischievously.

'No, I mean I'm glad the others aren't spooked. I had a horrible dread that we were going to be forced to move or that some of our friends would want to re-locate. It could have got awkward. I feel responsible in a way. It was my idea to buy the pub.'

Jessica put a reassuring hand on Deborah's arm.

'No-one was forced to do it. You were quite clear with your proposition, and as I've said before, everyone is content. Even me! Though I would like to get rid of that wretched ghost! Or ghosts!'

'I thought you said you were content,' Deborah laughed at the grim determination on Jessica's face.

'I am. But I'm not letting a destructive banshee mess up my seed compost. It has to go!'

By the time they'd finished their first course, there were many vacant tables. Half way through eating her apple pie and cream, Deborah's mobile rang. She struggled to get it out of her jacket pocket which was hanging over the back of her chair.

'Hello.' She glanced across at Jessica and silently mouthed, 'Dennis.'

Jessica frowned trying to think who Dennis might be. She listened to Deborah's side of the conversation and realised she was speaking to the landlord of *The White Hart*.

'So what did he want?' Jessica asked. She put down her desert spoon and wiped her mouth with her paper serviette.

'He said he's found the deeds to his pub and has written down the names of the previous owners over the last two hundred years. He's also got a map that shows the parcel of land where *The White Hart* was built and the landowners who bordered it.' She gave her friend a wry smile. 'One of the surrounding landowners was a wealthy aristocrat. I think he told us that to hook us in.'

'Hmm. As if we needed one. So are we going over there now to have a look?'

'I think we should. He said he'd email the list of names to me and that he'd scan the map so that we could have a copy of that too, but I think it might be better to see the hard copy, the image might not be so good on my lap top.'

'Right, but first of all let's see what we can find out about this place. It's almost deserted now. I wonder if the owner is around to talk to.' Jessica signalled to the original bar attendant, who looked far more relaxed. She brought them the bill. 'Everything alright?'

'Yes lovely thanks. We're just admiring the décor and all the pictures. Do you know much about the history of this place?' Jessica asked.

'Lots of customers ask us that. My dad has put together a little leaflet about the place. I will go and see if I can find one for you.'

Two minutes later she was back and handed over a folded A4 piece of thin card with a photograph of the inn on the front. Inside was a short account of the inn's history and Jessica's eyes latched on to the word ghost.

'So is this place haunted?' she asked, catching Deborah's eye.

'According to my dad's research it is. But I haven't seen anything. We've lived here for ten years now. My dad hasn't seen anything either, but he's hoping to,' she giggled. 'He thinks we may have disturbed it when we did the refurbishment and now it's sulking.'

They joined in her amusement, then Deborah asked if there was a story attached to the supposed haunting.

The young woman stood with her hand on her hip as she relished repeating the tale that she had obviously recounted on several occasions.

'The story goes that round about eighteen hundred and seventy some workmen were staying here. They were employed to do maintenance on the railway that used to run through Rossett and on to Chester. Apparently one of the men fell in love with some girl, I don't know who but she was rich and her parents forbade her to see him.' The woman sighed. 'Same old story, you know. The man wasn't good enough for her, blah blah! Anyway, one day the poor soul had an accident on the railway and was killed. That probably satisfied the girl's rich parents, but she was broken hearted and refused to accept his death. Some people say she kept hanging around here looking for him, clinging to the hope he was still alive. Eventually she was taken away to live with her married sister. I don't know what happened to her after that.'

'So where did her sister live?' Deborah asked.

'That bit I don't know.'

'What were their names?' Jessica asked.

'He was called James. I don't know hers.'

Deborah risked a quick glance at Jessica who had taken in a sharp breath at the sound of James' name.

'Is he buried in Rossett church yard?' Deborah asked suddenly.

The young bar attendant looked taken aback at such a question. 'You know, I really don't know. He might be. I've never thought about it. I'll have to ask Dad. He's busy in the kitchen at the moment. It's been frantic. I have to go now.' Before they could ask any more questions she left them to speculate.

Jessica let out a long sigh. 'Intriguing though it is, we're not getting much further forward. We know what happened to *our* James. It was a common name.' She seized her coat from the back of her chair.

'Come on, let's go and see what our friend Dennis has to say.'

On the way out, Deborah took some photographs of *The Trevalyn Inn* using her mobile. She took a few shots from various perspectives, angling her device in various positions. 'You can see where the alterations to the house were made,' she said pointing to the gable end of the old inn. 'Perhaps that's where the railway man's old room was when he worked here poor chap.'

Jessica contemplated the building sadly. 'More than likely he shared the room with other workers. Tragic. To be far from home and then dying in an accident at work.'

She started the car and drove two miles down narrow country lanes to join the Chester road. Deborah enjoyed the view through the window. 'To think all these fields and meadows have remained unspoilt over the centuries. I know that they were probably used for various types of crops as the years passed, but the overall scene is virtually unchanged. I never appreciated it until now, living so close to it.'

'I know what you mean. I began to appreciate it more when I returned to live in Pulford. Those twenty years living in London after I married Pete taught me that. I didn't realise how much I'd missed this place. I always thought we would return here together... But I was wrong!' She turned into *The White Hart* carpark, chose a spot and braked sharply. Deborah guessed that Jessica's aggressive handling of the handbrake was because she'd been reminded of her deceased ex-husband, who had deserted her for a much younger woman.

'Perhaps it's Pete who's haunting us. I hope he's rotting in hell!' Jessica laughed harshly and marched in to the pub, Deborah close behind.

'Ah, it's my two favourite ladies,' Dennis greeted them. Jessica turned to look around the deserted bar then back again, to meet the landlord's steady gaze.

'You can cut that crap for a start,' she admonished. Deborah put a warning hand on her friend's arm.

'I'm sure my friend didn't mean to speak so sharply,' she addressed Dennis. 'We're getting overwhelmed with things...'

Jessica shook her friend's arm away. 'Yes, yes I was a bit abrupt. Sorry.'

'No worries. I say these things without thinking. It's just a bit of banter with me. I can see you are independent women. No offence intended.' He held out his hand to Deborah and then to Jessica. To Deborah's relief she managed a genuine smile. For her part she enjoyed a little harmless flattery. Jessica on the other hand felt it was sexist.

'I know you're interested in what I have discovered about this old pub and the outlying area. Why don't we go over to that table in front of the window and I will bring out some of the stuff for you to look at, seeing as it's quiet in here for now.'

Within seconds of finding chairs to make themselves comfortable, Dennis sat down with an assortment of documents; some of them rolled up like wallpaper, others bound in the red tape ubiquitous of a solicitor's office.

'Here, first of all look at this,' he said. He unfolded the deeds to *The White Hart*. These documents are old and brittle, yet this section gives a fascinating account of previous owners from seventeen hundred and eighty six. Thank goodness everything is recorded on computers these days. The records for earlier are extremely brittle so I got a computerised version. As you can see over the centuries there have been several landlords. There seems to have been a long line of Baxters up to seventeen eighty six. Then the Trellicks and after them the Mathews. More Mathews then Rowlands and now Balantyne, that's me - Dennis Balantyne.

'Balantyne?' Jessica appraised him openly smiling. 'Do you mean like the whisky?'

Dennis's eyes gleamed. Not exactly the same spelling, I have no connection with that distillery, regrettably.'

'Shame,' Jessica muttered. Deborah nodded her agreement.

'Now look at this map that came with the deeds,' Dennis continued. He was clearly fascinated by the history, Deborah observed. She studied his thick black wavy hair interspersed with grey at the temples, as he bent over the document. A few more stray greys tufted over his ears. She felt a whisper of attraction to him that took her by surprise. She shook her head to make the feeling go away.

'Are you alright Debbie?' Jessica asked, looking up suddenly to witness her friend's flustered face.

'Yes of course. It's fascinating.' Deborah leaned over the map to follow the line that Dennis had traced with the back of a spoon handle.

'As you can see,' Dennis informed them, 'there are clear boundary lines between my land and the land of other households. To the South, more or less is the old mill, see here is the River Alyn, and to the east is *The Trevalyn Inn*. Now over here to the west is the boundary between my place and yours, as it was then. There's also a network of footpaths and country lanes between the four households. The Chester Road was just a one horse and carriage wide lane in those days just like the one leading to your old pub. I understand from the locals that it was called the *Peacock Grove*, yet it is marked here *The Peacock Poste House*.'

Both women frowned. '*The Peacock Poste House?* I thought it was *The Peacock Coaching Inn* before it became known *as The Golden Peacock Inn!*' Deborah looked up to catch Dennis's eye. His own eyes gleamed triumphantly lingering on Deborah's face a few seconds longer than necessary. Jessica was quick to witness the chemistry between the pair, and stifled a grin.

'It was indeed a coaching inn, but it was also used as a place for receiving and despatching mail. That's probably why this plan refers to it as the *Peacock Poste House.*'

'Wow! That's amazing,' Jessica enthused. Deborah agreed, genuinely interested.

'Now then look at this!' Dennis said proudly. He unsheathed the roll of parchment carefully. 'When I bought this place six years ago, my wife and I got very interested in the history, and we sourced these old maps. This one shows the original buildings and *The Golden Peacock Coaching Inn* is marked here.' The two women peered at the spot where Dennis placed his finger.

'Absolutely amazing. Thank you Dennis.' Both women acknowledged the man's efforts.

'Did you know that the picture of the peacock on the hanging sign is so that people could recognise that they were in the right place?'

'What do you mean?' Jessica asked.

'Pub signs were very important because most people couldn't read. So if they could recognise a picture, they would know they had found the right place.' He stopped, enjoying their ignorance. 'This is why you see so many *White Horses; Red Dragons; Golden Lions* and so on.'

'Well I never,' Deborah said. I've seen some strange pub signs too on my travels; like '*The Swan with Two necks; Axe and Cleaver and The Barley Mow.*'

Dennis smiled, 'there you go.'

147

Jessica shook his hand. 'Thank you very much Dennis.'

'Yes, thank you,' Deborah added. 'We are trying to get hold of our deeds so we can do some research too. We left them with our solicitor and so far they haven't released them. I suppose they will be too busy now, what with the lockdown and everything.'

Dennis nodded. 'More than likely. Have you paid for them yet? If your cheque hasn't gone through they aren't likely to send them soon.'

Deborah exchanged a worried glance with Jessica. 'I wasn't informed of a fee!'

Dennis laughed. 'If I were you I'd ring them, though as you say with the lockdown tomorrow, they may have other things on their mind. 'He began to carefully fold his documents away. 'Now then is there anything else I can do for you?'

They both shook their heads.

'I take it you haven't figured out who is haunting your house?'

Jessica laughed. 'You know something? I'd completely forgotten about that blasted ghost!'

'Ah ha. So I was right. You are haunted. Well I'll be damned! You might have told me.'

'We're sorry,' Deborah said. 'It's been a shock to us and we didn't want to tell too many people in case they thought we were barking mad.'

'And neither did we want nosey people turning up,' added Jessica.

'You can trust me. I'm naturally curious, but I wouldn't start a stampede. So why don't you tell me what's been going on, and I will try to find out more, maybe one of my regulars knows something?'

Deborah's glance at Jessica gave unhesitating consent. Between the two of them they related everything that had happened. Dennis was a rapt listener, and after they had finished both felt some relief. Unfortunately the pub began to fill up and so they couldn't discuss things further. Dennis was needed behind the bar. They decided to go.

On their way out of the pub, Dennis called to them as he pulled a pint for a customer. 'I have your contact details, so I'll get in touch if I come up with anything.'

Deborah sighed heavily as she got into Jessica's Mustang. 'Well, that was an interesting afternoon one way or another.' She checked her watch. 'Hell look at the time, it's quarter to five.'

'Do you fancy Dennis?' Jessica asked abruptly.

'Of course not. Why do you ask? Deborah kept her attention firmly on the road as her friend manoeuvred their way out of the car park.

'I thought I saw a flicker of interest between the two of you.'

'He's married.'

'He might not be. He mentioned a wife, but she could be in the past.'

Jessica scrutinised her friend's face and decided not to say anything more about Dennis. She changed the subject and discussed the information they had gleaned that afternoon.

Outside *The Golden Peacock*, Jessica parked her car next to Kirsty's Volkswagen as they arrived simultaneously. Jessica examined her sister's face.

'Have you been mucking out all afternoon?' She challenged her incredulously.

Kirsty flushed guiltily. 'There's a lot of work to do besides mucking out, and I have been for a ride too.'

149

'Don't they have paid help?'

Kirsty tossed her head, turning her back on her sister and Deborah to reach for her bag. She slung it over her shoulder then reached into the car again for her holdall containing her muddy boots from the back seat.

'Yes of course, besides Tina and Jeff, there's Rosemary, Donna and...Leslie.'

'Leslie? Who's Leslie? I haven't heard you mention him before? Or is it a she?'

Kirsty walked off in front of them to get indoors. She laughed as she called over her shoulder, 'Oh he's definitely male. He started working there a few months ago. Anyway less of the interrogation, I'm going to get out of this clobber.' She strode quickly through the kitchen to the hall and then ran up the stairs. Deborah felt there was something shifty about her behaviour. She brushed the thought aside, she needed a cup of tea.

CHAPTER FOURTEEN

Over dinner, Deborah and Jessica related what they'd heard at *The Trevalyn Inn* about the tragic death of the railway worker.

'I remember the old railway station in Rossett,' Simon remarked. 'I used to live on Station Road when I was young, before we moved to Gresford. It's all closed down now. Sad.'

'I think we all remember those days,' Deborah remarked, 'what about you Tony?'

'Yes, I spent most of my youth in the south of England, and I remember other railway stations meeting the same fate.'

'The question is, 'Joy asked impatiently; 'Is the poor railway worker connected in some way to our ghost? Maybe he and his lover met secretly here and are now haunting us? It would be useful to know whereabouts he was killed. If he was working near here, she may have walked to *The Peacock* to meet him.' She tapped her chin with her fingers and added, 'I don't think the railway line came very close to this house.'

Terry responded with his own theory. 'The accident may not have happened actually on the line. Railway maintenance involves all kinds of tasks. I think you might be right Love; I don't think the rail workers would have been working in the vicinity of this house. However, I'm wondering, that if some of the workers were staying at *The Trevalyn Inn*, that it's plausible that some of the others may have lodged here? They may have helped the lovers to meet secretly in *The Golden Peacock*?'

Terry's observation was met with some excitement.

'Do you think you could find that out Joy?' Jessica asked.

'I'll give it my best shot tomorrow. My last chance because the library will be shut tomorrow evening for the damn lockdown.'

'I'm sick of that word already, 'Shirley groaned. 'That's all I hear at work.'

'And tomorrow is the last chance to go to *The Miller* for lunch and do some more research,' Kirsty reminded them. 'Shall we all go? The pubs will be closed from six o' clock tomorrow night. Even if we don't find out any more information about our unwanted guests, we can at least have a last fling.'

Simon stroked his chin before he answered, 'Much though I'd like to, I think we ought to finish what we can with the outside work, and get enough material from the builders ready for the repair work in the cellar and so forth. What do you reckon Terry?' He shot a sidelong glance at Tony as he spoke. He knew that the man was not as mobile as himself and Terry, but didn't want to exclude him from their plans.

'Yes, I agree. What do you think Tony?'

'I'm happy to stay and help if I can. I'm not completely useless.'

'Are you sure?' Shirley said patting his hand. 'I mean about staying here not about being useless!' She laughed.

Tony smiled, 'of course.

'Do you think those sisters and their brother who lived at *The Miller* hold the key to our mystery?' Grace asked. She didn't wait for an answer though acknowledged Deborah's and Jessica's affirmative nod of their heads. 'I was thinking, if we knew their names, we could call out to our ghost tonight, when the wine bottle goes for a flight.' She giggled nervously.

'Good idea, Deborah said. 'If Joy could find out their names, it might help us solve the mystery. I was also thinking about the names of all the daughters and sons of those merchants who lived nearby during the time the railways were built. Shall we say... mid eighteen hundreds? That's if our assumption that the railway worker's accident has anything to do with our mystery spectres. It's a starting point anyway. Is that too much to research?' Deborah raised a quizzical eyebrow at Joy.

'I think that shouldn't be too difficult, the problem now, is time. If we're going to *The Miller* for lunch, I might not have enough time in Wrexham library. It could take hours to find what we are looking for, that's if there is anything to find. There's stuff on the internet but just snippets. I was hoping for something more.'

'Why don't we come with you to help?' Deborah suggested. 'If we go early in the morning, we would have a few hours before lunch. You'd have to point us in the right direction for the reference books. It could be fun.'

'Not me, Sorry. I've got two people coming tomorrow morning for haircuts. Their last chance before, sorry to mention - the dreaded lockdown, and all that,' Grace informed them. 'I can meet you at *The Miller* at one o' clock though.

'Thank goodness you're a hairdresser Grace, we'll all need our hair doing too, Jessica remarked.

'I will be in work of course,' Shirley reminded them.

The clock in the hall struck quarter to eight. The conversation came to an abrupt end as they listened to the chimes. Furtive glances leapt from one apprehensive face to another. Deborah sipped her red wine. Presently Joy broke the silence, uttering the words she knew most of them were thinking;

'Shall we sit in the piano room and see if something happens?'

They quickly cleared away the dishes from the table and took them to the kitchen. Jessica loitered in the conservatory and then made a snap decision. She removed her seed pots from the window ledge and put them carefully on to a piece of cardboard on the floor. Kirsty watched her with approval.

'Good idea. At least we won't have to clear up a mess in the morning, I hope.'

In the piano room everyone sat more or less in the same position as the previous night. Yet the tension was not so heavy as before, Deborah noted. The atmosphere was more like excitement. Just a few minutes before eight o clock, Jessica suggested they remove the bottle of wine from the table in front of her and put it elsewhere.

'Won't that aggravate the ghost?' Grace asked timidly. 'Isn't it better to leave things alone?'

'I just thought we could test it. See if it picked it up from somewhere else in the room,' Jessica said.

'Are you still looking for some scientific explanation for all this?' Terry asked her.

Before she could answer, or remove the wine, the clock struck eight. Jessica sat back in her chair holding her glass of wine. She decided to leave things as they were.

As expected, the bottle of wine glided to the end of the table, raised itself and sailed towards the door to the hallway. This time it had been left open. Just when the bottle reached the doorway, Grace's mobile chimed *Johann Strauss's 'Blue Danube'*. To the astonishment of all, the bottle swivelled around mid-air then hovered high over the coffee table where Grace sat. She took her mobile out of her pocket and turned it off quickly.

When the music stopped the wine bottle soared higher in the air, faster than usual on its journey to the conservatory. It tapped against the window several times, then, as previously it settled on the windowsill.

'It was more aggressive this time. Did you see how it hurled itself against the glass? I thought it was going to break the window pane.' Terry commented. He had been the first one to follow the bottle, Joy on his heels. She had intended to speak out again, but remembering her fright the night before, her bravado faded.

'Yes, I thought so too,' she said.

The others agreed they had noticed a difference in the wine bottle's performance. One by one they gravitated back to the piano room where Grace was reading her mobile message.

'At least our plants are safe,' Jessica said triumphantly.

'It's Dan, he's left me a message to ring him,' Grace explained as she turned to Simon. She keyed in his contact number and moved to stand behind the piano to talk to him.

'Do you think the ring tone on Grace's mobile has any significance to the change of direction of the bottle?' Shirley asked no-one in particular.'

'It could be just a coincidence,' Tony replied. 'We could observe the action more closely tomorrow, since it doesn't look like the bottle is going anywhere.' He forced a smile. 'Neither are we after tomorrow.'

Terry groaned, 'don't remind me. All our bowls matches have been cancelled for the foreseeable future.' Joy sighed, catching his disappointment. She sat cross legged on the floor.

'What about you Kirsty? Did you find out if you can still go riding?' Shirley asked.

Aware of her sister scrutinising her, Kirsty directed her response to Shirley.

'The riding school will close as from four o'clock tomorrow afternoon, but the horses still need to be fed and exercised and what have you. So I will go and help.'

'Is that allowed?' Jessica asked.

Forced to turn to face her sister, Kirsty nodded. 'Yes, obviously we will have to social distance, we have been doing that lately, anyway, and we started to wear masks.'

'But you are a volunteer, surely you don't need to go. Don't they have employees to do all that mucking out and things?'

'Yes, Donna, Leslie and Rosemary. However, Rosemary's parents are anxious about her working during the lockdown. She's only sixteen, and works part-time at weekends and after school. So she won't be coming. I said I would help. It's not as if I will be coming into contact with members of the public, because there won't be any.'

Jessica eyed her shrewdly, 'So this Leslie you mentioned and Donna will continue?'

Again Kirsty avoided eye contact with her sister. 'Yes. They work full time, and live locally, so they will continue. We can't neglect the horses.'

Before anyone could ask Kirsty any more questions, Grace moved closer to the group still clutching her mobile in her hand. Simon stood at the side of her and after a little hesitation informed them all that Dan had been furloughed from his job.

'Unfortunately, he's lost a place to stay too. The hotel have decided to take advantage of the lockdown to completely refurbish the place. This means that as from tomorrow night, he will have no job and nowhere to stay.'

'That's mean,' Jessica said immediately. 'What a rotten thing to do. We've all got to help each other. Couldn't they at least find him space somewhere in the hotel?'

'Apparently not. They're moving into their holiday cottage in Llandudno as from tomorrow afternoon, so that the builders, renovators or whatever, can start. Apparently they need a new roof and most of it will affect Dan's room. He lives in the converted attic.'

'I thought the construction industry were not allowed to work either. In the lockdown I mean?' Tony ruminated.

'Certain restrictions apply,' Terry said. 'It depends on the job. But generally they can continue to work.'

'I was wondering if Dan could stay here?' Grace asked quietly. 'Simon and I would pay his running expenses, and Dan would pull his weight with the domestic chores. He could cook for us too?'

'That's a good idea,' Deborah said instantly. 'I don't mind at all.'

Deborah's response was followed immediately with enthusiastic agreement from the others. Grace's relief was obvious as she smiled. 'Thanks everyone. It's good to know I have such wonderful friends.'

'Talking of Dan, didn't he say something about a friend of his whose father built conservatories?' Joy asked suddenly, looking up.

Deborah, roused from her thoughts about Dan's circumstances turned her attention to Joy's comment.

'Yes he did, and didn't he say he had a supernatural experience here when fitting the conservatory? I'd forgotten all about it.'

'We ought to try to get hold of him tomorrow,' Joy said.

Shirley sighed. 'It seems we've got a lot to do tomorrow. We should make a plan of some kind to make sure we don't waste time.'

Joy got up to get a writing pad and a pen. Setting up timetables and organising things was something she loved to do. 'Right, let's see. Plan of action; I will write down the things we need to do, the time needed and who is going to do it.' She looked up as she saw Terry make his way to the kitchen.

'Just getting more booze,' he called.

'With the information we have, I think we should concentrate on researching stuff from the early nineteenth century to present day. I reckon we should split into two's. Two of us need to spend at least three hours in the library; somebody, should make contact with the conservatory man, and then two of us go and see him.' Joy took a breath then focused on Deborah.

'Debbie, do you think you could follow up your phone call to our solicitors to ask about the deeds?'

Deborah sat up with a jolt. She'd forgotten again about ringing the solicitors. 'Yes of course. Someone remind me in the morning, I will do it first thing.'

'And hopefully you will be able to call tomorrow to pick them up, or at least get the info we want,' Joy continued.

'Anything else?'

'Food?' Grace suggested.

'I think we've got more than enough essentials and probably enough non essentials to last a couple of weeks,' Shirley advised. 'As most of you guys are seventy or thereabouts we would be able to get home deliveries if necessary. I don't mind going to get a few odds and ends if we need something.'

'The only thing I can think of is our health,' Tony said. 'Obviously we need to protect ourselves against this terrible virus, but I'm thinking of other stuff, like dentists and feet. As you know I am a qualified, though retired chiropodist. I have my tools, so if you need help with your corns and callouses or what have you, I'm happy to do what I can.'

'Hell, I hadn't thought of that, but thanks Tony. I appreciate it. Actually I think I have a corn coming on my right foot so maybe you can have a look at that some time tomorrow?' Jessica asked. She caught Joy's frown and shrugged, 'Time permitting!'

'And it goes without saying that I will do your hair, as usual. I had to say no to some of my old customers over the phone today. They wanted to come tomorrow night. I've already got Joyce and Alison coming at four-thirty and five-thirty.'

'It's going to be a busy day tomorrow one way or another,' Terry slipped his fingers under his baseball cap to scratch his head. Wisps of grey and blonde hair protruded from underneath.

'I've had to cancel my music classes too,' Deborah sighed.

'It suddenly makes you realise what's happening across the country doesn't it?' Kirsty observed. She poured herself another glass of wine. 'Let's hope the bloomin' lockdown works.'

'Thank goodness we've got each other,' Jessica said. She smiled at Deborah and raised her glass as a tribute to her.

'And the garden,' Kirsty reminded her.

'And very soon our own boules court,' Simon announced.

'We ought to explore the cellar too when it gets a bit warmer,' Terry remarked.

'Why? Are we running out of wine already?' Jessica chortled. 'I'm not surprised the way we drink it.'

'I'm intrigued about the cellar. Who knows what else we'll find in there. But don't worry about the booze. There's plenty to keep us going for a while. We might find some more.'

'I'll drink to that,' Simon laughed.

CHAPTER FIFTEEN

Grace phoned Dan the following morning, to tell him that he could stay with them until he was able to work again. During the conversation she found out the name of the man who installed conservatories.

'He's so grateful he can stay with us,' Grace told Deborah and Jessica with a wry smile as they cleared up in the kitchen. 'He's looking forward to cooking for us too. He said he'd found an interesting vegetarian dish that involves rum! I'm not sure that appeals to me but it might meet with Shirley and Tony's satisfaction. He also said he'd help us catch the ghost!'

'Oh God, we're not turning into ghost hunters now, are we?' Deborah giggled despite herself.

'It will be very satisfying if we do,' Jessica remarked putting away dishes in the cupboard. 'Catch the ghost, I mean. I don't want to do it forever.' It was her turn to giggle. 'Did you manage to contact the conservatory bloke? I've forgotten his name.'

'Yes, his name is Graham Bailey. I've tried ringing him, but it went through to his voicemail. I'll try again now.' Grace pulled her mobile out of the pocket of her tartan trousers and punched in the number again. 'It's ringing. I hope it doesn't go straight to the...oh hello Mr. Bailey?'

She caught first Jessica's eye and then Deborah's. They stood still to listen to Grace introduce herself. Her eyes widened as she listened intently. It seemed to her observers that it took a long time before she was able to speak. Eventually, with her hand over the mouthpiece, she informed them that Mr. Bailey was in a hurry to finish a job and wanted to know if he could call to see them later that day.

'I think it would be easier, if he came to talk to us rather than discuss things over the phone?' She tilted her head on one side as she checked for her friends' agreement.

'Yes, yes, that will be fine Mr. Bailey. What time do you think you can get here?' She faced her two friends as she repeated his suggestion; five-thirty? Both nodded. Grace finished the call.

'Gosh, in the time he took to ramble on about how busy he was and how the lockdown was causing him problems, he could have told us everything we wished to know about his previous experiences here, I'm sure,' Grace laughed.

'Still, if he comes here to explain to all of us what happened, it might be better,' Deborah assured her.

'The only thing is, though, I have a client for hair styling at five-thirty, so I won't be able to talk to him when he gets here.' Grace glanced at her short auburn hair in the mirror in the hall. 'Good job I had my own hair cut before we moved in,' she gently ran her fingers through it.

'No problem, we can do the talking,' Jessica assured her. 'That's worked out well. We've got more time now to do other things on Joy's list. She and Kirsty have already gone to the library.'

Grace dried her hands and opened the kitchen door to the hall, 'I've got to prepare things for my clients this morning. I'll see you all later for lunch.'

Deborah followed Grace out of the kitchen and sat on a chair by the grandfather clock to phone the solicitor's office. After a very lengthy discussion with one clerk in the office, then being passed on to a senior clerk, it was agreed that she could call at eleven-thirty to pick up the deeds.

'It feels as if we are doing something positive,' she confided in Jessica an hour later. They walked along the High Street in Wrexham to the solicitor's office.

'I've never been so interested in deeds before. I just thought they were a set of boring old documents necessary to purchase a house,' Jessica confessed. 'Actually they are boring if you aren't looking for the paranormal.' She grinned when they stood outside the polished front door to the Solicitor's office. It had once been a three storey town house.

Gittins, Worth and Smith nestled between a Chartered Accountant on one side and an Estate Agency on the other. Jessica traced her fingers over the brass plate that proudly told them the name of the legal agents inside.

'Come on. Let's see if we can shed some more light on our mysterious phantoms.'

In the reception area of the solicitor's office, Deborah pressed the buzzer at an opaque glass window set in the wall. She sniffed the air nostalgically whilst they waited. Despite the heavy use of furniture polish, it didn't disguise the odour of an old and musty building.

'Years ago, I came here with Clive when we bought our first house. You could smell leaden type, paper and ink then. These days they use computers and printers, yet that sense of mystery is still here. It reminds me of that small stationery shop that used to be on Regent Street.'

'Money. That's what you can smell,' Jessica replied.

'They say where there's muck there's brass. Just look around you. The floor boards are old and need

163

replacing, this hatch is probably left over from when the place was a house. At first glance you'd think the firm wasn't doing well, but the sound of activity coming from behind that glass hole in the wall belies that first impression.'

'You could be right.'

'Can I help you?' A young woman slid open the hatch.

Whilst Deborah stated their business, Jessica peered over the receptionist's shoulder to look into the office. Despite the dilapidated appearance of the décor and the bare floorboards, her roving inquisitive eyes approved of the modern equipment at the disposal of the staff. As well as the receptionist, three other employees filled the room.

Twenty minutes later they found themselves back on the high street with the precious documents safely ensconced in a brown envelope and lying flat at the bottom of Deborah's hessian shopping bag.

'That's one job done. We can either spend half an hour in the library with the other two or we can go for a quick coffee then join them at *The Miller*. What do you think?' Deborah asked.

'If it's alright with you, I would rather use the time to buy a birthday card for Richard. It isn't until next week, but I may as well get it now, whilst the shops are open. And I think there's an antique fair on in the market hall. I'd like to pop in there for a few minutes.'

'Fine by me. If you like I'll walk up to the library and join the others and see you up there. I hope they are having a fruitful search.'

As arranged, Deborah found her two friends upstairs in the reference library. Each occupied separate desks at some distance from each other. Joy was half sprawled over old maps that showed a network of disused railway lines that once connected to the coal mines around the Wrexham area. She'd set herself a task to find out how closely to *The Golden Peacock*, ran the Wrexham to Chester line.

'Hi, Debbie, I've got a bit side tracked,' Joy whispered, smiling at her pun. 'Do you want to have a look at this? I've got more reference books to look at over there on another desk. I've taken up a lot of space today.'

It wasn't long before Deborah also became fascinated with the old train routes.

At the next desk, Joy was searching for historic information relating to merchants' houses in Rossett.

Kirsty had been allocated the task of researching life in the eighteen fifties in Wales, hoping to find something relating to the Rossett and Burton area. She was absorbed in looking at pictures of *Rossett Mill* and *Marford Mill* when Deborah crept up behind her.

'Hi, those look interesting,' she whispered.

'Yes, these pictures have attracted my attention. There's one here of *Bradley Mill* too. Kirsty frowned looking over Deborah's shoulder as if she had lost something. 'Where's Jess?' she whispered.

'Getting a birthday card for Richard.'

Kirsty started to say something but changed her mind. Deborah assumed she was about to say she needed to get a birthday card for her nephew.

Joy appeared behind Kirsty, acknowledged Deborah with a nod, and then tapped Kirsty on the shoulder making her jump.

'How are you getting on?'

'I've got a bit distracted, but I think I've found some intriguing stuff which might help us. I must admit I am becoming absorbed with Rossett history. Did you know that nineteenth century artists used to come to Rossett and Marford to stay? Apparently they were inspired to paint scenes of the mills.'

'Any famous artists in particular?'

'It seems John Turner did. In fact, some of his works were bequeathed to Cardiff Museum.'

'Do you mean John Turner of the *Fighting Temeraire*?'

'The very one.' Kirsty grinned.

'Wow. That's interesting. I didn't know that.' Joy sat down and closed her notebook. 'I've made notes about some interesting facts I have found about Welsh gentry.' She paused to glance at her watch.

'I think we ought to make our way to meet Jessica and Grace at *The Miller*. It's nearly quarter to one. Jess is on her way to the car park now. According to this text I've just received from her, she was delayed in town so decided not to come here. She said she would meet us at the pub.'

Kirsty raised her eyebrows glancing at Deborah. 'Delayed? Hmm!'

In the car, Joy talked enthusiastically about what she'd discovered about the railways. As Kirsty drove them off, she was held up at the traffic lights. When the lights changed from red to amber, a man emerged from the nearby market hall. He strode off the pavement onto the zebra crossing in front of them, just as the traffic lights turned green.

'Isn't that Malcolm from the book club?' Joy stopped talking for a second, to focus on the tall man who had raised his hand to acknowledge the waiting car driver's patience. In the split second of the lights changing,

166

Malcolm recognised the occupants, but Kirsty had no option but to drive forward.

'Yes it is. What a coincidence, she said.'

Seated at the back, behind the driver, Deborah saw in the mirror, a smirk glide on Kirsty's face. She winked at Deborah which confused her. Joy continued her lecture about disused railway lines, and she soon forgot about Malcolm.

The River Alyn that ran parallel to the carpark of *The Miller* pub attracted their attention when Kirsty parked her Volkswagen. The three women leaned over the fence to watch the water flow past towards the old Rossett mill.

'Hi,' Grace joined them. 'I've just got here. One of my clients dropped me off.' She turned to admire the view. 'It's idyllic isn't it? This pub on the corner of the old stone bridge with the river running by makes a lovely scene. *The Alyn* pub on the opposite side is nice too. Didn't you go there for your birthday Debbie?"

'Yes, we had a lovely meal. I must admit, I've never been so fascinated about this part of the river before, until we started ghost hunting!' Deborah laughed. The others agreed.

'Neither have I, and when you think how many times we've stood here over the years. This is Station Road, where Simon used to live. We used to go for walks down here when we were courting.' Grace's face was dreamy. She let out a long wistful sigh.

Deborah smiled, 'you were childhood sweethearts.' She linked her arm through hers. 'Come on let's see what this place has to offer for lunch. I hope it's as good as *The Alyn.'*

The smell of hot food assailed their senses as they walked through the pub door. Jessica waved to them from a table she had reserved that morning. They spent a few minutes re-arranging an assortment of coats and bags before they eventually sat down.

Kirsty picked up the menu and sniffed the air. 'Chips. I fancy some chips!'

'I haven't seen one of these for a long time, Joy commented, eyeing the jukebox that had been set up almost alongside their table. 'Very retro.'

'Brings back some memories,' Deborah agreed.

'I wonder if they have sixties music in it?' Joy said.

'There's a lively atmosphere in here, Grace commented looking around. 'I wonder if this is because of the lockdown starting from tonight.'

'Probably. It was the same yesterday at *The Trevalyn Inn*,' Jessica confirmed. 'It was busy at *The White Hart* on Wednesday too.'

Deborah laughed. 'You know what, you and I have lunched out three times in a row. All because we are chasing phantoms.'

'Yes, but it's been pleasant all the same,' Jessica raised her glass of lemonade. 'Let's make a toast to the ghost!

'To the ghost!' A combination of glasses chinked together.

'What held you up in town?' Kirsty eyed her sister suspiciously. 'Did you meet up with someone?'
Deborah frowned as Jessica avoided her sister's eyes. She wondered if her friend had a secret lover. She dismissed the thought, yet she couldn't help thinking that Kirsty seemed to know something about her sister she wasn't sharing.

Before Jessica had chance to reply, heavy rock music drowned their conversation. A young woman with purple hair had fed the juke box with a pile of coins. Between records they managed to agree to postpone a discussion about their findings until they returned home. In any event their food order arrived and so they devoted their attention to eating.

When the music selections stopped, just the gentle hubbub of animated conversation spiked the atmosphere. Soon after, the purple haired woman, her two companions and several other customers left the restaurant.

'That table over there by the riverside window is free now, shall we move?' Jessica suggested. 'If someone else puts money in this machine we will never be able to hear ourselves speak.'

The waiter watched the five women move, waited for them to settle again and then ambled across. He began to take away the empty plates, piling them together with obvious experience.

'Can I get you ladies any more drinks or sweets?' He recited from memory a selection of deserts, then disappeared with his load of washing up and their order.

'Have you any idea if the owner of this place is around?' Deborah asked no-one in particular. 'It's a while since I've been here.'

'I believe it changed hands a year ago,' Joy said. 'Do you remember Grace, you and Simon came here with Terry and me after a bowls match, just after the new manager took over?'

'Yes. He and his wife seemed quite young. He's very interested in bowls as well as boules, I recall. He regretted that he didn't have enough land attached to the pub to compete with *Lavister Bowling Club.'*

'Is that him over there?' Joy said suddenly. They focused on a tall man smartly dressed in a suit. His loosened tie lying under the unbuttoned collar made him appear less formal.

Grace craned her neck to see him over the heads of people sitting at the next table. 'Yes, I think it is.'

'As you two have already met, do you want to remind him who you are and get him talking about his pub?' Kirsty suggested.

'I don't mind, but I doubt he's going to remember Grace and me. Still, I have discovered quite a lot about this place, so I could use it as an opening gambit. There's a possibility he's not interested in the history of the pub.'

Did you find out anything in the library about ghosts in the area?' Jessica asked, just when the waiter arrived with their desert order. He put each dish down in front of the correct person without having to ask who had ordered what.

'Good memory!' Deborah congratulated him. 'Thank you.'

'You're welcome.' He lingered for a few minutes. 'Did I hear you ask about ghosts in this pub?'

The five regarded him silently waiting for him to say something else. He looked uncomfortable. Deborah guessed he'd wished he hadn't spoken. She gave him what she thought was a disarming smile. 'This pub is ancient and we were just wondering about the history attached to it and if it is haunted. There usually is a ghost or two knocking around in old buildings isn't there?' Her companions leaned forward inspiring him to speak.

170

'Actually I think there is a ghost here.' He moved closer to their table, lowering his voice to almost a whisper. 'Ever since this place re-opened I've noticed strange goings on.'

'What kind of things?' Kirsty smiled.

'At certain times during the night I get this strange sensation behind the bar, and the floorboards creak all along the space where we store the drinks.'

'Couldn't that just be because the place is old?' Kirsty suggested craftily. 'Old floor boards do creak.'

'It only happens at a particular time though,' he insisted.

'What kind of sensation do you mean behind the bar?' Joy interrupted.

The young man turned earnestly to face her.

'It's like there's someone behind me whispering, and I get a sense of a breeze wafting past.'

'Are you sure it's not a draught from the door? A lot of people coming in and out could cause it,' Joy said. She tried not to look excited.

The waiter glanced over his shoulder as if to check he wasn't being watched. 'I'm positive it's something supernatural. It didn't happen before the pub's renovations. Believe me or not. I know something spooky is going on.' He made to move away.

'Before you go, is there a particular time when you get this... er sort of breezy feeling.' Joy delayed him.

'Yes, it usually happens between seven and eight o'clock. I have to go, I'm getting funny looks from the manager.'

'Well!' Jessica said, a spoon poised above her melting ice-cream. 'Strange things happening between the hours of seven and eight o' clock. Now there's a surprise.'

171

'That's too much of a coincidence not for it to be connected,' Deborah admitted. 'I think as soon as we've eaten our sweets we should look for the manager. Let's ask him if he knows something. Most of the customers have gone or in the process of leaving, so he should have time to give us.'

Ten minutes later, Deborah and Joy ambled their way to the bar to approach the manager. They were acutely aware of their watchful friends.

Adrian Harper recognised Joy. Her shoulder length strawberry blonde hair neatly cut and covered by her ubiquitous baseball hat made her distinguishable. Added to that was the equally identifiable sports jacket Joy mostly wore for playing bowls. She had chosen to wear it that day because it was the closest to hand, having left home earlier than usual and in a hurry.

Joy shook hands with Adrian and introduced him to Deborah. She turned her head to indicate they were with friends. Adrian waved to Grace and mouthed a silent 'hello.'

'You seem to be making a success of this place,' Joy started the conversation. She was impressed that he'd remembered her and Grace.

'Yes, we've had a good year. And now we have to close again because of the lockdown.' He sighed. 'I suppose you are hearing that word a lot. Not much I can do about it. I will just have to think of something to keep myself occupied. Mind you there's always work to do here. We have a huge function room upstairs which needs attention so Lara and I will get on with that.'

'A function room?' Deborah asked. 'I didn't know there was anything like that here.'

'Technically it isn't. But it was once, and will be again.'

'What do you mean?' Deborah risked a glance at Joy.

'The room hasn't been used for decades, possibly not since the early twentieth century. At least not for what it was intended, such as glittering balls for the landed gentry. It's been nothing more than a junk dump, since, we think, just after the Second World War. It was used by the military as a small hospital then. Lara and I want to restore it to its former glory and start to run events here.'

'What, you mean hold dances or discos?' Joy asked.

'Not exactly, though I won't rule them out. Lara and I like murder mysteries. We watch all the crime drama series on television. We want to organise murder mystery dinner evenings, or possibly exclusive murder mystery weekends.'

'Sounds exciting, I'd be up for that,' Deborah said enthusiastically. She had always wanted to go to one.

'Yes it does. Me too,' Joy agreed amiably. 'I suppose there must be a lot of history attached to this place if, as you say, there used to be balls here a hundred years ago?'

Adrian nodded. 'Yes, there is, Lara and I have been doing some research on the subject. We want to know as much as possible about our pub. Are you interested in history?' He searched their faces looking from one to the other with a whisper of a smile tracing his lips.

'Yes. We are, and our friends over there,' Deborah turned to indicate the table where their companions were stalwartly watching, 'are very much in to history. We are thinking of starting a history club.'

Deborah didn't know why she said that, but it seemed a good idea at the time. She caught Joy's surprised expression but chose to ignore it in case she started to laugh.

Adrian Harper leaned forward conspiratorially. 'That sounds like an interesting project, perhaps Lara and I could join. Presumably it will be about local history?'

'Oh yes, definitely local. At the moment we are concentrating on pubs and inns like this one. They witness so much life.' Deborah congratulated herself on her quick thinking. She enjoyed the fleeting look of admiration from Joy who nudged her slightly with her knee.

'So what have you found out about this place?' Joy gave Adrian her full attention.

'Well, as you know we have only been here two years, though open to the public just for one and there's been a lot to do. The place had been empty for many years. So far we've discovered the pub was a house before it became a hotel. It used to be owned by the people who ran the mill. If you would like to step around here I will show you some of the original flag stones.'

Joy turned quickly to wink at the trio still seated at the table, then followed Adrian and Deborah around the bar. An archway led them to a small anteroom evidently used as an overflow stock room for the bar. A side door opened up to reveal three stone steps leading down into a cold room not much bigger than two yards square. Adrian went down the steps, turned and bent down.

'See here. Seventeen hundred and ninety.' He leaned back proudly as first Joy then Deborah took it in turns to look at the stone.

'Interesting,' they both murmured.

'According to the deeds, the house became a hotel in eighteen forty-nine.'

They followed him out again to the bar area, Adrian continuing to inform them everything he knew. Most of it confirmed what they'd learned at *The White Hart*. Deborah formed the impression Adrian Harper wanted to show off his knowledge.

'So what about the family who lived here when it first became a hotel, and of course subsequent owners?' Joy asked.

'Ah yes, there doesn't seem to be much hard fact really. I've heard varying stories from the local villagers who remember the stories they were told when they were children. It's a bit like Chinese whispers. I've heard about a daughter who disgraced herself, because of an affair with a railway worker.' He stopped to take payment from a couple who wanted to settle their bill. Joy slipped back to the table to whisper to their friends that they were having interesting conversations. Unable to keep her curiosity at bay, Kirsty got up to accompany Joy back to the bar where Deborah was waiting to resume their conversation.

'We've also heard the story about a connection with a railway man,' Deborah prompted him.

'Oh I see. Did you also find out what happened to his lover after he was killed?'

'She went to live with her married sister?'

'Very convenient don't you think?' Adrian Harper said.

'What do you mean?' Deborah responded quickly, aware of gasps from her two friends. Even as she

175

spoke she realised what Adrian Harper was suggesting.

'Murder of course. He was out of his class. The girl wouldn't give him up, and what do you know, the next thing the man's dead.' The landlord again turned his attention to a customer. He poured a pint of beer whilst chancing a confident sweep of his eyes across first Deborah's rapt face then those of her companions.

'So if you think he was murdered what do you think really happened to the girl?' She must have been heartbroken,' Joy asked when they had Adrian's attention again. She hadn't considered the possibility of a murder.

Adrian Harper was happy to continue talking, 'From what I can gather, so far, the story goes that the heartbroken, bereaved girl was sent to live with a relative at *Marford Mill*. But every day she was seen hanging around *The Trevalyn Inn*. That's where her lover was staying you see when he worked on the railway.'

Deborah was unable to speak. This added to the story she and Jessica had heard.

'But I suspect something more sinister. I think the girl must have been demented to hang around her deceased lover's lodgings. What if she'd been sent to a mental asylum?'

'You mean like the one in Denbigh!' Kirsty breathed. 'But surely she'd have gone to her relative's house.'

'In the beginning, yes. But Marford isn't that far away from *The Trevalyn Inn*. If she was becoming an embarrassment..."

He held their attention as they digested this theory.

'As well as the bereaved woman, there were three other daughters and also a son. He was engaged to someone who lived at *The Peacock Coaching Inn*, but something went wrong with that alliance too!'

'So do you have any theories about that?' Joy encouraged him to say more, though he didn't need much prompting.

'My guess is, that there were rumours of foul play over the railway worker, so the Slaters of *The Peacock* didn't want their daughter to be associated with the Hayes who lived here. And of course there's the reputation of the hysterical daughter to contend with. It's likely they wouldn't have approved an alliance. Of course it's just my imagination running riot. But it is plausible don't' you think?'

'So have you investigated the possibility of murder?' Kirsty asked.

'Not yet, but give me time.' He winked. 'It's just a theory. I haven't anything concrete. Rumours, you know the kind of thing. But there must be someone who has a link with the past. We are only talking about a hundred and fifty years or so.'

A flurry of customers demanded Adrian's attention, so the three women aware they had taken up a lot of his time, returned to their table. A few minutes were spent disentangling coats, scarves and bags.

Outside in the car park Grace suggested a quick stroll down Station Road before returning home.

'Are you developing my fetish for railways Grace? Or should I say disused ones?' Joy teased her friend as they set off down the road.

'I haven't been down here for years, but used to come a lot with Simon. He lived in that old cottage there.' Grace pointed to a pair of whitewashed stone cottages facing the road. They were set beside a row of red brick terraced houses. 'I just want to remind myself of the walks we used to have.'

Deborah sighed, 'I used to go for walks with Clive along here years ago, there's hardly anything left to see of the old railway.' Her thoughts drifted back on her memories of Clive, but as they strolled, she couldn't understand why the face she visualised was Dennis Balantyne.

The road came to a dead end and the group stopped to face the spot where Rossett railway station had once stood.

'The station was closed to passengers in nineteen sixty-four,' Grace informed them.

'So is this going to be your Mrs. Mastermind topic?' Jessica teased Grace. Her comment was ignored as Grace pointed to some old tracks. 'Look, some old sidings, a relic of the past.'

Just then, a gust of wind made the little party shiver.

'This old relic is feeling the cold, and I think we should get back to discuss our discoveries,' Jessica remarked.

'Yes, I have a client at half-past four, and I'd like a cup of tea before I start cutting hair. It's already past three.'

CHAPTER SIXTEEN

Kirsty made several pots of tea and carried them to the piano lounge. Grace followed with a tray of mugs. Simon trailed behind with the biscuit tin.

'We've got a lot to tell you,' Joy said, reaching for a chocolate biscuit.

Deborah couldn't understand why Joy was so skinny, she'd just eaten steak and chips followed by vanilla cheesecake.

'Before we start, I should remind you we will have a visitor later on, from that chap who does conservatories.' Grace clapped her hand to her forehead, wrinkling her brows. 'Damn, I've forgotten his name. I wrote it down somewhere.'

'It's here Love. You wrote it on your notebook. His name is Graham Bailey.' Simon handed the notebook to his wife.

'Oh yes, that's it. Anyway he's coming at five thirty, but I also have a client at five thirty. So I will leave you all to talk to him. Shirley will be home then, so she can listen to what he has to say. We can fill her in with the other stuff later, and then you can tell me what Graham Bailey said.'

'Shall I go first and tell everybody what I discovered at the library?' Taking the silence as consent, Joy continued.

'I must admit, I got engrossed with the old railway lines, and a bit side tracked.' She tittered at her repeated pun as she heard the others groan. 'The upshot is, that none of the lines came close to *The Golden Peacock*. The network of lines served the coal

179

mines and the main station in Wrexham. The closest pit to here was Gresford. Curiously, there was never a pit in Burton nor Rossett.'

'And we know the closest railway line was, and still remains, the Wrexham to Chester line,' Simon finished for her. He folded his arms, deep in thought as he leaned against the doorway. Grace caught his muse. 'We strolled past your old house.'

Observing their expressions, Deborah could see the couple silently shared a memory. She used to enjoy that special telepathy with Clive. An image of his face flashed through her mind and her lips curved into a secretive smile.

'So, I think we can discount our ghost has anything to do with the accident on the railways in the eighteen seventies, or whenever that poor man was killed,' Joy said. She smoothed her hands across her notes laid out in front of her. Assuming the role of chair she invited Kirsty to relate what she'd found.

'Hang on a minute.' Kirsty topped up her tea, then burrowed in her capacious leather handbag for her spiral notebook.

'Right, here we are. Actually, I got a bit side tracked like Joy. I have to say that, although it is fascinating to read about glitzy balls, and dazzling clothes of the eighteen hundreds and so forth, I don't think I've learned much more than what we knew already. However...'

'You mean those of us who have read *Jane Austen*'s novels and the like,' Jessica said crisply. 'The books I had to read in school rather than the books I wanted to read.' She turned to face Terry who had let out a longer groan than Simon. 'I take it you had to read those books too?'

'Yep. I have to say I can't remember much about them.'

'Me neither,' Simon agreed.

'Well anyway, thank you for interrupting, but I haven't finished yet.' Kirsty waited until she had their attention again before continuing. 'I did manage to discover something that was closer to home. It seems, as you would imagine, that the landed gentry of this area, and there were a lot, what with the mill owners and the coal and lead mine owners; they frequently held balls. I mean, what else could they do with their time? They danced, played cards and played the piano or some other musical instrument.' She shifted her glance to Deborah who was sitting on her piano stool.

Terry laughed. 'If they were respectable! Didn't the men gamble, shoot birds and drink and womanise as well? I remember that bit from *Pride and Prejudice*!'

Kirsty glared at him. 'As I was saying! *The Golden Peacock* was one of the venues and so was *The Miller* as we have learned today.'

Taking advantage of a hushed atmosphere which Kirsty knew would break any moment in a babble of excitement, she pressed on.

'Furthermore, *The White Hart* and *The Trevalyn Inn* also hosted these balls…'

'Because the parents of the younger set were looking for marriage partners for their offspring,' Jessica couldn't resist adding.

Kirsty flashed a quick smile at her sister. 'Yes, exactly. I've also found out that certain people who hosted as well as attended balls, were actually named in some of the local journals I have read. Either because of notoriety or because they were rich, I don't know, but those four Hayes daughters and son of *The*

Miller get a mention, as indeed other wealthy women and gentlemen.'

Kirsty flicked the pages of her notebook enjoying the suspense she had created.

'I have also managed to discover a bit more about the sisters at *The Miller*. The one who lost her lover, and became hysterical was the youngest. She was called Martha Hayes; she was broken hearted and never recovered. Eventually her parents sent her away to a convalescent home on the North Wales coast. There isn't anything to tell us what happened to her after. My guess is she ended up in the mental institution in Denbigh!'

'Anyway, those are my thoughts. The oldest sister Victoria Hayes married a brewery owner in Oswestry and went to live there. Another sister Cecily Hayes married a coal merchant and lived somewhere around here, though I can't find out much more.'

Kirsty looked up to check her rapt audience before continuing with her report. 'Are you following so far?'

Encouraged by the response she went on. 'Now this is where it gets really interesting. The fourth sister, though actually she was the third oldest, but I have kept her to last, and you will know why in a minute.'

'Get on with it will you?' Jessica jibed, but good humouredly.

'That sister, was Emma Hayes who married one Sidney Mathews of the *White Hart* in eighteen sixty-nine.' Amidst breaths of incredulity which Kirsty enjoyed, she concluded her account.

'What's more, their brother James Edward Hayes was secretly engaged to the daughter Henrietta Slater of *The Golden Peacock Inn*. But it seems the parents of Henrietta did not approve of the engagement.'

182

'Blimey,' Terry breathed.

'But why?' Tony asked.

Before anyone could respond to Tony's question, the clock in the hall struck half past four simultaneously with the ringing of the doorbell.

'That will be my first client,' Grace said getting out of her chair. She had moved just two steps, when strains of the *Blue Danube* by *Johann Strauss* filled the air.

Patting her pockets to search for her mobile, Grace's fingers struggled to reach her phone. It was jammed in the lining of her trousers. As she pulled it out, a hard backed chair near the coffee table fell over for no apparent reason. Startled, and clutching her mobile, she righted the chair with her free hand then answered her call. Simon caught her eye; acknowledged her unasked question with a wave of his arm; then left the room to greet his wife's client waiting outside at the kitchen door.

'It's Graham Bailey,' Grace informed those gathered. 'He can't make five-thirty, but he can come at seven-thirty?' She leaned against the fireplace and held the mobile to her chest to muffle the sound. Upon gaining their agreement, her companions heard her confirm the re-arranged appointment. Then she walked out of the room to meet her client.

'Hmm that was strange, the chair toppling over like that,' Jessica commented. 'I didn't notice a draught or anything.'

'I think Grace knocked it over when she got up,' Tony said.

'Are you sure?' Deborah stared at the chair as if it could speak. She too, felt it had toppled over on its own accord, but couldn't be certain. She'd also felt a heaviness in the atmosphere but couldn't describe it.

Kirsty frowned. 'It did seem odd. Perhaps we're just suspicious because of other events.' She forced a laugh.

No-one offered an explanation about the chair toppling over. Joy was keen to dismiss it because she wanted to divulge another section of her research. So Deborah put it out of her mind as she watched Joy reach for another biscuit. After taking a bite she put it down whilst she unfurled her notes on an A4 pad.

'Right, well to add to Kirsty's findings about our wonderful home,' she said with a sweeping wave of her arm. 'It seems that *The Golden Peacock Inn* has undergone several alterations over the years. You will recall that before we bought it, the estate agent told us there was some dispute over the age of it. Some locals claimed it was thirteenth century, others said it was seventeenth or eighteenth, but no-one came forward to prove either. Well,' she paused for impact taking a nibble of her biscuit. 'I've found something that proves it is at least three hundred years old.'

'So it could be a listed building?' Tony frowned. 'Will we be in trouble for all the alterations we made?'

'No, don't worry. I'm coming to that. I have found a collection of various documents and journals written by some of the gentry themselves. A few of them not unlike the ones Kirsty has read. They give accounts of the local landmarks as well as snippets, gossip if you want to call it, about their peers. The earliest report is dated eighteen thirty, but the content refers to events and such like that go back as far as seventeen hundred and forty! Over the centuries, various local historians took it upon themselves to write accounts of Rossett. Some made very good sketches and those I have seen show variations in the size and shape of

The Golden Peacock Inn. This building had changed status and appearance so much over the centuries, that there is little resemblance to the way it was originally. That explains why it couldn't be a listed building.' Joy took a breath and waited for her words to sink in.

'Do you think that the renovations we made, may have disturbed the ghost?' Tony asked. He moved from the sofa to occupy an armchair. His new position enabled him to face Joy still sitting on the floor eating the remains of her biscuit.

'I... well, I hadn't really thought that far ahead. But let's park that theory for a minute. I wanted to concentrate on these artist sketches, which I photocopied at the library. From what I can tell, there used to be more space at the back of the building. It appears to have been annexed to this room. Then as the years went by it was extended; added to; knocked down again; rebuilt; extended and so on. They kept this section where we are sitting now but it was wider. It could have been used as a ballroom.'

As if coordinated, several heads turned to examine the dimensions of the piano room.

'It's getting dark in here.' Tony got up to switch on the light.

'Wow, that might explain why things keep happening in this room and the conservatory,' Kirsty exclaimed bending over Joy's shoulder to look at her documents.

'Yes, there's more. There used to be another building attached to the stables – probably the carriage house. It backed on to the narrow lane at the rear of the garden. From what I can see of this artist's impression, there appears to be some steps leading away from the carriage house that go down somewhere. Look there's a figure of a woman in full evening dress walking down the steps. Where is she going?'

Terry got up to bend over Joy's other shoulder. 'You're right Love! Maybe the steps led to a covered passageway at the back of the carriage house, for visitors to enter the building from the lane without getting wet or muddy?'

'Or maybe it was intended as a separate entrance from the coaching house, to avoid those travellers and the like on foot entering the front of the inn?' Jessica suggested. 'Plus they also had the mail to deal with. A separate entrance would be ideal for that kind of business.'

'It would make sense, I suppose,' Kirsty crossed her legs as she leaned back on the sofa putting away her notebook.

'It fits,' Terry agreed, turning his head to see Simon return to the room.

'What have I missed?' He helped himself to a biscuit and sat on the sofa next to Kirsty.

Having been brought up to date, Simon suggested that once he and Terry had finished constructing the boules pitch, they would return to the cellar and continue with their exploring.

'I have a feeling those steps in the wine cellar might lead to something else.'

Deborah fiddled with the brown envelope on her lap that contained the deeds to *The Golden Peacock*. 'I haven't had time to look at these, I thought we could wait until we all had a chance to do it together. 'But going back to what Tony suggested, that our renovations may have disturbed the ghost, what do you think?' Her eyes searched her companions' faces expectantly.

'Yes, it's a valid point,' Jessica offered. 'And, Deborah, if you remember, the waitress who served us at *The Trevalyn Inn* said something similar. At the time I thought she was just making a casual remark, but maybe there's some truth in it. That pub like this one, has undergone a lot of alterations over the years. I must say what Joy has discovered is remarkable. Who would have thought this house had been so large.'

A draught from the kitchen door followed Shirley's arrival into the house. They heard the familiar sounds of her dumping her brief case in the hall, kicking off her shoes then a sigh of relief before calling out, 'Anyone home?'

A few seconds later she opened the door to the piano lounge to find everyone seated where she expected. She squeezed herself between Tony and Kirsty causing Simon to move sideways to accommodate all four of them on the sofa. He glanced at the vacant sofa opposite but remained wedged where he was. Nothing like the body warmth of friends, Deborah observed wryly. She wondered how long it would be before one of them would move.

'We've got a lot to tell you,' Joy greeted Shirley, 'but at the moment we are about to learn what is in the deeds. Debbie has them on her knee.'

'Oh so you managed to get them from the solicitors then.' Joy passed her the biscuit tin.

Deborah broke the seal of the large manila envelope.

Shirley eyed the package eagerly. She couldn't resist saying, 'And the winner is…'

Amidst good humoured grunts at Shirley's attempt of a joke, they watched as Deborah removed the contents. The documents were in several bundles. Carefully she untied the pink tape from each frail and brittle parcel, gently unfolding and laying it out on the coffee table. At once, Deborah's companions crowded around her to view them. Simon gave up his tight spot to stand behind her. The remaining three on the sofa took advantage of the extra space and leaned forward impatiently, though unable to read upside down.

With enthusiastic companions hovering over her shoulder silently reading the legal documents at their own pace, Deborah read out loud the names of previous owners. Joy seized her pen and began to write down dates and names of each owner every time it was announced the building misrepresented d hands.

The fragile edges of the older documents in the bundle made it difficult to read without tearing them. From what they could gather their house had been known by several derivations of its name. *Purple Peacock, Peacock Grove, Golden Peacock* were the most recent. Surnames of the owners didn't vary much during the eighteenth century. Things changed from the beginning of the nineteenth century. By then, the building had undergone several alterations as well as ownership. It went to the Slaters in eighteen hundred and twenty-two.

'Well, there you go. The building was inherited by a Henry James Slater in the year eighteen hundred and fifty-eight,' Jessica announced. Shirley sat down again, this time on the chair that Grace had re-arranged after it had tipped over on to the floor.

'There seems to be a lot of Henrys and James' Slaters. They didn't have much imagination for names did they?' Shirley gently traced with her finger the repeated Christian names.

'Have you noticed that all the names of previous owners are male?' Joy leaned over Jessica's shoulders to get a better look. She scanned the deeds whilst writing notes in her notebook using Jessica's back for support. 'Nothing to suggest joint ownership except when brothers are mentioned.'

'Yes, that's the way it was in those days,' Jessica turned forcing Joy to slip to the floor.

'Oops. Sorry. Are you ok?' She helped her up to a standing position and handed her the biro which had fallen out of her hand.

'Yes, I'm fine. Thanks.'

'Anyway as I was saying. The only time a woman's name would appear on deeds, is if she were an heiress or, at best, a forward thinking male guardian ensured her name was on the documents, giving her joint ownership.'

'Keeping the family name tradition was an obsession. At least it gives us a link to the probably first born son who would inherit,' Deborah agreed. She tapped her lips with her finger as she tried to make a connection with what they had learned. She leaned over the deeds again then her heart thumped wildly as she noticed that in eighteen ninety-eight the building was inherited by a Henrietta.

'Look Jess, one of those Henry's is actually a Henrietta! A Henrietta Charlotte Slater-Hayes. We've assumed that all the names beginning with 'H' were men so didn't realise there was an heiress. It's very

189

faint the writing but it's definitely a woman's name. Have a look for yourselves.'

Again they crowded around Deborah and peered over the spot where she gently held down the fragile piece of paper. So here's proof that there was a link with the Hayes of *The Miller* and the Slaters of *The Peacock* despite the scandal.'

Deborah momentarily took her hands away from the delicate papers, then hastily replaced them to stop them rolling up.

Joy studied her pad for a few seconds, she frowned for a second then excitedly compared her notes with the document Deborah still held down.

'That's great, and I think everything we have learned so far has given us a solid starting point to find the identity of our ghosts.' She read her notes before continuing.

'Listen, we know what happened to the four Hayes' sisters, and we now know that three of them married around the eighteen sixties or seventies. But we don't know what happened to their brother James. Neither do we know what happened to Henrietta Slater. The Slaters were against the marriage.' Joy exhaled deeply.

'So, is Henrietta Charlotte Slater-Hayes the woman who inherited almost thirty odd years later our ghost? Was she a spinster denied of her love and only able to marry after the death of her parents? That would be a good reason to haunt the place, I suppose,' Deborah said slowly thinking over everything Joy had said.

Shirley's eyes sparkled. 'Are you saying she eventually married the Hayes chappie, what's his name...James Edward and they are haunting this place together? How romantic! They waited all those years. A true love story, and eventually she inherited the inn too. Obviously she was the only surviving next of kin!' Shirley's radiant expression mirrored Joy's, neither of them spoke.

It seemed to Deborah that the atmosphere was charged with speculation. She became aware of another draught as the back door opened and muted voices told them that Grace's client had gone. She re-entered the room bringing a faint aura of hairspray. Dan was behind her.

'Look who's here.'

'Hi folks, nice of you to let me stay. Just as well really, because my car failed its MOT this morning.' Dan plonked himself down on a chair opposite Simon who raised his hand to welcome his grandson.

'Bad luck. Will it cost much to put it right?'

Dan shrugged, crossing his legs as he made himself comfortable. 'Not really. Apparently an indicator light and the windscreen wipers need replacing. I can do that myself.'

'If you need help, you only have to ask,' Simon told him. Aware that Grace was hovering in the background he went out with her in the hall. Tony and Shirley followed them.

'Fag break!' Dan grinned. Joy rubbed the back of her neck with her hand. 'Yes,' she agreed sighing.

'Dan would you like a cup of tea?' Deborah asked. 'I think we could all do with another.'

The young man leapt to his feet straight away.

'Let me do it. I haven't come here to be waited on.' He began to stack the dirty mugs on a tray. 'By the way how's the ghost hunting coming along? Any clues?'

Joy smiled at him. 'Actually we've discovered a lot. That's what we are discussing now. We'll give you an update when you've made the tea.'

'And when the smokers return,' Jessica added.

Dan winked. 'Sounds good to me.'

Joy got up. I'll go and help him. Poor lad has only just got here and he's making us tea.'

Deborah laughed. 'Don't worry. He's eager to help.' But Joy was already on her way to the kitchen just as the doorbell rang. 'I'll get it,' she called. It's probably Grace's half past five client.'

'I would still like to know where our gravestone man fits in to the deeds. I know we've established he died in World War Two, poor man, so he isn't going to be our ghost. At least I don't think so,' Shirley cast her eyes around the room for support from her friends as they assembled again over mugs of tea.

In another attempt to solve the mystery Deborah picked up the deeds again and read out loud.

'In nineteen thirty-nine we have a George Tyler, he may have been James' father, because in nineteen forty-six... Joy you will be pleased to note *The Golden Peacock Inn* went to a Victoria Tyler! I wonder if she was the wife or sister of young James Tyler? She would have inherited it as next of kin?'

'Looks like she never married or re-married if she'd been widowed. Victoria's name isn't joined with another on the deeds.' Joy peered over Deborah's shoulder, and picked up where Deborah had left off reading out loud. 'The pub changed hands several times after that. In twenty-ten we get to our Mr. Gibson, the previous owner before we bought it in twenty-nineteen.' She leaned back satisfied, conscious that her companions exhaled sighs of relief.

CHAPTER SEVENTEEN

They brought Dan and Grace up to date with the rest of their findings over dinner. Dan was impressed with their discoveries. He was especially thrilled, that there could be two phantoms.

'There might be several ghosts prowling around. They just might be keeping quiet,' he said cheerfully.

''If they are, then let's hope it stays that way,' Jessica frowned at Dan over the rim of her glasses.

'With a bit of luck, things will become clearer when your friend Jason's father arrives at half past seven,' Grace assured him.

'You mean Mr. Bailey? Is he coming here?'

'Yes, I spoke to him this morning. He remembers you.'

'I haven't seen him for years. Cool. Did he say much on the phone? Does he know who the spooks are?' Dan's face was wreathed in smiles.

Grace put her head on one side and contemplated her grandson with a twinkle in her eye. 'He said a lot yes! But nothing about the spooks as you call them!'

'He'd better get a move on, otherwise he will be here when we get our entertainment for the night,' Jessica commented as the clock from the hallway chimed quarter to eight. A minute later Graham Bailey knocked on the door. His voice, continuously apologising about arriving late, reverberated from the kitchen door to the hallway and reached the conservatory, as he followed Deborah.

'This is Mr. Graham Bailey,' she announced politely. To her dismay the man started again to launch into explanations about his late arrival, but was deftly cut off mid-sentence by Jessica. She had already got out of her chair and was heading towards the piano lounge. Her friends gathered behind her. Grace, who had started to clear away dishes, rose to greet him, just as Jessica held out her hand to Bailey. He rubbed his own hand against his overalls before grasping Jessica's.

'It's very good of you to come at all, especially when the country is going into lockdown. This is Grace who I believe you may know? In any case you two spoke earlier?' Jessica asked.

Graham Bailey blinked as he counted the unfamiliar guests exiting from the conservatory. Taking advantage of a break in his relentless chatter, Grace held out her hand.

'Hello, good to see you again after so many years. You know my grandson Dan, and of course you've met my husband Simon?'

Momentarily derailed, Graham nodded whilst shaking Simon's hand and acknowledging Dan with a nod of his head.

'Why don't you come in to the piano lounge Graham? Your timing is ideal.' Over his shoulder, unseen by their visitor, Simon winked at the others as he led the way from the hallway.

Graham Bailey stood open mouthed, scanning first the wooden beams of the ceiling before focusing on the Victorian fireplace and then the piano. Deborah's eyes twinkled as she noted that for once the man was speechless. She wondered for how long.

'Why don't you sit here?' She indicated the only remaining armchair. Managing to take his eyes from the marble mantelshelf which had held his attention, Graham sat down.

'Wow you really have gone to town in here...,' he started to say. Over his head, Deborah shared a crafty smile with Grace as she rolled her eyes and checked her watch. 'Two minutes,' Grace mouthed. Deborah tilted her head slightly.

'Can we offer you a drink Mr Bailey?' Dan interrupted.

'No thanks, I won't stay long. I've been busy all day. I need to get home.' As if to prove his industriousness he wiped his sweaty forehead with his sleeve. 'You've made some alterations I see. A big improvement too.'

'Glad you like it,' Deborah smiled. She watched him switch his attention from the fireplace to glance furtively towards the conservatory. Moisture still glistened on his forehead. He fumbled in his pocket for his handkerchief and brushed it off properly, adjusting his focus again to watch Kirsty pour some wine for herself and Jessica. His eyes strayed to openly stare at her. He frowned, a puzzled expression flitting across his own face. Kirsty sat down beside her sister, putting the bottle deliberately in front of them on the coffee table. It was in full view of everyone now seated in the piano room. Aware of his scrutiny she looked up and smiled politely.

'Don't I know you?' Graham asked. He passed a puzzled look from Kirsty to Jessica and then back again.

'I'm not sure. You look familiar,' Kirsty smiled.

'Did you live near the Flash?'

'Yes, I did actually. At least not far away. On Pike lane. A long time ago though. I've moved twice since then. Did you live there?'

'Not exactly. Just around the corner on the main road, but I went down there a lot to go fishing in the *Flash*. I remember seeing you in your front garden when I passed. You and your husband.'

'You've a good memory. I'm sorry I don't remember you. So many people passed our cottage on the way to the fishing club, or out for a walk.' Kirsty avoided his blatant gaze and occupied herself with examining her glass of wine.

'One minute,' Terry said causing Graham to switch his attention from Kirsty to one of the sofas where Terry sat with Joy and Deborah.

'Sorry, I didn't mean to take up your time,' Graham began, then stopped when Grace shook her head quickly, forcing a deep frown and more sweat to nestle in the furrows of the bewildered man's brow.

Miraculously, Deborah observed wryly, he remained silent as the grandfather clock in the hall began to strike eight o' clock. His mouth gaped reminding her of a pike. Kirsty laughed when she told her later.

The man sat as if frozen, his mouth widening further when as anticipated by the residents of the house, the bottle of wine levitated itself high into the air. Graham Bailey's entranced eyes trailed its route to the conservatory. Joy, Terry, Shirley and Tony got up to track it.

Grace motioned Graham to leave his chair. His eyes wide and open mouthed he followed her into the conservatory. The others, as agreed earlier stayed behind, so that Graham could get a full view of what they knew would occur.

196

A few minutes later they returned to their seats. Joy and Shirley guided their dazed visitor back to his chair. Graham's face was drawn. Sweat glistened on his forehead. Instinctively he accepted the small glass of whisky handed to him by Simon.

'Are you alright Mr. Bailey?' Dan inquired. 'Have you seen anything like that before? I haven't. It's kinda wicked.'

Graham Bailey fixed his eyes on Dan's eager face. 'It's hard to take in. I saw something odd here when I built the conservatory. I thought I was dreaming. But it happened twice, and about this time.' He glanced at the small clock on the mantel piece. 'Yes, it was summer time, so there was still plenty of light. I wanted to finish work on the conservatory. The first time something strange happened, I took no notice, but I was rattled, I don't mind telling you. Then the second time, I suspected there was something spooky going on. But it wasn't like this.' He knocked his whisky back. Simon offered him some more, but he refused.

'I'll have another when I get home thanks. I'll need it after this. How long has it been happening?'

'We believe since we moved in,' Shirley said. 'Tony and I saw it first, but now everyone has seen it. What do you think it is? Any ideas?'

Graham shook his head. 'I didn't see any bottles flying around. I actually convinced myself that what I'd seen was the outline of a woman. Or at least I thought it was a woman. She was wearing a long flowing dress, but when I went to speak to her she vanished just as I was putting up one of the glass panels of the conservatory on the third wall.' He scratched his head and looked longingly at his empty whisky glass. 'I thought I was dreaming. Despite the lateness of the hour, the sun was still bright and I thought it had reflected something off the glass. I tried not to dwell on it, but it bothered me.'

Graham hesitated, trickles of perspiration slipped down his face and he mopped at it quickly with his handkerchief. For once the man was silent. Grace frowned willing him to speak again.

'So what happened the next night?'

Taking a deep breath, Graham continued.

'The next night was a bit cloudy, the weather had changed a lot during the day. But, I saw something I have never forgotten. A woman in a kind of evening dress came out of nowhere, I think from over there, in the corner near your fireplace. It was as if she was dancing or being lifted in the air. Anyway she came floating into the conservatory. By then I had just one more glass panel to fit and she seemed to vanish through the opening just where your plants are.'

'Was she holding a bottle of wine?' Dan asked.

Graham shook his head.

'Did you see her just now?' Deborah asked.

Again Graham shook his head.

'And you didn't see anything else come out of this room when you saw the woman?' Dan asked.

'No. But this room isn't the same as it was when I built the conservatory. There used to be little compartments in here, cubicles or small booths if you like. Not too enclosed, but nice and cosy like. You could get six or more people in each little section. The floor was also on different levels too. You might remember it, from before you did your alterations?'

'Yes we remember,' Deborah spoke for all of them. They'd had long conversations on how to remove the wooden partitions and to level off the floor to make the space they had now.

'After I'd finished the conservatory, I didn't visit here very often. But one night, I came for a pint. I remember the landlord saying to me that a few customers had experienced something spooky in one of the booths close to the conservatory, so he'd reconstructed the booth and closed the conservatory off to the public. I think the booth was where you two ladies are sitting.' He pointed to Kirsty and Jessica.

'Hmm that might explain a few things,' Simon commented.

'The landlord manufactured some story about a man called James up to his tricks. In fact there used to be a headstone from a grave in the fireplace. Have you seen it?'

Graham got up to examine the Victorian mantelshelf over the fireplace as he spoke. He smoothed his hand over the marble mantel. 'This is a nice piece of stone. I don't think it's the original though I think the fireplace is. The building has had lots of alterations over the centuries you know. There's not much of the original left according to what I read in the *Wrexham Leader*, which is why it wasn't given listed building status. Still, I'm glad you managed to save it from demolition.'

Their visitor had regained his composure and with it his tongue, Deborah noted with some amusement.

'Are you aware of other changes over the years?' Joy ventured to ask, hoping to keep Graham focused. 'Outside for example.'

'Not much. I've lived around here since I was a lad. When I was old enough to drink I came here a few times with my dad. I recall a large hall at the back of this room. My dad told me it was where they used to hold dances and in the past, they used the space to sort the post that came from the carriages. The stables were at the back you see with a place for the owner's carriage.'

Grace realised that Graham was getting distracted. 'That's very interesting. Do you know anything about the people who lived here?'

He shook his head. 'No sorry. I remember the Daniels family who had it before they sold it to the Gibsons. I hear they've gone to Spain. Lucky devils. I wouldn't mind going to Spain myself. But who knows now with the lockdown and everything...'

'So what do you remember about the Daniels?' Deborah asked. 'That would be early nineteen nineties? I used to come here myself then, but I can't think of anything in particular about them. The pub was run efficiently though.'

'That's right. They were very efficient. Business like, but hard to get to know personally. Some people said they were too business like. They went all of a sudden without a word to anyone. I often wondered why.'

Graham got out of his chair and handed his glass to Simon. 'Thanks for that. I'm looking forward to another when I get home.'

Taking advantage of the fact that Graham was already on his feet, Grace thanked him for coming and started to usher the man to the door. Deborah, catching her drift, stood up too hoping that their visitor would take the hint. It took another ten minutes and the back-up from Terry and Simon getting to their feet, before they finally managed to edge Graham to the back door. Even with one foot over the threshold, Graham continued to talk. His final lament was that his favourite pub *The White Hart* would be closed to the public.

Deborah and Grace returned to the piano lounge and slumped into chairs.

'Oh please pour me a glass of wine,' Deborah laughed.

'Me too,' Grace added. 'What an extraordinary man!'

Dan smiled. 'Yeah, Jasie said his dad goes on a bit.' Simon and Terry returned to the room carrying cans of *Wrexham lager*.

'Interesting chap,' Terry commented. 'At least we have just a little bit more detail to go on. Tomorrow morning when it's light I will have a look around the ground close to the conservatory to see if I can find any evidence of another building. If what our friend tells us is correct, and it seems obvious from the deeds, that it is, I think we may find the foundations of what used to be a ballroom.'

'That chap Adrian Harvey at *The Miller* said that there was probably a ballroom here.' Joy reminded them.

'Dennis Balantyne at *The White Hart*,' mentioned ballrooms too.' Jessica stole a glance at Deborah waiting for some kind of reaction. Deborah busied herself with helping herself to a larger than intended handful of salted peanuts.

'These old pubs have got a lot of history to tell. If only they could talk,' Shirley said. 'We still don't know what happened to the peacocks. I noticed that sometimes peacock is mentioned in the deeds and other times the name has been dropped.'

Dan was enthusiastic when Jessica explained what they'd discovered about pub names. He spent the next half an hour trying to outdo his grandfather with unusual names for pubs. Simon, being over fifty years older was able to recall many. Deborah suspected he'd invented the names of some of them to impress his grandson.

'I'd like to have another look at the plans that came with the deeds, to see if I can find the exact location of the ballroom,' Joy said suddenly. 'Have you got them to hand Debbie?'

'I think I left them on the piano before we had dinner.' She got up to retrieve them then unfastened the pink tape that bound them.

'Let's see, Joy said. 'I also want to check the name of the owner for eighteen ninety-eight. I'm working on another theory. When did it change hands after? I've forgotten.'

Deborah eagerly sat beside her and traced her finger down the parchment. 'Nineteen thirty-nine it went to George Tyler.'

Jessica stood behind them cupping her wine in one hand. 'Here what's that?' She bent down over Joy almost tipping her wine over her head.

'Hey, careful.'

'Oops, sorry.' Jessica flashed an apologetic glance at Joy, 'but just look at the description of the property, *Peacock Inn, Cobblers Lane.* I didn't know this lane had a name. Does that mean there was a cobbler here at one time?'

'I would have thought there was more likely to be a farrier, kind of the same thing. Horses, you know,' Kirsty smiled when her sister raised her eye brows.

Joy flicked her eyes over the plan that was attached to the deeds. 'Never mind the cobblers. Look at this again.' She pointed to the diagram that showed the inn passed to Victoria Tyler in nineteen forty six.

'According to this rough sketch, it looks like some of the buildings altered shape again. The ballroom or post room or whatever you want to call it, is half the size as it was on previous plans.' Joy started making notes, every now and again checking dates and names.

'Who bought it after Victoria Tyler?' Shirley asked getting up to have a look. 'I can't keep track of these dates and people.'

Deborah raised the document for her to see not expecting to have it lifted out of her hands. She sat back in her chair and watched as Shirley took the deeds to a sofa, where she showed it to Tony, the rest of the group crowded around her as they examined the document.

'The Marshalls. We'd be too young to remember anything about them. Not even Simon who lived closest to this place.' She glanced at him as he watched her scrutinise the document.

'I don't know anybody of that name.'

'So who bought it next?' Dan asked reaching for another can of *Wrexham Lager*. Deborah felt gratified that the young man was engaging in the history of the building. She sipped her wine catching Grace's eye. As if she had read her mind, she tilted her head and smiled.

'Right, Dan now we're getting to the nineteen seventies,' Shirley announced. 'A time for change for all of us.' She scanned the faces of the listeners. 'Some of us getting married or thinking about it; some of us leaving Wales; going to work in London; others going to universities and so on.' She wound her beads around her finger.

'In nineteen seventy-six Mr. Edward Hopkins bought the place, and extended the hall again. Probably for discos that were so popular then. Hopkins sold the pub in nineteen ninety-five to James Daniels,' Shirley announced

'Oh no. Not another James.' Dan groaned.

Joy looked up from her notes, 'and he in turn sold it in twenty ten to our Mr. Gibson. It looks like by the time he got his hands on it, the previous owner Mr. Daniels had done some major alterations too,' Joy added. She bent down to catch several loose sketches that fell from the folds of the deeds.

'And when we bought it, we added to the changes,' Deborah supplied.

'Are you working on the theory that all those alterations over the years has disturbed the ghosts?' Dan asked Joy.

'Yes, it's what we considered earlier, and I'm becoming convinced that's what happened. I just need to figure out when, 'Joy said, with a twinkle in her eye.

'Ghosts don't like change!' Shirley said mischievously.

Dan's blue eyes rounded. He stared at her for a moment then grinned.

Joy moved towards the fireplace for more space, kneeling down she lay all the various sketches side by side on the rug.

'I'm going backwards in time now. If you look at these little plans, you can see how it altered over the last two hundred years.'

Terry joined her and with creaking joints that weren't as supple as his wife's knelt down beside her. He cast his builder's eye over the drawings. After   a   few seconds wherein, the rest of the companions remained sitting in their more comfortable seats, he turned his head to face them.

'It looks like Jessica and Kirsty have erected their two greenhouses alongside the site that would have been part of the ballroom. It extended from this room, to right across that section of the garden.'

Joy looked closer. 'What's bothered me ever since I saw that sketch with a woman going down some steps from a carriage is; where were the steps, and where did they go? If, as Terry suggested earlier, that there must have been a walkway leading from the old carriage house, which isn't there any more...could it go through...'

'Under that crumbling old building next to the wine cellar!' Jessica interjected.

'It's possible it went into a kind of subway,' Terry said slowly.

Simon got up to have a look. 'You could be right.'

'Do you mean there's an underground passageway?' Joy's eyes were bright.

'Yes.' Terry put his hand on Joy's shoulder to lever himself to a standing position. He held out his hand to help her up.

'I suppose walking from the carriage house to the ballroom over a muddy field would have meant dirty feet and clothes. An underground entrance would have avoided that.' Joy was ecstatic.

'Marvellous,' Shirley said. 'It's so romantic!' Deborah sat snugly in her chair. 'But how is this going to help us find the ghost?'

'I think the ghosts are looking for the tunnel.' Dan said.

'I think you're right Dan. If we find it, we might get rid of them,' Kirsty said.

Shirley was excited. 'So are we going to look for the secret passageway?'

Simon shrugged. 'It might have been filled in, or it could have caved in years ago. Still, we can have a dig around the area to look for some clues.'

'I hope that doesn't mean moving the greenhouses,' Jessica said. Her consternation was echoed by Kirsty.

'No, of course not, but if we can find it, or at least some of the remains, it would be interesting don't you think?' Simon faced the sisters with a reassuring smile. A murmur akin to agreement circled the room.

'Fine. Just so long as we are agreed on that.' Then Jessica added as an afterthought. 'But if it means we're getting closer to ridding ourselves of those blasted ghosts, I might change my mind.'

CHAPTER EIGHTEEN

Saturday mornings had followed the same format for Kirsty for several years. The lockdown made no difference to her routine. She heard the clock in the hall chime six thirty as she quietly tiptoed past. She carried her heavy hacking boots, freshly polished, to the kitchen to make herself toast and tea before heading for the stables.

'Off to see your fancy man?' Jessica, came up behind her making Kirsty jump. The knife in her hand shook as she cut a thicker than intended piece of Grace's home-made bread.

'I don't know what you mean.' Still with her back to her sister, she asked her if she wanted a piece of toast.

'Yes, two please. I'll make some tea.' Deciding not to tease her sister further, Jessica changed the subject.

'I thought that when you come back from the stables, we could go outside to do some digging. The weather is quite clement and we need to double dig the ground ready for planting. The garden is much bigger than I originally thought, even with the greenhouses.'

'Fine by me. I thought you might want to help the others look for secret tunnels.'

Jessica shrugged. 'Exciting though it might be, I'd rather concentrate on growing vegetables. Who knows how long this lockdown will last. There might be shortages.'

'Do you think finding the passageway will help solve the ghost problem?'

Another shrug. 'It's possible I suppose. I had a quick look at those sketches that Joy was on about. I think the passageway travels underground at the side of the greenhouses and not directly underneath. Not that I'm worried we would have to move them.'

Kirsty checked the bread on the grill.

'Your toast is ready. Do you want butter and marmalade?

'Thanks. Yes both.'

Jessica poured the tea. 'If the underground passage is in some way connected to the ghosts and we can stop the floating wine bottles, it will be a relief.'

'Amen to that.' Deborah sauntered into the kitchen, still wearing her dressing gown. 'Any tea in the pot? I've run out of tea bags in my room. I overheard what you said about the ghostly events as I came down stairs. I was wondering whether the phantoms really could be James and Henrietta and that they are trying to reach each other. Perhaps they got separated because of our renovations.'

'To be fair, these ghostly apparitions started before we moved in. That's if the rumours we have heard are anything to go by,' Kirsty said. She handed Deborah a mug of tea. 'Mind you we could have made it worse. If your theory is true, that they're lost lovers, let's hope we can re-unite them. I would hate to get in the way of a couple in love.'

'Neither would I,' Jessica agreed, meeting her sister's tenacious glare.

'It would be awful if we discover they died like Romeo and Juliette,' Deborah said lightly. She looked from one face to the other, getting a sense of some tension between the sisters.

Kirsty got up. 'I must go.' She pulled on her boots leaving her slippers in a shoebox in the small recess by the kitchen door. An assortment of boots and shoes had been carefully arranged on shelves initiated by Grace. 'See you later.'

'Have you two fallen out?' Deborah asked cheerily.

Jessica laughed, 'No, she knows I'm on to her. I think she's got a secret lover!'

'What?' Deborah spluttered into her mug of tea. 'Who?'

'The guy at the stables - Leslie I think she said his name is.'

'Did she tell you?'

Jessica laughed. 'No, but I can tell.'

'Good for her.'

'I couldn't agree with you more.'

It seemed to Deborah, that each time the clock in the hallway chimed a half hour, two more of their housemates drifted into the kitchen seeking tea and toast. At nine o' clock still in her dressing gown, she mooched back to her room to get changed. She'd arranged to Skype with her son in France and didn't want to face him still wearing her nightwear. Once she'd got used to the technology involved in setting up her computer to do video calls, she looked forward to her Saturday morning catch ups with Steven and his family in France. Deborah kept in touch with David by email or an occasional telephone call.

After she'd given Steve the latest news about the UK lockdown, she began to tell him about the strange happenings in the house, and what she and her friends had discovered. When she got to the bit about the occurrences in the conservatory, Zoe had pulled up a chair to sit next to her father.

'See, I told you that I'd seen something spooky Granny.'

Deciding to take the bull by the horns, Deborah asked her grand-daughter what exactly she had seen. She avoided the incredulous expression on her son's face.

'A woman in a long evening dress. It was beautiful. I couldn't see her face, she had her back to me, but her long hair was floating and she was carrying a little bag.'

'When did you see that?'

Before the girl could reply Steve intervened. A frown etched his face.

'Are you sure it was a ghost and not one of your granny's friends?' Zoe's father was sceptical.

'Surely Mother, that's impossible!'

But Deborah was determined to pursue Zoe's story.

Zoe didn't need much encouragement. With a defiant look at her father she carried on.

'I told you all at breakfast in the conservatory that I'd seen something spooky the night we came back from taking Granny for dinner. Nobody believed me, and I wasn't sure myself. Uncle David said it was just the lights flickering. But I saw it again the night before we left. It was different that time, and the image was clearer. I'm certain it was a ghost.' She checked her father's reaction before continuing. Steve frowned and stared at his daughter in disbelief. Deborah could see that she was in earnest.

'I thought she was one of Granny's friends at first, dressed up to go out in an evening dress. That's why I wasn't scared. I would have spoken to her to say how much I liked her dress, but she seemed in a hurry. I watched her go into the conservatory and then she vanished. That's when I wondered if she was a ghost.'

Deborah tried to cast her mind back to the night before her son and his family had left to go to France. That was the night when Shirley and Tony had witnessed the wine bottle phenomena.

'Zoe, are you sure? That same night Shirley and Tony said they saw something, but they decided to wait until the next day to tell us.'

'Yes, I am sure and Granny, I remember seeing Shirley and Tony. They seemed to be agitated about something so I said nothing. They both went into the conservatory after the woman. That's what confused me. I thought the three of them were together and then the other woman kind of disappeared.'

'I wanted to say something the next morning, but we had to leave so early. Anyway, I started to wonder if I was imagining things. Nobody believed me before so I decided not to bother. But now it all makes sense.' She giggled. 'Or really it doesn't make sense.'

'What were you doing down there anyway?' Steve stared incredulously at his daughter.

'The first night, I wanted to get my book from the library tele room before going up to Granny's. You lot were still talking in the kitchen, so I didn't bother saying anything. Anyway, I knew you wouldn't believe me.'

Deborah dipped her head slightly. She remembered that Zoe had said something about getting her book and that she and her family had lingered in the kitchen chatting on their return from *The Alyn*.

'The second night, was the same. I'd left my book downstairs again. When I came out of the library tele room, the ghost came past me and floated down the hall to the conservatory.'

Zoe finished talking with a triumphant glance at her father. Steve frowned.

'Mum I'm sure there must be some explanation for all this. I can't believe the place is haunted!'

'Honestly Steve, I didn't want to believe it either, but now I'm convinced we have some kind of spectre here. We've all seen it. Well, not exactly seen the ghost, but we've seen something odd! So don't think I'm losing my marbles, because I'm not.'

'I believe you Granny.'

'Actually from our research we think there maybe two ghosts, so Zoe might have seen just one of them.' Deborah wasn't sure why she admitted this, but she needed to convince Steve that something paranormal was happening in the house. Not, she reflected that he could do anything about it.

'Two! Cool!' Zoe squealed. 'I wish I was there with you Granny to help you catch them.'

'I don't want to catch them, I want them to go away!' Deborah laughed despite herself. Steve's horrified face also amused her.

'So what's the plan Mum? Exorcism! Can you get a priest in lockdown?' He tried to smile.

'Nothing so extreme. We're going to try to find the source and persuade the ghost or ghosts to go down another route.' Deborah had no idea what they were going to do, but thinking on the spur of the moment, she realised it was actually a good plan.

'Persuade it to go down another route? What are you going to do? Build a motorway?' This time Steve did laugh.

Deborah and Zoe joined in his mirth.

'I'll keep you posted.'

'Please do, and Mum please take care of yourself. Have you got everything you need?'

'Don't worry. Take care of yourselves too.'

Having made arrangements to Skype again the following Saturday, Deborah went downstairs to find her companions occupied in pulling on coats and shoes.

'What's happening?'

Joy enlightened her. 'Jessica's working in the garden; Shirley and Tony are going for a walk; Terry, Simon, and I are going down the cellar to look for some clues. Grace and Dan are in the kitchen concocting some special meal for tonight. Do you want to come with us?'

'Yes, I think I will.'

The door leading from the hall into the back garden, opened out onto a red quarry tiled path. The worn tiles were broken in places leaving gaps for moss and other weeds to force their way through. As they progressed down the long stretch that led to what was once the old stables, the remains of a flower bed became evident. Deborah bent down to lift the heads of some overgrown purple hellebores.

'They're lovely aren't they?' Joy stopped to examine them. 'Such a deep purple almost black colour. I haven't seen these shades before. I used to have some pink ones. There's some more over there, tangled up in ivy and fern. We'll have to give Jessica and Kirsty a hand out here. We've got a lot to do. They want to concentrate on growing veg at the moment.'

Both women glanced across the large expanse of land where Jessica was battling with weeds.

213

'I don't think the previous owners did much to keep it going once they decided to sell, but Jessica said it won't take long to get it back into condition. The soil is good apparently,' Joy said.

'I don't mind doing a bit of weeding. I quite like it really. If I do just a little bit at a time,' Deborah confided. 'Good exercise. It will keep us fit.'

Following Terry and Simon down the crumbling steps into the old stable was an exercise of a different kind. The uneven stone steps were worn smooth making them slippery to tread on.

'Best to keep as close to the wall as you can for support. The balustrade, if there ever was one, has gone,' Terry advised taking hold of Joy's arm as she stepped down first. He helped her to the bottom then held out a steadying hand to Deborah.

Simon shone his torch through a gap in the wall to the right of him. She could see the remnants of a door and two steps leading to an anteroom with racks of wine. The wooden shelves were sturdy in comparison to the brick wall. In their excitement to reach the wine, the men had cleared away the cobwebs and dust to reveal the layers and layers of stock.

'As you can see we've probably got enough to last until next Christmas!' Simon enthused proudly.

'I must admit I hadn't realised how much was there when we saw it last time,' Joy said. 'You've obviously cleaned up a bit in here.'

'Only where it mattered,' Terry confessed. He shone his torch beyond the last rack of wine. 'The flimsy door hadn't been hung properly, just wedged against the wall with those bricks you can see over there. On this side there's some fallen brickwork and a mass of old mortar. It looks as if it hasn't been touched for years. We ought to clear that away to make the place more accessible and safer. Then we can start on this side.' Terry turned to shine his torch on the opposite wall where another doorway was partially bricked up. 'We might be able to salvage some of the materials to make a small shed. Jessica and Kirsty are looking for somewhere to store their gardening tools.'

'Do you think you could restore the old stable for them?' Joy asked.

Terry shrugged. 'Depends how badly damaged it is. If the foundations are still good, we might be able to build on it. But aren't we here to find a ghost?'

'Lay one, more like,' Simon said. His eyes twinkled. 'Come on let's start shifting this rubble. I've brought some sacks. If you and I start shovelling, perhaps Joy and Debbie can hold the sacks upright so the rubbish can go straight in. Then we can lift them up the steps.'

'Good plan,' Terry replied. 'Is that alright? He raised a querying eyebrow at the two women. Neither disagreed.

An hour later, Grace and Dan called down to them that coffee and homemade biscuits were waiting for them in the yard. Glad for a break the four grimy workers, climbed up the steps. Terry put a plank of wood across two bags of rubble to form a seat.

'Thanks Grace. We're making good progress.' Simon sipped his coffee. He leaned with his back against the ivy strewn brick wall of the dilapidated building.

'So am I,' Jessica informed them walking across in her muddy wellingtons. 'The ground is quite soft after all the rain we've had. It makes pulling up weeds easier.' She sat on the makeshift bench next to Joy.

'We've got the clean jobs - in the kitchen,' Dan grinned. He and Grace maintained a little distance from the grubby workers. Dan leaned against the wall with his arms folded. One hand held a mug of coffee, in the other was a half-eaten biscuit.

'Did you make these Florentine's?' Jessica asked.

'Yes, a speciality of mine,' Dan confessed. 'I love making biscuits.'

'And I love eating them,' Jessica winked. 'So carry on the good work.' Her remark was reinforced with similar compliments from the others.

'He's also made quiches for lunch,' Grace said proudly.

Dan's face coloured slightly. 'Have you made any discoveries down there?' He unravelled his biscuit arm to point down the steps of the ramshackle building. Simon gave an update just when Deborah heard *Beethoven's Ode to Joy* on her mobile. She searched her pockets trying to find where the source was coming from. Finally locating it, she noted the call was from her older son.

'It's David,' she informed them and moved away slightly to take the call. She smiled wryly anticipating what he was about to say.

'David, good morning? Or is it still?' She glanced at her watch to note the time was five minutes to noon. 'Just about. How are you?' Absently she blew away some dust off her hand.

Once the pleasantries were out of the way, David plunged into the real reason for his call.

'Mum I've just had a Skype with Steve...'

'How nice. I'm glad you're keeping in touch. I Skyped with him this morning too. They're in lockdown in France you know.'

'Yes, yes, I know that Mum. I'm a bit concerned over what he told me about you.' He hesitated.

216

A smile flicked Deborah's lips as she waited for him to explain. Her smile broadened when he eventually broached the subject.

'Mum, Steve said that you've been seeing ghosts.'

'Yes, that's right. Though I have to say I haven't actually seen the ghost, just its antics.'

'Its antics? What do you mean?'
Deborah took a deep breath and told him everything she had told his brother.

'Yes, that's what Steve said. Are you sure you aren't making this up? Mum I'm worried about you.'

'Don't worry about me. Look why don't you talk to Jessica, she's here, I'm sure she will tell you I'm fine.'

'Yes, good idea. Put her on.'

Deborah turned around to see Jessica making her way back to the vegetable plot. 'Oops she's gone back to the garden, I'll put Joy on instead.'

When Joy handed her mobile back to Deborah after her conversation, David seemed even more troubled. Having listened to the detailed account Joy had given him, she wasn't surprised.

'Mum if this is some kind of joke, I'm really worried. I just wish I could come there and sort something out. This flaming pandemic!'

'For goodness sake, David, I'm fine. We're all fine. Look perhaps you will feel better if you talk to Dan. He's Grace's grandson, staying with us because the poor lad has been furloughed. Though actually, I think it's more likely he has lost his job. Anyway we will see.'

'Yes, put him on.'

Listening to Dan's cheerful conversation with her son, Deborah couldn't help thinking what a relief it was, to have the young chef staying with them. His

217

lively attitude and energy was welcome more than ever, now they had a ghost or two to locate, and deal with lockdown. She chuckled, and she had her sons to contend with.

'Satisfied now?' she asked, when Dan handed back her mobile. She watched him and his grandmother retreat to the house.

Joy was using hand signals to indicate that work was about to begin again in the cellar. She whispered she was willing to talk to her son again if necessary.

A long sigh came from David. 'Mum this is a lot to take in. I don't know what to say. But please take care.'

'Don't worry. I will. Give my love to Lucy and the boys.'

Returning down the steps, Deborah told her friends about the reactions from both of her sons regarding the phantoms.

Terry, his face covered in brick dust, chiselled at the remains of broken plaster that covered over what remained of a doorway as he listened.

'We haven't told our two kids what's going on in fear of the same reaction.'

Joy nodded as she swept up some debris into another black bin bag. 'We'll have to tell them eventually, if we don't sort it out. Actually, I think Fay would enjoy the mystery, I'm not sure about Amy.'

'Grace and I haven't told Katie, Simon said.' He chuckled, 'though I suspect Dan has kept his mum in the loop. Katie would find it all exciting. She loves things like the paranormal. It's rubbed off on to Dan. That's why he's taking it all in his stride. He's a sensible lad for a twenty year old who likes his beer.' He swept his torch over their handiwork. 'Now we've cleared all this rubble out of the way, we should be able to see what's behind this bit of crumbling plaster and brickwork.' He carefully chiselled away at the barrier and was pleased that it fell away without a lot of time and effort.

'If I'm not mistaken, 'Terry said, 'we've found the remains of a door. It's pretty rotten in places.' He prodded it with the end of his chisel. The rotted wood fell away in bits revealing green and black mould. A putrid stench took away their breath as it surged through the hole.

'Christ what a smell.' Both men choked and stepped back quickly with their arms across their mouths. Joy and Deborah had already retreated up the steps desperate to get fresh air. Within seconds Terry and Simon joined them. All four sat on the plank seat to get their breath.

''I suppose we should have expected that,' Terry said. He pulled out his handkerchief to wipe his face. Simon did the same. The two women got to their feet with the intention of cleaning themselves up inside the house.

'It's getting close to lunch time anyway,' Joy said.
Half an hour later, they sat in the conservatory to eat the food prepared by Dan and Grace.
Freshly showered and looking radiant from her horse ride, Kirsty glanced furtively at Jessica before sitting down with her back turned away from her.

Deborah wondered if Kirsty was avoiding her sister. She guessed Jessica would want to know about Kirsty's so called love affair. She loved to tease. Yet Kirsty hinted the other day that Jessica might be having a fling with Malcolm from the book club? Thinking about romance, caused Deborah's thoughts

219

to turn to Dennis. She was astonished at how her mind had wandered and gave herself a little shake.

'Penny for them,' Jessica said.

'Nothing much. I was just wondering what might lie behind that door in the cellar. The odour was horrendous.'

'Just bad gasses escaping, I shouldn't wonder. No doubt when the complete doorway has been cut away, the air will be sweeter.'

From the adjoining table Terry leaned over to agree with Jessica. 'But we will take masks with us when we go down again. I suggest we leave it until tomorrow.'

The strains of *Johann Strauss's Blue Danube* floated through the conservatory. Grace got up to look for her mobile.

'It's in the piano room Gran. I saw it this morning when you went in there to tidy up. It was on the mantelpiece.'

A minute later, Grace's scream from the piano lounge sent them all rushing after her.

The piano stool had been upturned, and several of the lighter armchairs had been pushed to one side. Deborah's metronome was ticking furiously even though she was convinced she'd put the pendulum back in its place.

'What's happened?' Grace put her hand to her throat ignoring her mobile vibrating on the top of the fireplace. Within seconds of her shouts, she was surrounded by anxious faces. Dan picked up his gran's mobile just as it went into voicemail. He checked the caller.

Joy got hold of one of the chairs to put it right again. Deborah seized the piano stool and sat on it dumbfounded.

'It was Mum,' Dan said cheerfully. 'She's spooked us.'

'Don't be ridiculous. Katie's done nothing of the kind.' Grace managed a grin, though she wasn't sure it was for her own benefit or that of her grandson's.

Shirley and Tony, returned from their walk, helped to re-arrange the furniture. Once order was restored, everyone tried to come up with an explanation for the commotion. Grace remained standing as if frozen.

'I think it's the music,' Kirsty said.

'What music? Deborah asked frowning.

'*The Blue Danube.* It's on Grace's mobile. It's her ring tone.'

'What about my ring tone?' Grace frowned at Kirsty, then wheeled round towards the fireplace where Dan was leaning, with the mobile still in his hand. He passed it to her. She took it from him gingerly.

'There's a missed call from Mum,' he reminded her.

Kirsty ignored Dan, jumping in to explain before Grace managed to speak again.

'I noticed yesterday when we were looking at all the documents relating to *The Golden Peacock* that when your mobile rang, a couple of chairs began to rock forwards.' Kirsty took a breath surveying the listening faces around her, 'it was as if they were swaying in tune.'

'Swaying chairs. I've heard everything now.' Simon scratched his head. He tried to reassure Grace with a smile, but she was distracted reading the text message from her daughter.

'Let's try again. Gran why don't you play the ring tone on your mobile? Then we can see what happens.'

But Grace had moved to the back of the room keying in a text to her daughter. Deborah lifted the piano lid and began to play *Johann Strauss's Blue Danube.*

For a few seconds, nothing happened. Then Dan who was still standing in front of the fireplace shook his head as he felt something gently caress his skin.

'It's here. I can feel it,' he said, unable to keep the excitement out of his voice.

Deborah felt something too. The back of her neck tingled, she didn't know if it was fear or exhilaration. She continued to play from memory, enjoying the music and the atmosphere in the room. She was oblivious to Dan's shout that he could see something shiny gliding across the room. She was only inspired to play harder, hitting the keys louder and then pressing the pedals with her feet for good measure.

Entranced, Dan drifted towards what he later described, was a kind of watery image of a young woman in a soft silky dress. His arms were positioned as if in a waltz. To the housemates, he appeared to be dancing by himself. Shirley, who had stood to pass a cushion to Tony, found herself ensnared into an unseen web. She also began to dance. Transfixed, the others, powerlessly looked on, as the two dancers with invisible partners were twirled towards the conservatory.

Deborah performed as if possessed. Her exhilaration increased the tempo of the music as it got louder. She knew she'd lost control, but helplessly played on. The metronome's pendulum swung rapidly to and fro urging her to play faster. She saw the spring sunshine glinting on the keys and felt heat rush through her fingers. But it wasn't the warmth from the sun that made her hands uncomfortably hot. She was unable to

222

stop, an unknown force compelled her fingers to recite the notes.

Tony and Terry struggled to get up. Both had the intention to follow the dancers with their unseen partners as they were spun into the conservatory. As soon as the two men were standing shakily on their feet, they were immediately drawn into a vacuum of energy, pivoting them towards the conservatory door.

Terry later said he felt he was fighting an unseen power that tried to force him into the conservatory and against the glass walls. He was afraid that the panels would smash but had no strength to resist.

Tony also felt as if he was being manipulated. It had taken him a few seconds longer than Terry, to get up from his seat, and he had seized hold of one of the chairs to anchor himself. He'd tried to put his free arm out to hold Terry back, but a stronger power dragged him into the potent vortex. He'd found the strength to shout, 'stop! stop! Debbie stop!' before he too was propelled towards the conservatory. But Deborah couldn't stop. She was compelled to go on.

Joy's legs felt spongy. She'd been sitting in a chair behind the piano. In an effort to help her husband, she'd got up and like the others, immediately became caught in an energy that forced her towards the conservatory. But she had to pass the piano. Feebly, she tottered around it, holding on to the sides of the piano for support. When she levelled with the keyboard, there was nothing to cling to; she lost balance and fell sideways on to Deborah. Joy's weight toppled Deborah backwards. Instantly her hands left the keyboard and she clutched Joy's arm to save herself from falling. Joy recoiled with a scream, when she got a burning sensation from her friend's touch.

Deborah's eyes were glazed, she rested her hands on her knees then bowed her head.

'Are you alright Debbie?' Joy tentatively put her arm around her friend's shoulder, half expecting another burn, but Deborah's body had returned to room temperature. With a concerned glance over her shoulder, Joy was relieved to see Terry and Tony leading a disorientated Shirley and a mystified Dan back into the piano lounge.

'For crying out loud. What was that all about?' Jessica spoke for them all. 'I don't know about you guys but I feel as if I've just stepped out of a tube of glue! It looks like your theory was right, Shirley. That music on Grace's mobile has sparked something deeply disturbing.' She got up to go to her room. 'I think we could all do with a drink and I don't mean tea. I've got just the thing.'

CHAPTER NINETEEN

'That was sick. Did you see her?' Dan shook his head when he was offered some whisky. He swaggered to the kitchen to get some *Wrexham Lager*.

'I couldn't see her face properly but she looked young and she was smiling,' he called over his shoulder.

Whilst moments before, Deborah had experienced a burning sensation thrilling her fingers, Dan's announcement sent contrasting cold ripples of shock through her body. Examining the widened eyes on the faces of those around her and the tense body language, she guessed that her own bewildered appearance was the same.

Dan sauntered back from the kitchen, his eyes sparkled. Shirley waited for him to settle on an armchair, before questioning him.

'Did you actually feel anything? I mean physically?'

'Yes. It was very slight. I had a sensation of dancing with air, yet I felt her dress, kinda silky on my hands. Weird.' He lifted the pull ring on his can and bent his head down to suck the froth that fizzed over the top, 'Did you?'

'I think so. It all seems so hazy now even though it was just a few minutes ago. I couldn't see anything really, nor feel anything. But subconsciously I was aware I was dancing with a man dressed in an evening suit. At least, somehow, I was conscious he was wearing a dinner jacket. Sorry to be so vague. It sounds daft now.' She turned to Tony who held her hand encouragingly. She took a sip of her whisky, then pulled a face at the taste and reached for an ice cube. She risked a glance at Jessica, expecting a disapproving rebuke, who despite catching Shirley's eye, refrained from mouthing the expected 'sacrilege' castigation.

'What about you, Deborah? What happened to you? It was like as if you were glued to the piano. Are you feeling alright now?' Joy had guided Deborah from the piano stool to sit on a sofa next to herself and Terry, then handed her a glass of whisky.

Deborah nursed the drink in her hands as she spoke.

'As soon as I started playing those notes, I felt as if I was bound up in another era. I could hear an orchestra playing and the sounds of people dancing, but I couldn't see anything. Then somehow, I was being forced to play faster, although my fingers were burning hot. I couldn't stop. If you hadn't pushed my hands off the keyboard, I don't know what would have happened.'

Joy slowly ran a finger around the rim of her tumbler as she studied Deborah. 'It took an effort for me to physically move. I felt as if I was being pulled, but I kept close to the piano and when I heard Tony say stop, I knew I had to resist, to get to Deborah. I think all of us were under some kind of a spell.'

'Some kinda energy was dragging me too.' Dan added. 'The funny thing was, I felt as if I couldn't let go. But I didn't want to. Weird. It was only when the music stopped that something snapped. Cool though.'

'But what does it all mean?' Shirley asked. 'Debbie I don't think you should play that tune again. At least not until we've figured out how to solve this phenomena.'

'Do you think I should change the ring tone on my mobile?'

A unanimous 'yes' responded to Grace's question.

'Try to find a modern tune rather than a classical one,' Kirsty advised her. She fumbled in her jeans pocket. 'Talking of which, I don't know where my own mobile is.'

'Probably in your riding jacket pocket?' Jessica suggested. 'Your jacket is hanging up by the back door in the porch where you left your boots. At least, it was before we had lunch. Are you expecting a call?'

'Not really, but I would like to know where it is.' Kirsty got up and made her way to the porch. When she reached the hallway, the kitchen door bell rang making them all jump.

'Anybody expecting callers?' Kirsty turned round to check, then made her way to answer the door. A few minutes later she returned with her jacket in her hand and her mobile in the other.

'Deborah, you have a visitor. It's Dennis from *The White Hart*. He's insisted on waiting outside.'

'I wonder why he's here.' Deborah got up exchanging a puzzled look with Jessica.

'Go and find out. I'll come with you. You've had more than enough shocks today.'

Dennis stood a few metres away from the door.

'Hello, I'm sorry to disturb you. I'm keeping my distance don't worry. I just thought you might like copies of these maps and plans you were so interested in the other day.' Dennis indicated a supermarket carrier bag he'd left on the doorstep. A few rolls of paper stuck out.

Deborah blushed despite herself. She found it difficult to keep eye contact with Dennis much to

Jessica's amusement. He looked uncomfortable. Deborah wondered if he'd regretted calling.

'Thank you that's very kind of you,' she managed to mumble, suddenly at a loss of what else to say. She was conscious that she might smell of whisky and didn't want to give him the wrong impression. For some reason she couldn't fathom, it seemed important to her to let him know that she wasn't a habitual day time drinker.

'I'm sorry we've been drinking whisky. It's been a funny day you see... 'She stopped awkwardly as Jessica pinched her sharply on her back side. Dennis stared at her with a furrowed brow and made a half-hearted attempt to move away.

Jessica on the other hand, felt this was a good opportunity to make strong ties. Never stuck for words she immediately took over the situation. It was unfortunate that they weren't able to invite him in for a drink. She actually said as much, but was determined to delay him somehow.

'How are you and your wife coping with the lockdown?'

Dennis shrugged. 'This is only the first day. It was difficult not opening up at lunch time as usual, but hopefully it won't be for long. I suppose I will get used to it, for a short while. Like I said I hope it won't be for too long.'

'And your wife?' Jessica persisted.

'My wife, died two years ago. It's just me and my daughter and son-in-law running the pub. Fortunately they have other jobs, so it won't be too bad for them.' He stood awkwardly staring at both of them.

'I suppose I'd better go. See you again hopefully when this pandemic is done with us.'

'Yes. Thanks again.' They both stood on the doorstep for a while to watch him walk down the drive to his car.

'Keep in touch. You have my mobile number.' Deborah surprised herself, blurting out that last remark. She was rewarded when he turned to smile.

'Yes. I will do that. Let me know if you want anything else?'

'There, I told you he fancied you.' Jessica bent down to pick up the bag of maps then closed the door. She linked her arm through Deborah's as they walked back to the piano lounge.

'Rubbish. He's just being kind. He's probably bored already with nothing to do.'

'I wouldn't be so sure about that. There must be plenty of work to keep him occupied even without customers. At least, for the next week or two. Anyway let's look at what he's brought.'

They explained the nature of Dennis' visit to the rest of the group.

'Interesting that the landlord of *The White Hart* has documents relating to *The Golden Peacock*,' Simon commented.

'How come?' Dan asked.

'It seems that, at one time the owner of both pubs was the same. Most pubs are owned by breweries, but some of them were sold off to private landlords,' Deborah explained.

Joy agreed. 'Believe it or not, the breweries were essential to the town's economy. *Border Breweries* used to be the biggest in Wrexham, but it stopped trading long before you were born, Dan. In fact I could tell you a lot more about the need for pubs on market days and all that, but maybe another time.'

Deborah took out the documents from the plastic supermarket bag and laid them out on the coffee table. There were four pieces of paper. Attached to one was a note to Deborah saying that they should be joined together with some sellotape to be able to make any sense of them.

'We can do that later. Let's see if we can learn anything that might help solve our mystery.' Terry assembled the documents side by side, then re-arranged the drawings to show the foundations of *The Golden Peacock Inn*. The lines were faint in places, and some words so worn away that it was difficult to read.

'Look at this!' Terry bent eagerly over the centre where two pieces joined. 'If I'm not mistaken that bit over here on the right is our cellar. Here is the stable. These two lines represent a subway of some kind.' He traced the lines with his finger across the page. 'This is a much better plan than the one we had with our deeds. It clearly starts from the end of the garden where it meets the back lane, as we supposed. From there it goes under what is depicted as a field, and is now our garden.' His finger stopped at the edge of the paper. It finishes at the gable end of the house, the side of this room in fact. There's also an intersection to the cellar. Hmm.'

'An underground tunnel?' Dan said. 'Cool.'

'Fascinating, but what's that got to do with our paranormal experiences?' Grace asked. She held her mobile in her hand and kept rubbing it with her fingers as if she expected it to burst into flames.

Terry scratched his head. 'I'm not sure, but I have a sneaky feeling there is a connection.'

Simon examined the documents again, Grace leaned on his back to study them over his shoulder.

'I think you've got a point Terry. We'll have to get started on that door we found tomorrow, and see what's behind it. If we discover the tunnel we might unravel our mystery.'

Joy knelt down in front of the documents to get a closer look. When she raised her head again her face was beaming. She looked straight into Deborah's anxious eyes.

'I think I know what it is.'

'What?'

'A few years ago when I was working full time at the library, I discovered some old books referring to the history of the breweries in Wrexham. Some of the old pubs have underground passages, created for the delivery of barrels of beer to the publicans. Many of them were wide enough and high enough, to take the fully loaded wagons straight to the cellars. I wouldn't be surprised if the horses went down there too.'

'They were huge horses too. Probably Shire horses if I'm not mistaken,' Kirsty added.

'Hell, I've just remembered something. Sorry to interrupt Joy, but I read something similar to this in the *Wrexham Leader* not long ago,' Shirley covered her mouth with her hand and nodded to Joy to go on.

'Anyway, I was thinking that *The Golden Peacock Inn,* or whatever you want to call it, must have had a tunnel to take delivery of the beer.'

'Cool. Dan said again.'

'Yes, it is cool as you say Dan, but what's that got to do with our ghosts?' Grace smiled at her grandson as she asked her question again.

'I think the tunnel was used by the gentry who came here to dance,' Joy speculated. 'It's like we surmised earlier. They wouldn't want their finery to be soiled by the mud and what have you outside, so the carriages would draw up at the end of the lane and they would walk underground to the ballroom which would have been about here.' She pointed to the bit on the map and leaned back so the others could see.

'This is astonishing, but it fits perfectly, Deborah said.'

'If we can discover the tunnel we might be able to figure it all out.' Simon picked up two of the documents that showed the cellar, then with a glance at the walls of the piano room he walked to the fireplace.

As if reading his mind, Terry got to his feet, groaning about the ache in his knees. He stepped over to join Simon. A few minutes after checking the document, they both nodded as if reaching a conclusion.

'It's likely that this fireplace was the original, just as Graham Bailey suggested,' Terry said, straightening up again. He put his hand on his back and stretched.

'Whoever played the music at the dances, may have been playing exactly here, where Deborah's piano is situated now,' Simon added.

'Think about it, if a pianist's hands are cold, it would be difficult to play?' Simon jerked his head in Deborah's direction and she nodded.

'There would have been a blazing wood fire, the pianist would have felt very hot.' Simon folded his arms. He looked pleased with himself. 'You said you felt there was an orchestra around you?'

Deborah nodded, her wide eyed shock was mirrored in those of her companions.

'Wow!' Dan enthused.

Simon and Terry then moved from the piano to the corner of the room. After a few seconds they turned to face the wall that separated the room with the conservatory.

'And the conservatory, as we suspected, would have been part of the ballroom,' Terry concluded.

'Yep, that tallies with the plans.' Simon pointed at the assorted documents strewn on the floor.

'Cool,' Dan was ecstatic.

Shirley grinned. 'This is fascinating!'

Grace knelt down and carefully rolled up the documents then handed them to Simon for safe keeping. 'So are you saying if we find the tunnel, we will find out why we are being haunted?' She asked.

Simon turned to his wife. 'Perhaps. I can't honestly say for sure.'

'I'm going to make some tea.'

'I'll help you Gran, we can try some of that lemon drizzle cake I made this morning.'

In the silence that followed Dan and Grace's departure, a faint rumbling sound became evident.

'What's that?' Kirsty clutched her throat. 'Surely not another ghost!'

Shirley laughed, 'It's Tony. He's snoring. He usually has a nap around now. Ever since his knee replacement op he's rested in the afternoons. All this excitement has sapped his energy. He ought to go upstairs for an hour.' She nudged him gently, then helped him out of the room. Simon followed them on his way to the television lounge. From the hallway they heard the clock chime four thirty.

Deborah slumped on the sofa and put her feet up on the small stool.

233

'I could do with a nap myself, I feel drained.'

'We're going for a walk before it gets dark, anybody else want to come? I need to stretch my legs,' Joy bent down to rub her knees.

Jessica poured herself another glass of whisky, 'Not for me thanks.' She offered the bottle to Deborah and Kirsty who both accepted a small tot.

'And then there were three,' Kirsty laughed.

'It was good of Dennis to bring those plans around for us.' Jessica turned to Deborah with a meaningful expression, but Deborah merely nodded as she sipped her whisky.

'He seems a friendly sort of bloke,' Kirsty agreed. 'It's nice to have a link with *The White Hart,* so romantic.'

Grace and Dan brought in a tray of tea and cake and left it on the coffee table in front of them.

'We've got another tray for us and Simon,' Grace said. 'We're going to watch a quiz show on the TV before supper. According to Simon, there's a good film on at eight o 'clock. We are going to watch it, because I don't feel like staying in here for another ghostly performance. Once a day is enough.'

At five minutes to eight the entire group except for Kirsty, seated themselves in front of the television. Kirsty, had gone upstairs to Skype with her son living in Edinburgh. She was looking forward to the marriage of her son Mathew and his partner Keira. She hoped to be able to help plan their wedding.

Downstairs, an intense crime thriller on the television held the attention of the rest of the occupants. So not only did they not see Kirsty slip out of the house through the back door, but they also missed the two ghosts waltzing across the piano lounge towards the conservatory.

CHAPTER TWENTY

That night, Deborah couldn't sleep. Her sleeping pattern had altered as she'd got older. She often woke in the small hours, which was bad enough, but sometimes, despite being tired she couldn't drop off. The strange events that had transpired during the previous afternoon played on her mind. Each time she tried to push the thoughts away, strong images of herself and Dennis dancing kept forcing themselves into her consciousness.

At two o'clock she'd had enough. She got out of bed and filled her small kettle to make tea. A hot drink and reading for a while usually helped her to relax. Realising she'd forgotten to bring some camomile tea bags upstairs with her, she flung on her dressing gown and slippers to go to the kitchen. She'd almost reached the end of the landing corridor and about to go downstairs when she heard a groan coming from Kirsty's room. Deborah assumed she was having a bad dream. At least she was able to sleep. She tiptoed past the door but then heard the bed creak and footsteps. Maybe Kirsty was awake after all. Perhaps she'd like some tea too. Gently she knocked on the door then without waiting, opened it. The room was illuminated by the bedside lamp.

'Kirsty, I was going to make tea…Oh!'

A semi naked man flung himself under the duvet as Kirsty dived towards the door wrapping her silk dressing gown around her totally naked frame.

Deborah gaped.

'Hell, so sorry.' She turned away edging out of the room.

'No, don't go,' Kirsty whispered.   She smiled sheepishly. 'This is Leslie, Leslie this is Deborah.'

Despite the unusual encounter, and the time Leslie grinned.

'Pleased to meet you.' He spoke in a low voice.

'Hello,' Deborah managed to say. She avoided Leslie's eyes and focused on Kirsty's glowing face.

'Would you like some tea?' Deborah's lips twitched.

Unsurprised that they declined her offer, she returned to her bedroom with a few teabags in her pocket plus a glass of whisky, both provided by Kirsty. Only when she was propped up in bed sipping her version of a toddy did she start to laugh.

Leslie quietly slipped unseen out of the house the following morning. Kirsty breakfasted early and was on her way out when Deborah entered the kitchen. Kirsty winked, just as Shirley and Tony walked in.

'See you later,' Kirsty called, closing the back door.

At ten o 'clock, Simon and Terry decided to resume their work in the cellar. Dan passed them in the hall as he appeared carrying a plate of toast and marmalade. He offered to help.

'I'm not sure if I can be of much use, but I can try, just as soon as I've finished this.'

'We can all do something to help, I'm sure,' Joy said.

Terry shrugged, 'If you don't mind a bit of dust and getting dirty again.' He took in Joy's and Shirley's old clothes. They'd already dressed appropriately. Terry glanced at the inadequate garments of the rest of the women gathered in the hallway and shook his head.

'Oops. I forgot about the exploring. I didn't sleep well last night, I'm a bit tired. If you don't mind I'll just watch.' Deborah yawned as if to prove a point.

'You still need to wear some kind of overalls, there will be a lot of dust.'

Jessica looked down at her woollen skirt and Fair Isle sweater. 'I forgot to put my old clothes on. I'm looking forward to this project.'

'I'll make the coffee later,' Grace offered. 'Unless you can find me a job to do in the cellar. There might be too many of us down there for comfort.'

Upstairs, Jessica confided in Deborah that she'd heard some strange voices in the night.

'I had a feeling it came from Kirsty's room, but I might be mistaken. I hope it wasn't another ghost. Mind you if there is another one up here, I wish it would talk to me, I'd like to have a chat with it. Perhaps it was Joy's jewellery pilferer.' She opened the door into her room and Deborah, choosing not to enlighten her, walked past to get to her own. She hated keeping secrets.

In the cellar, the smell was as acrid as the previous day. Joy handed Shirley and Jessica a pot of Vaseline.

'Smear some above your top lip, it helps to stop you retching. You might as well have some too Debbie, even if you aren't coming all the way down.'

'Yuk, it's horrible. I don't know how you can stand it,' Jessica smeared more of the cream on the tip of her nose after just venturing down a few of the steps.

'Nearly through. Just have to get these rusted old hinges off the wall. Stand back, I need to use the angle grinder.' Terry shooed everyone away to a safe point.

237

Simon hoisted up a large sheet of plastic sheeting and hammered it in to the top of the cellar opening to shield those outside from the dust. He held one side in place and Dan the other.

Within minutes the hinges fell off and the door slumped towards Terry knocking him backwards. A lunge from Simon saved him from falling. The pungent smell from the fungi growing around the door frame was stronger. Bits of rotting wood and mould tumbled out of the hole. The three men recoiled as the odour over powered them.

'Let's get some fresh air before we do any more.' Simon advised.

Outside they gratefully leaned against the brick wall of the cellar taking deep breaths. Simon turned as he saw Grace walk towards them. She looked upset.

'I've got some bad news. Barbara's been taken to hospital with suspected coronavirus. Derek's just phoned me. He's devastated.'

'That's awful. I suppose Derek's not allowed to stay with her.' Deborah sympathised.

Grace shook her head. 'Unfortunately, no he's not.' She sighed. 'We must all be careful. Minimise our excursions and such like. When was the last time you saw her? We've been so busy lately with the move and everything, Simon and I haven't seen them since Christmas. If one of you saw her in the last two weeks we might all need to self-isolate, although it might be too late!'

'I saw them at Barbara's seventieth birthday party middle of February,' Deborah said.

'Yes me too,' Joy nodded. I haven't seen her since.'

'Is she on a ventilator?' Jessica wriggled on the heap of bricks and stones she'd made into a seat, trying to make herself more comfortable. 'I haven't seen her since her birthday either.'

Grace shrugged and replied she didn't know.

Terry sighed, 'not much we can do about it, I'm sorry to say. Let's hope she pulls through.' Deborah silently hoped that as well as Barbara pulling through, that she and her friends would be safe from the pandemic.

'Have you made much progress?' Grace stood where she was, taking in the filthy faces of the workers.

Joy explained. 'The smell in there is putrid, it seems to be coming from the rotting door and the fungi attached to it. If we can haul it out somehow, the rank atmosphere in there, will reduce and make it less uncomfortable to work.' She glanced at her husband for confirmation. 'Besides we're itching to see what's behind the door.'

'Right. I'll make some coffee and bring it out here. You all deserve it.'

'I'm sure between the three of us we can drag the door out here to the open air,' Terry indicated himself, Simon and Dan. 'With a bit of luck I think that rancid stench will go.'

Tony got up to help but Terry stopped him.

'It's not safe in there for you Tony. There is too much rubble underfoot. The last thing you want to do is damage your new knee.'

Tony gave in. He knew Terry was right. Shirley squeezed his arm.

Ten minutes later the heavy oak door was lying outside, flat on the ground. Black fungi mingled with wood lice and splinters of wood hung around the sides. The group moved away from it with their hands

239

covering their noses. Fascinated by the array of fungi, Dan held his arm over his face and stooped over the door for a closer look. Meanwhile inside the cellar, Terry and Simon were excited by their discovery. Through their dust smeared faces their eyes shone.

'We've found the tunnel,' Simon coughed as he spoke and Terry took the opportunity to add 'and it looks like it goes towards the house!'

Grace arrived with a tray of mugs and set it down on a pile of bricks, then caught sight of the door a few metres away. Dan was still examining it. He'd wrapped his scarf over his nose and mouth, so he could bend over the door to have a closer look.

'Yuk what is that? Grace wrinkled her face.

'It's the smelly oak door,' her husband smiled at her. We should take a photograph of it. Has anybody got their mobile with them?'

Dan was already taking pictures. Shirley wriggled out of her over-sized jumpsuit. 'My mobile is in my jeans pocket. I can't reach it through all this clothing. I'll take some pictures too and then, I'll come and wash my hands. I can help Grace to bring out the coffee pots.'

'Can we see the tunnel?' Deborah asked.

'Why don't you let us clear the entrance a bit to make it safer under foot, then we can all explore?' Simon advised. 'Anyway we may as well have our coffee first and enjoy the fresh air. Not that there's much seating here.'

As he spoke he balanced a few extra planks over some sacks of sand and gravel put aside to make the boules pitch. With the help of the other makeshift seats, there was enough space for them all to sit down. Grace returned with Shirley, carrying the cafetieres and a cake.

Deborah, enjoying the warmth of the spring sunshine and the coffee felt a surge of love for her companions. Their years of friendship had always been strong, but since they had moved in together it had strengthened. It could have so easily destroyed them. Yet even with the intrusion of the phantoms and the terrible pandemic, they had drawn closer together.

'Any coffee left for me?' Kirsty joined them still in her riding clothes. A whiff of horse manure reached their nostrils. Deborah thought it was quite pleasant in contrast with the decaying door. It seemed her opinion was shared.

'That's a welcome smell from what we've just experienced,' her sister informed her. The others grinned.

'What, do I smell horsey?'

'Of course you do. You always do. That is to say, when you come back from the stables.'

Grace handed her a mug of coffee with a bottle of hand sanitiser and a damp towel. 'I hope it's still hot.'

Kirsty stuffed her riding gloves in her pocket, then cleansed her hands. 'Thanks Grace, you think of everything.' She took a sip of the coffee, declared it was warm enough and reached out for a piece of carrot cake.'

'Is this home-made?'

Grace nodded. 'A new recipe. It has less fat.'

'Gorgeous. So what were you saying about the terrible smell?' She took another bite of cake and examined one dirty face after the other.

'They've managed to remove that rotten door,' Deborah told her. 'That's what caused the bad odour.'

'Plus we've made a major breakthrough.' The thick dust and mildew embedded into Simon's laughter lines gave him a gruesome appearance. 'We've found the tunnel!'

'Wow. Can we have a look?' Kirsty looked down at her clothes. 'I'd prefer to change first though, I don't want to look like the rest of you.'

'Fine. We'll make the entrance a bit safer, then wait for you. In any case we are at a point where we can brush up some of the dust. We can all explore the inside together.' Simon put down his coffee mug and made his way back to the cellar entrance followed by Terry and Dan.

'Right, I'll get changed then. Thanks Grace for the coffee and cake. Just what I needed.'

'I'll come with you, I need to go to the bathroom.' Deborah followed Kirsty inside the house.

Out of earshot, Deborah told her the news about Barbara. Kirsty stopped at the foot of the stairs a concerned expression on her face.

'That's worrying. Poor Barbara!'

Deborah nodded. 'Yes, it is terrible news. The thing is we were all worried about whether we'd been in contact with her, recently, which we haven't, though I'm not sure if you have?'

Kirsty frowned. 'I met her for coffee at *Cwtch Ceramics* about a month ago, so I'm sure if I had caught the disease I would know by now?'

Deborah nodded her head with relief. Then she hesitated before broaching another subject that was bothering her.

'The thing is, according to the government guidelines we shouldn't make contact with people outside our homes, and now I'm a bit worried about... you know...'

'You mean Leslie! Oh hell.' Kirsty clamped her hand over her mouth. 'I'm sorry Debbie, I wasn't thinking. Neither was Leslie obviously. We've been working closely together for several months and our relationship got even closer over the last few weeks. Last night wasn't... you know... the first time, you know, that he's been here.' She blushed. 'If one of us were to develop symptoms, we'd have noticed by now. Wouldn't we?'

Deborah gazed into her friend's distressed face. 'I don't really know. I suppose so, but I'm not an expert.' She faltered... she didn't want to have to ask Kirsty not to see her lover again, yet...

Fortunately, Kirsty realised what she should do.

'It's ok Debbie, it's too big a risk. We're all at a vulnerable age. I won't invite him here again. I can still see Leslie at the stables. We keep our distance there anyway, because those are the rules that Tina and Jeff have stipulated. It's only fair.'

Deborah was aware how uptight she'd been feeling. She breathed out heavily. 'Thanks Kirsty, I hated mentioning it.'

Kirsty hugged her, 'we're friends. Thank goodness we have each other. All of us. This idea of yours of living together has saved us.'

CHAPTER TWENTY ONE

'Take care of the steps Gran. There's about fifteen of them and they're mega crumbly.'

Grace hung on to her grandson's arm as he guided her down the dilapidated steps. It was the first time she'd been to the bottom. On the last step she turned to her right and gasped as she saw the rows upon rows of wine that Simon and Terry with a bit of help from Dan had cleaned and dusted. To her left was the gaping hole where the door had hung. Thick cobwebs drooped over what remained of the rotten frame.

'The air certainly smells a bit better.' Deborah wrinkled her nose as she followed Grace down the steps.

Terry and Simon waited at the entrance for everyone to assemble. Both carried heavy duty torches. Dan tested the torch on his mobile.

'Ready? Let's go,' Terry stepped through the gap in the wall first, followed by Simon. He issued a warning to everyone to go slowly.

'I've had a look at the ceiling and it seems to be safe, but take care. There's about five steps down." He shone his torch over their heads every step to make sure they were safe.

The tunnel was wider and higher than Deborah had expected. She'd imagined having to stoop to make her way along, but she found she could stand straight with plenty of headroom. There was at least another twelve inches above her five foot six. The air was damp and the further they crept along, the oppressive mugginess increased. Eventually they came to what

Deborah could only describe as a junction. Terry who was in front, chose to go left and they followed him. It was in the direction of the house.

'Look at these wall brackets or whatever you call them!' Shirley shone her mobile phone's torch at the metal pockets rusted and thick with white cobwebs. She let the beam wander ahead. 'There seems to be a lot of them.'

Joy's eyes were bright in the semi darkness. 'I think they were for chandeliers or candles,' she whispered.

'Why are you whispering?' Deborah asked.

'I don't know.'

'She's afraid of disturbing the ghosts,' Jessica whispered back.

'Now you are whispering.'

They tittered nervously.

'We've come to a brick wall,' Simon announced. He held his torch high for them all to see and let out a sigh of frustration.

'How far do you think we've come?' Where do you think we are in relation to the house?' Deborah plied Simon with questions. He scratched his head and through the dim light raised a quizzical eyebrow at Terry.

'About a hundred metres in the direction of the conservatory. I'm wondering if this was built to block the tunnel leading into the house.'

'Shall we see where the tunnel leads in the opposite direction?' Dan asked.

They trudged back to the intersection and then followed the damp walls as it curved to their right.

'We seem to be going in the direction of the back lane as we suspected. This should take us to the carriage house.' Terry lifted his torch to address the onlookers.

'I think this is the spot we had ear marked for the boules pitch.'

The tunnel finished sharply with a stack of rubble consisting of old mortar and broken bricks. Older intact bricks had been stacked up haphazardly against the rubble. Beyond the rubble, the stubs of worn out steps were still visible.

Dan who kept exclaiming how 'cool' everything was, took more photographs.

'How long do you think this end of the tunnel has been blocked up Grandad? Someone must have been down here to do it.'

'I think you're right. Whoever piled that rubble up, did it for safety and blocked the stairway, what's left of it. Probably the same person who blocked up the cellar. If my memory serves me right from looking at those plans of the house, this would be where the original coach house would have been. This part of the tunnel would be used to take barrels of beer to the cellar avoiding the house.'

'These are probably the steps that Joy showed us on that old sketch!' Shirley's eyes sparkled.

Outside again, Terry and Simon walked across the ground, in an attempt to calculate the curve of the tunnel underneath. Intrigued by their discovery, the rest of them followed. When Terry and Simon stopped, Dan drew alongside them.

'I'm pretty sure this spot is the entrance.' Terry said. 'Here are the bricks and stones we dug up last week. They are what was left of the building. Joy's phantom steps must be here somewhere.' He pointed to a pile of pieces of building debris.

Joy walked over to the neatly piled wedges of brick and stone as if trying to get some answers. 'So this is where the guests came into and out of the house to go to the ball.'

'It looks like.' Terry agreed.

'And two of them never left,' Shirley added thoughtfully. They must be our ghosts.'

'If this is the way the wretched ghosts come in and out, I would like to know how we are going to re-route them?' Jessica said. 'I can live with my pots of compost going amok, but what if it gets worse? No wonder that Mr. Gibson wanted to sell up. Deborah can you try to get hold of him again?'

'Yes, Jess, I will get on to it as soon as we get back into the house. Remind me.'

'Good idea, see if he can think of anything to help us,' Terry agreed. 'In the meantime, I want to look at the plans again, and I need a comfort break.'

Later that afternoon, Deborah sent a text to Mr. Gibson and was relieved to get a message back within ten minutes.

'This isn't a great help,' she told Joy who happened to be sitting on the sofa bed in Deborah's bedroom at the time.

'According to this Gibson guy, he said that although he'd had some paranormal occurrences in the lounge area, it was worse in the conservatory soon after he'd built it. When a couple of punters had complained they'd noticed their wine bottle moving, he decided to close the conservatory from customer use and just used it for himself and his family.'

'So why didn't he tell us?' Joy threw up her arms in mock despair.

'Probably thought we wouldn't buy, I suppose.'

'Would you, if you'd known?'

I think so, because I wouldn't have believed him.'

Joy laughed, 'me neither.'

'It's interesting that he noticed something amiss when he built the conservatory. And if you remember, that bloke what's his name, the builder, said he'd seen something odd when he built it.'

'Hmm, and didn't he suggest, or somebody did, I think it was Terry, that because of the alterations we'd made before moving in, that we may have upset the… ghost's route, for want of a better phrase.'

Deborah eyed her friend thoughtfully. 'You could be right. But if that's the case, are we going to have to undo things?'

Joy sighed.' We don't know for certain that the tunnel has anything to do with our phantoms. Yet I have a feeling it has. I think Shirley is right.'

'Simon and Terry will know what to do about the alterations. If our theory is correct, of course. What are you doing?'

'I'm ringing Mr. Gibson. I'm fed up of texts and emails. He was so difficult to get hold of before, but now he seems to be accessible, perhaps he's managed to get a better Wi-Fi deal. If I can get hold of him, it may be worth a chat. I want to know who saw the bottles moving and what happened when he closed off the conservatory.'

'I bet he's been avoiding us in case we want to sue.'

Deborah laughed. 'I can't see that argument holding up in court.'

'Stranger things have happened.'

Mr. Gibson answered the call. Deborah pressed the speaker on her mobile for Joy to hear the conversation.

248

'I was wondering if it might be better to talk to you and you've beaten me to it. I'm sorry I've been out of touch. I've been having a lot of communication problems.'

Whilst exchanging an eye roll with her companion, Deborah got straight to the point. 'Thank you for your recent text, I have a few more questions. First of all when you closed the conservatory off to the customers, did you get occurrences with the wine bottles moving from the main lounge?'

They heard Gibson sigh.

'Ah well, not exactly. We tried to contain it as best we could.'

Deborah stared at Joy open mouthed.

'There was a corner in the lounge adjacent to the conservatory wall. It had a dropped floor – where a few steps led down to it. We put a little table in there and half a dozen stools. It was popular with a small group of our regulars who liked to play cards or dominoes. Sometimes they started at eight o'clock and sometimes it was later. Occasionally, one of them said that strange things were floating around, but they laughed it off. After a while my wife and I decided to close the corner completely. We put up a wooden partition and then filled up the space to level the floor. The domino players moved to another corner of the pub, so everybody was happy.'

Another exchange of shrewd glances. Joy whispered that she wanted to say something.

'Mr. Gibson, I have a friend here with me, she has some questions too, Deborah said.'

'Fine.'

Joy leaned forward to speak. 'Hello Mr Gibson, I wanted to ask, did those strange occurrences happen

249

only after you constructed the conservatory? And that little snug you referred to, did filling in the space make a difference?'

Mr. Gibson laughed, 'Not for my wife and me. Actually we re-constructed that snug at the same time as building the conservatory. Before we made the alterations it had been an awkward shape. There wasn't much space either because at the back was a large cupboard. We had no use for it so we took it away and boarded up the wall to match the rest of the décor. If you remember there was a lot of wooden panelling in some sections?'

Deborah had a clear picture in her mind how it used to be. 'Yes, that's right.'

Mr Gibson took a deep breath and continued. 'When we first bought the pub, we arranged individual tables spread across the main lounge to accommodate the odd and uneven surface of the floor. In fact there was a lot of uneven levels to the flooring. We levelled off some of the floor with boards, but in that snug no matter what we tried, whatever it was that haunted us, it refused to go away. Then things changed.'

Joy's puzzled expression matched Deborah's. 'What happened?'

Another laugh. 'We were always aware that there was something amiss. Some customers reported they'd seen a ghost disappearing through the walls or down the steps. Funnily enough the customers used to like the idea of a ghost. But later after the re-construction it got worse. Not many people noticed, but we found broken bottles on the floor every night, always in the snug area, and always just before or just after the card players arrived. That's when we decided to fill in the snug and put up the partition.

'As far as the customers were concerned, we heard no more comments about ghosts. But they didn't see what we saw on the other side. In the space between the partition and the conservatory wall, all sorts of things such as a vase, or a candelabra went flying around. My wife got fed up and moved everything out of that area. It was similar in the conservatory. It happened usually at the same time in the evening.'

Deborah shared Joy's astonished face.

'Why didn't you tell the estate agent this before we bought it?' Joy asked.

'And risk my sanity being questioned?'

'It might have been useful information for us!'

'Is there anything else?' Mr. Gibson sounded agitated.

Deborah leaned over the mobile again.' Are you aware of any tunnels under the building?'

Gibson sighed. 'I saw on the deeds that there was something, but I didn't spend much time looking. I think there used to be a tunnel under the old stables and harness room. I wondered if there was a room underground where the stable lads used to sleep. Possibly the stagecoach driver too when they used it as a coaching inn or post house. By chance, I came across some steps near the back lane, but they didn't lead anywhere. I think whatever was underneath had caved in, so I topped the gap up with bricks.'

'Wow.' Joy leaned back as she whispered the words.

'Is there anything else you need to know?'

'Just one thing. What do you know about the gravestone of James Tyler?'

His laughter irritated Joy and she frowned waiting for an answer to her question.

'I was surprised to hear that it's still there, I asked the estate agents to get rid of it.'

Deborah's frown matched Joy's similar expression. 'It is still here.'

Gibson sighed again, 'we found it in the garden, when they dug footings for the conservatory. My wife hit on the idea of putting it in an old fireplace with a flower arrangement half concealing it. So when anyone said they'd had a spooky experience, she would point to James Tyler and say it was him!' Another laugh. 'It seemed to work.'

'And what about the cellar? Did you ever go down there?' Joy's eyes were dark as she met Deborah's anxious ones.

For once Gibson was serious in his reply. 'No, I had a quick scan down the steps, but it seemed past repair. Everything looked on the verge of collapse. I didn't want to risk breaking a leg. I had plans to do something with it, but never got round to it. My wife and I spent a lot of time renovating the house, and we had a pub to run. We didn't get chance to do much to the outbuildings, they were in such a bad state. Probably worse now. I doubt you'll find anything interesting in there. But I advise you not to go in them. You need a builder or someone who knows what they're doing.'

Both women stifled their glee.

'What about Mr. Daniels. You bought the inn from him didn't you? Did he mention the cellar?' Joy asked.

'Ah yes. Daniels hopped it pretty quick.'

'What do you mean?'

'I think he got himself into a bit of trouble with the police. I'm only repeating what I've heard.'

'Oh. That could mean anything,' Joy persisted.

'You know as much as me. I don't look for trouble.'
He forced a laugh. 'Anything else?'

Deborah sighed. 'No, that's fine for now. Thanks.
You've been very helpful.'

'Not as helpful as he could have been,' Joy muttered
after he'd gone. 'Still at least we know what we've got
to do.'

'Do we?' Deborah was perplexed. She reached for
the kettle. 'Tea?'

'Changing the subject completely, I think we ought to
send a get well card to Barbara from all of us,' Joy
said, prodding her teabag with a spoon.

'I can't help thinking, that if we had asked her and
Derrick to live with us, we might have been infected
too,' Deborah said.

'Hard to say. Did she come to your birthday party? I
don't remember seeing her.'

'No, they couldn't make it. They'd already arranged
to have a week-end away in London. They wouldn't
have got back in time.' Deborah felt guilty that she
hadn't contacted Barbara after their move. It had
slipped her mind, when she had so many other things
going on in her life to think about. So she had been
pleased when two days after her birthday, Barbara had
sent a text to say that she and Derrick had family
visiting them and they couldn't visit. They would come
and see everybody some other time, when they were
settled in their new home.

'It's been a busy few months for us all.' Joy stifled a
yawn.

'Yes. It certainly has.'

There was a light tap on the door, then Kirsty, not
waiting for an invitation, appeared wearing a mask. In
her hand she had two more.

'I've made these for when we go shopping or whatever. Do you want one?'

'Wow. Thanks. Joy took one and handed another to Deborah. They both immediately put them on.

'You might need to adjust the elastic to fit.' Kirsty stood behind Deborah to retie it.

'How many have you made?' Deborah's voice was muffled through the fabric.

'Just these three at the moment. I will make more tomorrow. I've got plenty of fabric in my room. I may as well put my sewing machine to good use.' She sat down on the edge of the bed. 'Did you manage to get hold of that Gibson chap?'

CHAPTER TWENTY TWO

Terry and Simon were studying the floor plans again when Joy and Deborah joined them in the piano lounge. Deborah relayed their conversation with Mr. Gibson.

'I wonder what kind of trouble Daniels was in,' Terry replied as he walked a few paces towards the window.

'It might explain why we have a cellar full of wine,' Simon grinned.

Terry turned a few paces to form a small rectangle. The others watched and waited for him to speak. Eventually he raised his head.

'I remember when this area used to be the kind of private cubicle for playing dominoes that Gibson described. If I'm not mistaken, underneath this spot where I am standing is where the steps lead down to that snug he was on about. I wouldn't mind betting there is a hidden stairway underneath that joins with the tunnel. If he filled the cubicle with hard core and then put these boards over the top, it shouldn't be too difficult to remove.' He jumped up and down on the floor boards as if to demonstrate.

Joy rested her chin on her hands reminiscing. 'There were lots of little cubicles, all semi-sectioned off with latticed woodwork. I used to think it was quite romantic. I especially liked all the different floor levels, you could imagine how it might have been in bygone days.'

Deborah nodded. She and Clive had often thought the same. He'd been such a romantic. She sighed involuntarily and as if guessing her thoughts, Simon laid a gentle hand on her shoulder. He turned towards Terry who was kneeling on the carpet trying to find a groove where he could loosen the fittings.

'The thing is Terry, if we get rid of the hard core, it will only get us down to the way it was when Gibson first had it, and he still experienced ghostly manoeuvres. 'We'd have to get down to the next level to reach the tunnel. It sounds like we need to find the awkward space where Gibson said he'd removed a cupboard. I wouldn't be surprised if there is a wall that conceals the entrance to the tunnel. We'd have to knock it through. If I am right.'

'Do you think we could do it?'

'It's a lot of work and it's going to be messy, but I think if you and Dan are willing to put in some muscle, we can do it. Once we remove the carpet, the floorboards and the hard core, we'll just have to see what we get. '

'I think Gibson said he'd replaced the cupboard with wooden panels, Deborah said.'

'Yes, they were fake. I remember looking at them myself years ago when we used to sit down there. We can easily get rid of that. The thing is, do we all agree to do it?' Terry searched each face from one to the other. 'There's no guarantee that all this work will get rid of the ghost. Gibson still had problems, like Simon has already pointed out.'

Simon nodded, 'that's true, but he didn't bother to try to find the tunnel. That could be the answer.'

Terry shrugged. 'It's worth a try. Let's see what the others think.'

'I can't see anyone objecting, but we'll check when everyone comes down for dinner.' Deborah walked to the piano as she spoke.

'At least we won't have to shift this. It's a good distance away. These musical instruments are very sensitive to moves you know.' She stroked it lovingly; her friends smiled as they watched her.

'There'll be a lot of muck flying around, you'd better cover it up when we start working,' Terry advised.

As Deborah supposed, no-one objected to the work. On the contrary there were eager offers of help. Grace immediately made plans to pack away her treasured ornaments that contributed to the decorations of the room.

'Start as soon as you can, as far as I'm concerned,' Jessica said. 'It would be nice to be able to put my seedlings on the windowsill without worrying if they'll land on the floor by morning. Plus there's always the possibility that one day one of those ghosts may re-live a day when a bottle of wine was dropped! Imagine the mess!' She laughed. 'Ban the banshees, I say.'

'And I would like to have *The Blue Danube* back on my mobile,' Grace lowered her voice when she mentioned the music and looked furtively over her shoulder.

Dan laughed, 'don't worry Gran,' I think the ghosts prefer the music not the mention of it.' He began to whistle it then stopped as she gave him a withering look.

'Oops sorry.'

'What I don't understand,' Shirley laced her hands around her wine glass and hesitated before she spoke again... 'My understanding of ghosts... not that I'm an expert...,' she hurried on, aware that her words had invited curious looks in her direction; 'is why does altering the route from the tunnel make any difference?

Surely ghosts can walk through walls and windows and such like? As we have more or less witnessed.'

Deborah had been harbouring similar thoughts and was pleased that Joy came up with a theory.

'Yes, I can see what you mean. All the films and books about the supernatural, suggest that is what they do. Some articles I have read, say that where there is a haunting, the phantoms repeat the same event each time.

'My guess is, that our particular ghosts are re-enacting a particular point in time. They are so familiar with the route from carriage to dance floor that they prefer to use that method of entering and leaving the building. I also think that when a succession of owners altered the route, they were reluctant to find an alternative, hence the disruptions. Unfortunately their route is now through the conservatory." Joy took a breath as she warmed to her theory. 'So yes, I believe they can walk through walls and glass, but they prefer to go the original way.'

Joy sat on an arm chair pleased with her analysis then added, 'Shirley, you said to Dan the other day that ghosts don't like change. I think you might have been joking, but now I think you are right. In other words, they are creatures of habit and…'

'Phantoms of habit more like!' Dan interrupted with a laugh.

'So we're back to our original question? Why choose that route in the first place?' Deborah said.

'Perhaps our ghosts were in a hurry,' Shirley said.

'Surely they would want to go back the way they came?'

'Something stopped them, maybe a fire?' Kirsty suggested.

'That would make sense,' Jessica said, turning to her sister.

'Why?' Deborah asked.

'There had to be an emergency of some kind.'

'Did they ever dance in the afternoons as well as the evenings?' Dan asked, changing the direction of the conversation. 'The *Blue Danube* incident was in the afternoon.'

'Afternoon tea dances,' Kirsty advised him. 'They were very popular in Victorian times.'

Dan's mention of their paranormal experience the day before reminded Deborah of something she had intended to check. She removed the lid of her piano stool to search through pieces of music which she kept there. Finally she found what she was looking for. She held up the manuscript for them all to see.

'This is the music for *Johann Strauss's Blue Danube*. It was written in eighteen sixty six. It became a popular waltz and still is.'

Kirsty took the manuscript from Deborah to read it. She was unable to play any musical instrument, however she was fascinated by the sheet music.

'That means our unwanted visitors wouldn't have heard the music until much later, so it puts them around eighteen seventy or a bit later? This, and the names we found on the deeds for round about that time should confirm the identity of our phantoms! It's looking more and more likely, that they are James Hayes and Henrietta Slater.'

'Wicked.' Dan began to whistle *The Blue Danube* again and stopped. 'Sorry.'

'You know something? I've just realised your name is half the name of *Danube*.' Shirley winked.

'Sick.'

Grace gave Shirley an eye roll though appreciated the titters from the others.

Tony checked his watch. 'It's ten to eight. I think I'll go upstairs and watch my own TV. I can lie on the bed. My leg is aching. I've done a bit too much walking today.' He got up to take his and Shirley's plates to the kitchen. She stopped him. 'Leave those, I'll sort them out. I will join you in a few minutes.'

'I'll give you a hand Shir, then I'm going to make some more face masks. Any requests on colour, I've got a lot of scraps of material.' Kirsty turned back from the door.

Simon scowled. 'I don't really care, I just wish I didn't have to wear one.'

Terry shrugged. 'I'll leave it to you Kirsty. Thanks.'

Jessica followed her sister in to the kitchen. 'Sounds like you're on a roll.'

'I believe I am. It's quite satisfying.'

'I've got some old pillow cases if they're any use, Deborah offered. 'I kept them for dusters but masks would be appropriate.' She glanced at the kitchen clock as she spoke. The others followed her gaze.

'Eight o' clock and all is well, in here at least.' Joy laughed. She'd slipped into the kitchen behind Deborah. 'It looks like no-one is bothered about watching the spectacle tonight. Everyone's left the piano lounge.' She laughed again. 'As it happens there's a drama just starting on Channel Four, so if you want to see it from the beginning, you'd better come now.'

Deborah hadn't intended to watch the drama, she'd planned to send a few emails and then read her book. However, she decided the emails could wait. She followed Joy into the television room, dubbed as such despite Joy's attempts to call it the library. Two episodes of the drama were broadcasted back to back and didn't finish until eleven o' clock.

Deborah was tired when she eventually went to bed, but to her annoyance she woke up at two o' clock wide awake. Sighing and wondering if this was going to be the pattern from now on she got up and filled her kettle. She realised she hadn't replenished the herbal teas after making drinks earlier for Joy and Kirsty. Pulling on her dressing gown and slippers she moved quietly along the landing. Outside Kirsty's door she stopped and listened. Nothing. She grinned. Poor Kirsty she'd have to wait a bit longer to enjoy Leslie's embraces. She passed Jessica's door with a smile. Even if she was seeing Malcolm from the book club on the sly, she doubted she would risk smuggling him in for a night of passion.

At the end of the landing she reached for the dimmer switch turning on enough light to help her see down the stairs to the hall.

In the kitchen, Deborah yawned then turned on just one of the small spotlights near the door and opened a cupboard. She grabbed a handful of herbal tea bags and put them in her pocket. Turning off the light she moved towards the hallway when she heard footsteps and a rustling noise. It seemed to be coming from the piano lounge. She held her breath, hoping the ghosts weren't up to mischief. Curiously she wasn't afraid. So far the ghosts hadn't harmed any of the occupants of the house. Rationalising that if one of her friends had come down for some reason, they would have turned on a lamp, she considered the possibility of an intruder. She stretched out her arm for the light, then changed her mind. If it was a burglar she didn't want them to know where she was. Her mobile was in her room, but there was a land line near the stairs and if necessary she'd scream for help.

Deborah didn't stop to think about her safety, stealthily she crept towards the sound. As she got to the end of the hall she heard music coming from the piano lounge. It must be one of her friends, who couldn't sleep and listening to a CD. Then she recognised the notes of *The Blue Danube.*

Puzzled, Deborah took a few more steps. She could barely see in the darkness, but she continued to move. Suddenly a figure loomed in front of her its arms stretched out in a threatening manner.   Despite her mystified state she sensed danger. Reaching beside her for a suitable weapon, she picked up a rubber plant, complete with pot and hurled it at the figure.

'Ow!

The music continued and seemed to emanate from the figure sprawled on the floor. In the dim light, Deborah bent over the figure.   She recognised the face, conscious of the spellbinding effect the music was having on her.

'Dan?' she said feebly.

'Oh my head.' His voice was slurred. 'Thank God it's you Deborah.'

'What's going on?' Her own voice was shaky. She felt dizzy whilst something brushed the back of her neck. Instinctively, she reached up a hand to push it away, but felt nothing there.

Dan didn't answer, he stretched sideways to grab his mobile which had fallen from his grasp when he fell. Quickly he pressed a button and the music stopped. Deborah felt faint and slumped across his chest. Dan groaned again feeling her weight. He helped her to sit up properly on the floor.

'Are you hurt?' she asked.

'Yes, but I'm glad you turned up when you did.' He pulled himself to a more comfortable sitting position and turned on the torch on his mobile to help locate the nearby table lamp. He got up and helped her into an armchair, then flopped down opposite her on a sofa. He rubbed the back of his head with his hand.

'I'm so sorry. It's just that I couldn't get that music out of my mind. I was lying in bed and couldn't sleep, because that *Blue Danube* tune kept coming into my head!' He exhaled deeply.

'Like an earworm thingy?'

'Yeah, it's like it was haunting me. So I decided to come downstairs and get a drink or something.' He averted his eyes and looked sheepish. 'I thought the best way to get rid of it was to listen to something else. I came in here to sit down and flicked through the options on the music app on my mobile. Then I started thinking about that bloody tune again…sorry. I suppose I just wanted to see what would happen if I selected it…' Dan looked sheepish as he confessed to Deborah.

'I admit, I was curious all day yesterday. I couldn't stop thinking about it. At first nothing happened. Then it started again.'

'What started?'

'The same as before.'

'You mean the dancing thing? Again?'

'Yes. I was waltzing with a young woman. The same one as before. She was pretty, actually and I didn't mind. Then the dancing got faster and I felt as if I was being forced to go through to the conservatory.

Try as I might my legs and arms wouldn't go where I wanted them to go. My mobile was still in my hand, but I had no energy to press stop and then you knocked me on the head.'

Deborah wanted to laugh. She managed to keep a straight face as she saw Dan's perturbed expression. A fine dusting of compost balanced on his eyelashes, some strayed on his cheeks, and she suspected more had found its way down his neck. The rubber plant lay on its side, the plastic pot had rolled across the floor and landed near the pedals of the piano. Deborah retrieved it, though it was cracked in several places. Nevertheless she re-potted the rubber plant as best she could.

'Are you in pain?'

'Not now. Just a twinge on my temple. It's amazing what damage you can do with a plastic pot.' He rubbed the spot on his head with the back of his hand.

She observed him wryly.

'Let's hope Jessica and Kirsty will be sympathetic. It was the closest thing to hand. At least it was heavy enough to knock you out of your enchantment! I think I was getting pulled in to it too. Come on I'll make you some camomile tea. That might help you sleep.'

CHAPTER TWENTY THREE

Everyone saw the funny side when Dan and Deborah told the tale at breakfast the next day.

'We ought to consider installing a burglar alarm, just in case that really does happen.' Joy paused, with her mug of tea held mid-air, 'we could also get one of those security cameras too,' she added.

'It was brave of you, or stupid,' Jessica said shocked. 'What if it had been a burglar and you were attacked? What were you thinking?'

'I thought it was best to check what was happening first before raising the alarm,' Deborah said in her defence. 'I admit I acted on impulse as if I were dreaming.'

'It worked anyway,' Simon laughed, winking at Dan.

'You could get a dog,' Dan suggested. 'I could take it for walks if you didn't want to,' he added seeing that his suggestion was not met with enthusiasm.

'Debbie, it's possible you were becoming influenced by the music,' Shirley said. Whilst she waited for everyone to digest that thought, she turned to ask about Dan's dancing partner from the night before.

'What was her dress like and what did she look like?'

'She was very pretty, but when I looked into her eyes, it was like they were dark holes and I couldn't tear my own eyes away. Yet, I can't really remember her face. But it was like as if she was urging me to go somewhere with her.'

'You were bewitched!' Grace sent an indulgent smile to her grandson.

'But can you recall her dress?' Shirley persisted.

'Not really. Just silky, very thin, I could feel her ribs and yet it was like touching flimsy paper. Weird.' He blushed at the memory and gave his attention to his beans on toast.

'It should have been whalebones,' Deborah said with a smile.

'It's fascinating that he felt anything at all,' Shirley said. On catching Dan's discomfort, she decided not to pursue her inquiry.

Joy fingered her gold necklace. 'You may be interested to know that when I got up this morning, my expensive jewellery was scattered all over the floor. Strangely enough my dress jewellery was untouched.'

Joy's announcement was greeted like a bombshell.

'That suggests the ghost is agitated. The mistress of the house would likely have had jewellery, and may have slept in your bedroom. Could Henrietta have stolen it? It must be connected with what happened to Dan last night?' Shirley suggested. She eyed him thoughtfully. He kept his head down.

'It's not usually that bad is it?' Deborah asked.
Joy shook her head.

'It seems to me that we need to get rid of this phenomena or whatever you want to call it, as soon as we can!' Jessica fiercely spread some marmalade on to her toast as she spoke. 'There is something menacing underlying all this. If Deborah hadn't disturbed things last night, who knows what would have happened to Dan.'

'And if I hadn't stopped her playing the piano the other day, what would have happened to all of us?' Joy chipped in. They turned to Deborah as Joy finished speaking, and she suddenly felt as if she was to blame.

266

'I'm sorry about all this, I ...'

'No, no don't worry, it's not your fault Debbie,' Kirsty assured her.

Jessica got up to put her arm around Deborah. 'In no way was I suggesting this is your fault. I'm just saying we need to face facts. Things are getting out of hand. What if that blasted music is played on the radio or on the television without any warning. Who knows what might happen?'

'I agree. And I was thinking I would like to play it on the piano and teach it to my students. It's a popular waltz.'

Shirley laughed. 'Debbie, I'm having the best time here. I've always wanted to go ghost hunting. So just to endorse what everyone else is saying, I'm so glad you asked me and Tony to come here.'

The rest reiterated Shirley's sentiments and Deborah felt better.

Joy held her ground. 'Just to go back to what I was telling you about. All that, coupled with my messed up jewellery, I have a theory.' She waited for the chatter to die down and to listen. 'What if the daughter of the house was planning to elope with her lover from *The Miller*?'

'Perfect!' Shirley clapped her hands. 'That would explain the urgency of trying to get me and Dan through the invisible door in the conservatory.' She caught his eye and after a wide-eyed incredulous expression, inclined his head as he realised what Shirley said made sense.

Deborah stared at her friend open mouthed thinking back to what they'd read on the deeds of the house. 'That would explain why we don't have a James Edward Hayes on the deeds. They were either both caught and prevented from seeing each other again, or they escaped and were both subsequently cut off? She inherited thirty odd years later.'

'Or perhaps after they eloped,' Jessica cut in, 'and when James Edward Hayes inherited *The Miller*, he took his bride back there? Henrietta would have to wait a long time for her inheritance! If you consider, that the Slater's were opposed to the marriage and not the iffy Hayes...' she broke off and frowned trying to make the bits of information fit her theory. Her eyes met Shirley's whose own eyes gleamed.

'Yes, I agree partly with that Jess. I think they escaped. They smashed the window to get out! Henrietta had nipped upstairs, stolen the jewels, then at the ball, they both slipped out together. They couldn't escape through the normal route, so they found another way out. It explains why we were being urged to the conservatory. We know that the building had changed shape over the years!' Shirley grinned, pleased with her theory. 'But, they couldn't go back to the Hayes' place because they'd stolen the jewels.'

'Yep! I'll go along with that,' Dan agreed.

'I think that's it.' Kirsty said. Her sentiments were echoed by the others.

'Perhaps you could do some more digging Love? Terry raised a quizzical eye towards his wife. 'You could try one of those websites that traces ancestors and the like.'

'You have to pay for that, but I'm happy to do it,' Tony offered. 'I found out quite a bit on one of those websites about my family.'

'Actually it's not a huge amount. Anyway, I've already signed up for it. I pay monthly because I've been doing some research of my own. I'll get started on this later.' Joy smiled, she was looking forward to her task.

'In the meantime, we need a plan of action,' Terry declared. 'After we've got rid of the breakfast dishes, we need to clear all the furniture near that haunted area so that Simon and I can loosen the floor boards.'

'Then everybody can help shovelling the hard core underneath, so we need buckets and as many shovels or spades as we can muster,' Simon added.

He turned to Deborah, 'You had better cover up the piano now; the dust will be thick. And Kirsty, if you can make some more masks so much the better. I've got about half a dozen heavy duty ones in the shed. I'll keep them back for Terry, Dan and myself. I'm guessing your home-made ones will be better than nothing for the rest of you seeing as you won't be on the front line, so to speak.'

Kirsty was delighted to help. 'I'll run up a few more when you start on the floorboards, it doesn't take long to make one. I've already cut out a few more. I'll make them quadruple ply. Luckily I've got loads of elastic. I haven't got anything to make a filter though.'

'Aren't you riding today?' Jessica asked. She scrutinised her sister's face as Kirsty looked away somewhat abashed.

'No, I think I'm needed here more urgently today.' She got up and followed the others into the kitchen leaving Jessica and Deborah still finishing their tea in the conservatory.

'That's weird. I think Kirsty is hiding something.' She met Deborah's eye who looked away guiltily.

'Now you are acting weird. Is there something I should know?'

'I think you should talk to Kirsty,' Deborah said lamely. She swallowed her tea and got up quickly.

'I'm going to find something to cover the furniture.'

Jessica remained alone, realised there was more tea in the teapot and poured herself another drink.

In the kitchen a mobile rang. Kirsty picked it up thinking it was hers. She saw 'Malcolm' on the screen and realised he must be calling about the book club. They'd hoped to do it via zoom, though they hadn't sorted it out yet.

'Hello.'

'Hello, how are you getting on? I've missed you.'

'What? Have you? Oh you mean the book talk?'

'No, you of course. I enjoyed our chat, at that antiques fair on the day of the blasted lockdown.'

Realisation dawned on Kirsty, and she allowed herself a smirk. She stepped back to the hallway with the mobile in her hand to search for her sister.

'Malcolm, it's me Kirsty. I've picked up Jess's mobile. She left it in the kitchen.'

'Aah.'

'Here she is. Jess, Malcolm on the phone for you. He's missing you.'

It was Jessica's turn to look embarrassed. Kirsty hung around the doorway forcing Jessica to get up and walk away to the piano lounge. With a backward smile at her sister, Kirsty chuckled as she retraced her steps to the kitchen.

CHAPTER TWENTY FOUR

It didn't take long to get the floorboards up after they'd rolled part of the carpet away from the wall. They stacked them neatly on one side creating a convenient resting place.

The mound of hard core began to diminish quickly as everyone except Tony pitched in. His task was to provide everyone with mugs of coffee and biscuits whilst they kept working. By mid-day they had revealed half a dozen steps running down to what Gibson had called the snug.

'That's not a bad morning's work,' Terry commented sitting down beside Simon on the makeshift seat of the heaped floorboards. He rubbed the sweat off his face with the back of his sleeve. 'I was worrying that it might not be hard core underneath but a thick slab of concrete. I dreaded having to use complicated drilling equipment to get through it.'

Simon agreed. 'I'm thinking about the next stage. I'm hoping it won't be concrete that's behind that wooden panel. I'm hoping it is another flight of steps to the tunnel. We don't know for sure what faces us on the other side. I'm also afraid we might create a hazard and the whole thing will collapse.' He got up and went down the six steps to examine the space, small stones crunched under his boots. He squinted to try to see over the slight gap above the imitation wood.

'It's a bit of a bodge job if you ask me. That Gibson chap obviously wasn't a handyman.'

Terry laughed. 'Don't be too hard on the man. If he had been curious and with time on his hands, he might have found that stash of wine! Lucky for us it was concealed behind that crumbling door.'

'Can we have a look?' Joy asked, turning to her husband. Jessica leaned behind her.

'Yes but take care you don't slip on these stones.'

'I've got a brush here, let me go down first. I can sweep it up as I go.' Grace sidled past and made quick work of the task she had set herself. One by one the others examined the old snug whilst they held mugs of coffee.

'This brings back some memories,' Deborah said. 'Clive and I never saw anything weird in here.'

'I'd forgotten all about it,' Jessica admitted.

After several more hours, all the rubble had been cleared. The fake wood was easily removed to reveal a brick wall.

'These bricks aren't the red Ruabon bricks.' Simon said. 'What do you think?'

Terry nodded. 'They're older. Probably from one of the other brickworks in the area around here during the eighteen fifties. Possibly they are from Ponciau or from the Aberderfyn brickworks. A lot of them have gone now. As soon as we get one out we can have a look at the stamp on it.'

Despite being exhausted, Simon and Terry chiselled away a few bricks at the centre of the wall so that they could make a gap big enough to look through. Simon held up a brick 'here we are, it's stamped *Ponkey.*'

Through the gap, they saw the remains of a balustrade. It clung precariously to loose concrete attached to the side of the wall where another stairway was revealed.

272

Simon moved aside to let Dan have a peep. 'I believe that is our tunnel down there.'

Dan being taller than his grandfather crouched slightly to peer down the dark stairway.

'Wow this is wicked,' Dan turned to lean on Grace's broomstick. He turned his dust streaked and animated face upwards to meet a line of equally dirty, yet excited faces peering down from the top of the six steps.

He bent to brush the last of the tiny stones into his dustpan.

'It is amazing,' his grandmother agreed. 'Who'd have thought that this existed?'

'When you stop to think about railways and the coal mines, the land must be riddled with underground passageways.' Grace moved away from the opening in the snug to let Kirsty peer through the hole in the wall. The others took it in turn to look too.

'You know, I've been reading about sink holes in Rome. It's a wonder that there haven't been any in Wales when you consider all the tunnels Grace is referring to.' Joy sat on the floor resting her back against the piled up floorboards. Terry perched himself behind her and used a grubby hand to flick grit off her denim covered shoulders.

'I'd like to go to Rome one day. Perhaps we could go for our fiftieth wedding anniversary.'

'Great idea.' Joy leaned her dust speckled head against Terry's knee.

Shirley smiled at them as she passed. 'I'm going for a shower folks. Tony said he's got quiches in the oven.'

Later that evening, Deborah made herbal teas for Kirsty and Jessica who had settled themselves on the two seater sofa bed in her room.

'You'll be relieved to know, Debbie, that I've told Jess about me and Leslie,' Kirsty said sipping her drink.

Deborah was startled, though instantly felt relieved. 'Oh, that's good.'

'And you may as well know, I've been seeing Malcolm from the book club,' Jessica confessed with a grin.

'Ah, now that all makes sense.' Deborah sat back in her reclining chair and smiled benevolently at her friends.

'Not that we can see much of each other now with this pandemic,' Jessica sighed. She turned to her sister. 'At least you can get to the stables to see Leslie.'

Kirsty nodded.

'So is it serious?' Deborah looked from one sister to the other.

Kirsty shrugged, 'I doubt it. Who knows? But it's nice to have the attention.'

Deborah didn't know what to say to that. She stared at her friend open mouthed then turned to listen to Jessica's assessment of her own lover.

'As for Malcolm, it's just a bit of a fling. That's all. He won't be moving in, if that's what you think.'

'What about you and Dennis? How are you going to handle that?'

'I don't know what you mean.' Deborah refused to be drawn by Jessica's questioning look who upon getting no reaction kindly let it go. Jessica didn't know that earlier that evening Deborah had chatted with Dennis. Ostensibly his call had been about the house and an inquiry into her health, but she sensed there was more to it than that. She wasn't at a point where she could confide in her friends. Memories of Clive still muddied her thoughts.

Joy knocked, then pushed her head around the door eyeing the occupants with a smile.

'I've made a fascinating discovery. I've already told the others.' She sat on the edge of the bed. 'I'm pretty sure now that our ghosts are Henrietta Slater and James Hayes. Just as we guessed! They eloped and went to Gretna Green to get married. I've found their records. I went on to the Gretna Green web site. They got married in eighteen seventy-one. It all ties in. It was their daughter who inherited the *Peacock* in eighteen ninety-eight. Henrietta Slater died at the age of forty-one in Glasgow. Her husband died a year later. They had one daughter born in eighteen eighty. Her name was Henrietta Charlotte Slater-Hayes!'

'Wow. Well done. So that banging on the window must be the lovers trying to escape!' Deborah said. Shirley's theory is correct. They obviously managed to get away.'

Joy nodded. 'Yep. That has to be the explanation. If you hadn't told me about the year *The Blue Danube* was written I might not have found them so easily. That date was a good starting point. Another exciting bit of information is the second Henrietta married George Tyler in nineteen ten. They had two children, sadly they both died in infancy. This is where it gets complicated. James Tyler was George Tyler's nephew and his wife Victoria Tyler inherited in nineteen forty six.

'That's amazing. I'm glad you've cleared up that mystery,' Jessica said. 'What a star.'

Joy beamed. 'It's nearly eight o' clock, I was wondering if you feel like coming downstairs to see if our work today has made a difference to our ghosts.'

They followed Joy to the hallway to find the rest of the group huddled in the doorway that led in to the piano lounge. 'It won't be very pleasant to sit in there, because of the dust, but if anything happens, we can see from here.'

As the clock struck eight they fell silent, though Deborah doubted the quiet would make a difference. After a few seconds nothing moved, though a strong odour of horse manure wafted through the air.

'It's probably drifted up through the tunnel because we've got rid of a lot of obstacles from the past.' Kirsty whispered.

'It's floated up from a hundred and odd years ago, you mean,' Jessica whispered. 'A century and a half of old horse shit.'

'So do you think they are there?' Deborah whispered back. Despite her anxiety, she felt a desire to laugh at Jessica's comment. 'And why are we whispering?'

No-one answered as at that moment they saw a wine bottle float into the hall and then a pot fall from the windowsill.

'Don't worry, it's an empty bottle and there's nothing in the plant pot. I put them there deliberately to see what would happen,' Joy explained.

'Good idea. So we know that we haven't made a difference yet. Let's see what happens tomorrow when we tear down that wall,' Kirsty enthused.

*

Early the following morning, Terry complained of a bad back. He struggled into a chair for his breakfast and apologised that he wouldn't be able to do much work. Dan said he was sure he and his grandfather could manage.

Terry thanked him. 'Sorry to leave it to you guys. The thing is I can hardly walk, and even if I don't do any heavy work, I would like to do something. But I'm not sure what use I would be.'

'Maybe I can help with the pain, Tony offered. 'I find that a simple massage usually does the trick. Don't worry, I am qualified. I did a course on Reiki.' He met Terry's startled eyes.

'Yes, and he's good too!' Shirley recommended. 'Try it Terry.'

'Yes, it's worth a go,' Joy encouraged her husband.
To everyone's relief, especially Terry's, the pain in his back was eased to such an extent that Terry had only the slightest of twinges.

'Wow, that's marvellous, cheers Tony.'

'You're welcome.'
Meanwhile, Simon had been to the shed to get his lump hammer. He positioned himself at the bottom of the steps in the snug and bashed at the small opening he'd made the day before. Soon several more *Ponkey* stamped bricks were knocked out making a much bigger gap to look through.

'I can see another wall down there! But it doesn't go right up to the ceiling. I think it's concealing a door behind it. His face wreathed in smiles he gingerly knocked away a few more bricks on the edge of the opening.

277

Simon's excited audience, perched on cushions at the top of the short, stone stairwell behind him, leaned forward to see.

'I just hope it hasn't been bricked up on the other side of the door. I can't remember what we saw when we went down the tunnel.'

'I can. It was bricked up. I'm sure of it,' Deborah said. Joy backed her up. They sat drinking coffee as they watched him work.

'That's a pity. Though if it is as easy to break down as this one, it won't take long. Then we can see what kind of condition the door is in. The hinges might have rusted.'

Another half hour of meticulous chiselling away at the brickwork, revealed the stairway down to the tunnel. Simon turned a satisfied face to the cluster of friends behind him.

'Shall we go down?' Dan said. He busied himself stuffing heavy duty bin bags with the rubble that Simon had created.

'Let me go first,' Simon advised. 'Dam, I haven't got the torches.'

'I'll go and get them,' Terry said. 'We left them in the tool shed.'

'Here, Grandad, take my mobile.'

Simon cautiously descended the stone steps.

'It seems ok, filthy and smelly as you can imagine,' he called.

Unable to wait for Terry and the torches, Shirley, Joy and Deborah utilised the beams on their mobiles and followed Simon down the steps. Dan gingerly trailed behind. Kirsty, Jessica and Grace looked frantically for their own mobiles, but gave up when Terry returned with stronger lamps.

Ten metres along the passageway, they confronted the brick wall, Simon had seen earlier. He sighed. 'We'll just have to get this down now. I'm hoping this is the opposite wall to where we walked yesterday on the other side of the tunnel.'

'Let's have a snack and tackle it later,' Terry suggested.

Two hours later, the brick wall was down and the debris swept away.

Again the rest of the housemates trooped down to see that this time a pair of wooden doors blocked their path. The old oak was bathed under a thick lacework created by decades of spiders. Grace used the brush to push some of the cobwebs away, and they admired the carved decoration on the doors.

'They're magnificent. What a shame they've been covered up for so long,' Deborah enthused. Simon tried the door handle. It wouldn't budge.

'I'm not going to argue with it until we've checked the other side. Anybody coming with me?'

Eager helpers trailed behind him back up the steps and then outside to the entrance to the tunnel from the cellar. Despite the early evening light fading, their quest to expel the phantoms, spurred them on. Besides that, Deborah told her sons much later, they were enjoying their adventure into discovering the old inn's history and secrets.

Tony stayed near the cellar entrance.

'I'll be the lookout. In case a pretty lady in a silk dress comes this way.' He winked at Dan then blew Shirley a kiss accompanied by a warning to take care.

Armed with torches and what they hoped would be adequate tools, they made their way down the tunnel until they reached the brick wall.

Simon and Terry replaced their heavy duty masks and told everyone to stand back as they began to carefully chisel at the mortar. The wall, just like the previous two walls, was constructed of just one layer of bricks. Once they had carefully removed some chunks of the blockage, they were rewarded with a glimpse of the mystifying concealed oak doors.

'It won't be long before we will be able to test the hinges,' Simon informed the earnest watchers.

'If the dancers managed to come up this tunnel to the ballroom, we need to find out why they didn't come back this way instead of making a big fuss in the conservatory.' Grace leaned against the tunnel wall with her arms folded as she spoke.

'It was the alternative escape route,' Shirley said dreamily. 'They were trying to elope. Something went wrong and I think they had to find another way out.'

'It's such a romantic idea and I love it,' Kirsty said. 'But if we don't find out why something went wrong, we may never get rid of the ghosts. Even if we knocked down the conservatory. They will re-live the situation every night.'

'I agree,' Joy said. 'We need to look for clues.'

The last of the *Ponkey* bricks fell with a clatter masking the expletives that were forming on Simon's lips. Terry brushed away the remaining bits of mortar and dust with his arm.

'There's the answer!' Simon said with glee. 'The doors were locked on this side. They couldn't get out. Look. It's one of those old locking devices that bolts into the ground. They wouldn't have been able to budge it from the other side. The door is as solid now as it was then.'

He tried to raise the handle upwards to pull it back so that the dropped bolt would be lifted from its cradle in the ground. But it was too stiff.

'These doors haven't been opened for over a century.'

'A hundred and forty nine years to be exact, if we're correct in our assumption, declared Joy. Her eyes shone.

'We need a lubricant of some sort I think,' Terry said. I'll go and get some.'

'So somebody deliberately locked them in,' Deborah breathed. She examined the pair of doors more closely. 'There's another bolt across the top and another across the middle. Whoever it was, went to great lengths to prevent the poor lovers leaving.''

'Who? Her father?' Kirsty said.

'Someone knew of their plan and was trying to stop them escape!' Shirley said. Somebody at the ball betrayed them. Dan's experience the other night was the same as mine. He felt as if he was being urged to go somewhere. Grace's mobile music must have been playing that night and they planned to go during the ball. Henrietta would have helped herself to her mother's jewellery so they could sell it.'

'Cool.' Dan stared open mouthed at Shirley and then Kirsty.

'*Johann Strauss* will never be the same for me,' Deborah declared. That statement made Jessica and Grace break out into hysterical laughter.

'You mean the *Blue Danube* won't!' Jessica shrieked wiping tears of mirth from her face. 'No wonder those blasted tomato seeds took a bashing!'

This made Grace sink weakly to her knees laughing. She ignored the dust and cobwebs that clung to her cardigan as she slid down the grimy wall. 'Too right!' she spluttered.

Terry returned with the oil, some cloths and a smaller chisel. He began to work at the bolt locked in the floor. Soon decades of gunge and chips of solid mortar fell away revealing the end of the rod stuck fast in its aperture. Carefully he cleaned away the debris with a rag then sprayed the tip of the rod with oil. After applying more oil on the bolts that locked the top and middle of both doors, then the hinges, he rubbed the greasy liquid into the metal with another cloth. Straightening up with a groan about his back, he nodded to Simon to try drawing the bolts. There was just a little resistance and then the metal slid across the doors to rest in its mounting.

'One.' Simon pulled another across.

'Two.'

Cautiously, he pulled back the lever on the top of the dropped rod then holding the lever steady attempted to lift the rod out of the hole where it had been embedded in the ground. It required the combined effort of both Terry and Simon, to pull the steel rod up then force the lever to the side. Exhausted with the effort they eased the doors open. The squeaks of the rusty hinges heralded a strong gush of air that wafted through the gap. Its potency catapulted Deborah and Joy into each other. Clinging together they slumped against the side of the tunnel. The force of energy had the same effect on their companions who were thrust against each other on the opposite side. Simultaneously they heard thuds of urgent footsteps, swishes of heavy garments, sighs and whispers gliding through the tunnel. The sounds vibrated with an intense vigour that diminished as suddenly as it had

282

arrived. Drifting soft echoes of horse hooves and exultant laughter became less audible as a soothing stillness filled the atmosphere.

'Did you feel that?' Deborah was breathless. She and Joy were still backed up against the wall where they felt as if they'd been physically thrown. Their bodies supported each other from slipping down the muck encrusted wall of the tunnel. Both women were reluctant to move.

Various gasps and whispered exclamations and observations from their companions confirmed to Deborah that she hadn't imagined the feel of silky cloth brushing past her cheek. The strong passing smell of manure had gone. She stared wildly at the huddled heap of her friends. Cast together by the supernatural force they clung to each other to anchor themselves. Kirsty's long blonde hair had woven with Jessica's loose tresses to form a dusty veil over their faces.

'Did you see anything?' Shirley whispered. She was the first to move. In an attempt to disengage herself from Grace's vice like grip she tapped her friend's hand to free herself. Looking down she noticed a large spider scuttle away behind the small mound of mortar. 'It was like a stampede. We've let out not just the lovers but all the ghost dancers who couldn't get home the normal way.'

Simon straightened himself and took Grace's arm into his own. She was shaking. He put his other arm on his grandson's shoulder and managed a grimy smile.

'Are you alright lad?'

Dan was wide eyed.

'I saw both of them, a man and woman dressed for a ball, they came out first then they vanished,' Dan burst out. 'This is so cool.'

Silently they smoothed down their clothes and hair before staggering to an upright position.

'Are we going to go through?' Dan couldn't wait for an answer, he pushed the two half opened oak doors completely back. Holding a torch he waited patiently for his companions to follow. Slowly he led the way along the tunnel until he reached the bottom of the steps that provided access to the house. There he waited again. Overawed, the others trailed after him. Breathing heavily they climbed up the stone steps into the piano lounge. Deborah collapsed on a plastic dust cover that protected an armchair. She didn't mind that she was sitting in brick dust. She was filthy anyway. The others found similar seats. Simon and Grace utilised the heap of wooden planks as a temporary resting place.

'I think we did it,' Joy said gleefully. 'Well done you three men. You've worked hard all day. It's half past six. I think you deserve a drink.'

Terry planted a kiss on Joy's forehead. 'Good idea, a nice cool beer, but first I'm going for a shower.'

Simon and Dan looked down at their dusty overalls and followed him to their respective bathrooms.

Deborah had been thinking about Shirley's last remark. 'Those locked doors forced the elopers to find another way out. After they'd gone the other guests were in the same predicament. That might explain the flying bottles and other objects. In their haste to leave, they broke a window in a room near the hall. They were probably angry.'

'Yes, that makes sense,' Joy enthused. 'And I bet the Slaters held no more balls after the elopement! Think of the scandal and the ruined clothes having to go across a muddy field?

'I think we should put some Champagne on ice,' Jessica said. 'Let's dress up glamorous. As if we are going to a ball,' she added mischievously.'

'Hell. Poor Tony. He's probably waiting for us at the cellar. I'd better go and tell him the good news.'
Shirley grabbed a torch and ran outside.

'I don't want to dampen anyone's spirits, but do you think we are being a bit premature?' Deborah was nervous.

'Are you suggesting we play the *Blue Danube?*' Grace asked anxiously.

'Something like that. Or at least wait until later to see if the empty plant pots goes awry again.'

Jessica nodded. 'You're right we ought to do some kind of a test, but there's no reason not to celebrate what we've done so far. It's been a fascinating few days and a historic discovery.'

Deborah got out of her chair. 'I would love a cup of tea but first I'm going to get cleaned up. I will make one in my room.' Her movement had a domino effect.

Over some quickly cobbled together sandwiches, they discussed how best to re-construct the floor. In the end they agreed to replace the floor boards with a trap door and a ring to open it, to preserve the history.

'But that will have to wait until another day!' Simon said.

'Do you think Henrietta's father bricked up the tunnel?' Kirsty asked. She munched on a sandwich.

Terry nodded. 'After the scandal and the loss of his daughter, I reckon Mr. Slater had the tunnel bricked up

285

on both sides of those oak doors. There wouldn't be any more balls. He would still have been able to take delivery of beer from the other section of the tunnel that gave access to the cellar.'

'I wonder when the haunting started.' Shirley mused.

'Presumably after Henrietta's death?' Deborah suggested. 'They would have to be dead.' She couldn't help smirk at her comment.

Shirley grinned. 'I think it would be when Henrietta's daughter inherited the inn,' she speculated.

'It could be that when both Henrietta and James died they wanted to see their daughter living in the house they had to flee in order to marry. So the only way they could do it was to re-live the night of their elopement.'

Shirley warmed to her theory. 'They had to keep repeating the elopement, because Henrietta had never been able to return to her childhood home.'

Deborah sighed. 'It sounds plausible, but I suppose we will never know for sure.'

When the piano lounge had been tidied up, Grace ecstatically vacuumed the area and replaced her ornaments. Everyone was in high spirits. Deborah felt their optimism.

At ten to eight Jessica retrieved two bottles of Champagne from the fridge and took them to the piano lounge. She deliberately placed them on the coffee table where the ghostly occurrences had taken place. Kirsty placed a tray of glasses alongside the Champagne and watched Jessica expertly open the bottles. She poured an amount into each glass, then let the sparkling bubbles settle before topping up.

'To us! Jessica said. They waited anxiously for the bottles to move and at quarter past eight nothing had happened.

'We did it!' Grace smiled triumphantly.

'There's just one more test to be sure.' Shirley turned to Deborah, 'I think you should play *The Blue Danube.'*

That idea had been in Deborah's mind and she hurried to the piano. She'd carefully removed all the covers and for good measure had polished the instrument to make sure it was still in good condition.

'Wait!' Kirsty stood up. 'We need to be on guard. 'If by some awful chance we are wrong, we need to be on hand to help Deborah get away from the piano. I will anchor my foot under her stool, then I can give her a shove.'

'Right and I'm going to stand at the back of you,' Dan said.

Deborah cast her eyes around the room, 'Ready?'

She began to play. After ten minutes she stopped.

Everyone was smiling.

Deborah raised her glass. 'There's one other mystery to solve,' she said wickedly.

'What's that?' Dan said edging his way back to sit on a chair.

'Whatever happened to the peacocks?'

THE END

A note from the author

I hope you enjoyed reading this novel.

Waltzing with Ghosts is loosely based on a spooky event experienced by three of my old school friends.

The Golden Peacock Inn was inspired by an old pub in Rossett which sadly has been demolished. Apparently a gravestone was at some time, featured in the lounge area of the pub. For the sake of the novel, I created the fictitious name James Tyler.

I'm very pleased to say that *The Alyn, The Golden Lion, and The Griffin* still remain in Rossett. As indeed *The Trevor Arms in Marford and Rossett Hall hotel.* These pubs and hotels inspired the stories surrounding the fictitious *White Hart, The Miller and The Trevalyn Inn.*

Lavister Bowling Club, Randalls Music and Crispin Hotel are also fictitious. However, *Cwtch Ceramics* is a lovely café in Rossett.

All the names of characters in this novel are fictitious.

After the Beeching Report of 1962, several train stations were closed during the nineteen sixties. Many village stations closed on the Wrexham to Chester line. This is still lamented by those who can remember.

The Gresford colliery explosion occurred on the twenty second of September nineteen thirty-four. It had a huge, emotional and financial impact on the people of Wrexham that shook the mining industry across the whole of United Kingdom.

In my research about brickworks, I was surprised to find there used to be so many in the area. To match up with the time period for the novel I chose Ponkey bricks.

After publishing my first novel **Bluebells and tin hats** in 2017 and then the sequel **Rhubarb without Sugar** a year later, I had no intention of writing a ghost story. However, inspiration came to write my first ghost story, **Restless Yew Tree Cottage**, and then **Text me from your Grave.** I am currently writing a follow up book to *Text me from your Grave.*

In the meantime I am working on my first crime novel *The Keeper* which I hope to publish in October.

Text me from your Grave
by Pamela Cartlidge

Rachel hovered at the edge of the broken stone wall that circled the abbey cemetery. She was waiting for her mother to come away from the funeral. She glanced around her. No-one had noticed her hanging about. Only once, at a burial, had someone perceived her presence. When Rachel had realised that, she had spirited herself very quickly to another spot.

Some of her friends advised her not to linger too close at funerals but she was fascinated observing the behaviour of the bereaved. She liked listening to the snippets of gossip shared amongst those who attended. It was a good way of finding out what was happening on the 'other side'.

Rachel's mother was taking her time getting away. Always gregarious and sociable, Anna Bellis was behaving true to form. She weaved in and out of the mourners; examined the names on the wreaths and silently sympathised with family and friends. Her wistful gaze followed each of the bereaved as they left her grave side to get to their cars. Finally Anna drifted across to join Rachel.

"Hello darling. I would love to give you a hug." Anna gesticulated a greeting. Her raised arms, swathed in the blue silk sleeves of her cocktail dress, fanned thin air.

Rachel nodded. "Me too. Her eyes roved over Anna's clothes. I see you have come out in style mum. Did you choose that get up?"

"Yes. Your father followed my instructions to the letter." She gazed down at her outfit taking joy in her white nylon tights and blue shoes that matched her dress. "I hoped you liked those clothes I chose for you. It was such a horrible, terrible time. Planning your unexpected funeral was not easy. It isn't nice for anybody in those circumstances, I know. But you were young. You shouldn't have gone so soon."

Looking down at her ripped jeans and her 'Save the Orangutan' T shirt Rachel grinned. "I was chuffed with your choice. Thank you. But Mum, why did you put my mobile phone in the coffin? Surely you didn't think you could contact me in the grave?"

"I did ring you. I could hear it calling you."

Rachel stifled a grin. "I didn't hear it, but I saw the 'phone vibrate and the light flashing telling me there was a call coming through. Not bad considering I was buried six feet under. But obviously I couldn't respond! There was nothing I could do about it. I was unable to touch it let alone answer or make a call."

Anna pursed her lips. "Well I instructed your dad to put my own mobile in my coffin just to see if I could communicate with him. Anyway I wanted him to make sure I was dead. I had a fear of being buried alive."

This time Rachel burst out laughing. "Oh Mum, I'm so sorry, but that wasn't going to happen. I'm sure dad would have checked everything. There is no way he was going to let you be buried alive." She softened her voice then added, "I don't think he will try to use the mobile."

"If he follows my instructions he will. He promised!" Anna retorted assuredly.

Rachel smiled at her mother. She let that comment pass. "Mum I am pleased to see you even though I'm sure you would have preferred to be on the 'other side' a bit longer. You aren't that old. God, fifty five. I wasn't expecting to see you again so soon!"

"I know. I thought I would have had at least another twenty years, but that heart attack left me very weak. However, I had time to make some plans and leave instructions. I have left unfinished business."

"Have you asked dad to carry on investigating my murder? I heard him swear to me at my own funeral that he would get justice for what they did to me. He visits me a lot. Gavin comes too."

"Yes of course! He will. It was my dying wish." Anna hesitated. "Please tell me. Did you know the brutes who killed you?"

Rachel shook her head. "No. They were complete strangers."

"Well that's some relief. I always dreaded that it might have been someone you knew. Anyway Gavin will help your father to try to find your killer, as soon as he flies back from Budapest. He will be leaving shortly after the wake."

"Budapest! What is Gavin going to do there?"

Anna smiled. "He is going to see if any of your friends can help. They will be endowed with some power just like you. He knows someone who is a psychic. His name is Phil. Do you remember him? They were in college together a few years ago. Apparently he and his then girlfriend went on a ski-ing trip there and fell in love with the place. They're married now living in Transylvania of all places! They keep in touch with Gavin by email and face book.

Rachel frowned. "Yes I remember Phil vaguely. But I don't have any friends in Transylvania nor anywhere in Romania. And I don't have any power."

"Your *special* friends. You know like you are now. In fact like me too." Anna chortled somewhat nervously.

"Oh I see. Just because we are all dead doesn't mean we are all 'universal friends' you know. And in any case I don't think those dead people in Romania or Transylvania have any more power than us either. All that vampire stuff is just a myth. Besides that, I can't get there to find out for myself. You need special agreements to go there. It is a very complicated system to get permission. In fact it is also very complicated to get permission even to venture outside your relevant zone."

"Zone? What do you mean by zone? I thought ghosts could go anywhere they like."

"That's just it. We aren't ghosts. We are spirits. We are only ghosts when we get the powers to re-visit a place and, in rare cases, be seen by someone living."

"I'll soon get the powers. I'm quick to learn."

"It doesn't work like that."

"What do you mean? Now I'm dead, I can do what I like."

"Sorry Mum but you can't."

"I don't see why not." Anna looked earnestly at her daughter.

"You need permission to be a ghost."

Anna frowned. "So do you mean to tell me that even though I am dead, I need some kind of agreement to allow me to go wherever I want?"

"Sort of. It depends on your death. I qualified to be a temporary ghost because I was murdered. You wouldn't be able to be a ghost because you died naturally."

"That's a shame." Anna sighed. "I was planning on haunting a few people I don't like.'

Restless Yew Tree Cottage

Chapter One

Sara signed her name quickly at the end of her note then folded the single sheet of paper in to three creases before putting it in to the white envelope. She had already written the name of her son Preston on the front of the envelope. All she had to do now was to seal it. The envelope had been lying around the house for a while and was not one of those self-adhesive types. Her lips were dry and so she moistened them with a sip of whisky from the glass at the side of her. With her tongue she licked the tacky edge of the envelope and then for good measure dipped her finger into the whisky tumbler and ran the tip of her finger across the sticky trail of the envelope. Pressing it down firmly the envelope was now sealed and ready for delivery.

Sara clutched the envelope to her chest. It contained instructions for her funeral. She sat back in her arm chair then surveyed the room. She had done everything she needed to do. Her eyes travelled over the empty whisky bottle on the sideboard then fell on to the near empty tumbler at her side. With an effort she stood up to place the envelope beside the whisky bottle. Leaning against the sideboard her eyes roved the room for the very last time. She noted the door from her sitting room that led into the hall was ajar. Through the space between the door and its portal she could see the narrow hallway where her bookshelves leaned against the wall. Her gaze shifted across the array of books, some of them stacked wantonly on top of each other. For a few seconds she contemplated these books and struggled with her conscience as to whether she should sort these books out before she went. One of the books wasn't a book at all. It was a tin that looked like a book. In the tin she kept all her personal letters and various other documents. For a few seconds Sara considered sifting through the tin box, then as if convincing herself there was no need, she shook her head. Sitting down again Sara drained the rest of her drink. She decided to leave things as they were. She neither had the energy nor the will power to do anything else. Putting down her glass for the last time she saw that Alwenna had arrived. The sunlight glided over her pale face as she positioned herself with her back to the fire place. Her long golden hair shimmered over her shoulders and down the back of her green woollen dress.

Sara pulled her blue cardigan tightly around her. "Time to go." She said.

Bluebells and tin hats – Pamela Cartlidge

Chapter One

April 1933

"Pass me the spanner." Harry demanded authoritatively. His oil smeared hand was already outstretched in readiness.

Louisa quickly did as she was told. She gazed at her brother in admiration as he wielded the spanner around the nuts to reposition the pedal on her bicycle. After a few minutes, Harry straightened up and with a bent arm pushed back his thick brown hair from his forehead and surveyed his work. He wheeled the bicycle around the yard, then he swivelled the pedals to test them. Satisfied with his task he handed the machine back to his sister with a warning grin.

"Quick. Try it out before they get back!" He urged her. Harry's grin broadened and his blue eyes twinkled as he watched Louisa leap on to the saddle. She gingerly placed one foot on the repaired pedal and tested it for reliability. Immediately assured that the pedal was safely repaired, she pushed herself forward and away from the garden shed. Her confidence in the machine now restored, she pedalled along the gable end of their terraced home towards the lane. "It works Harry!" She called over her shoulder. "Thanks."

"Look where you are going, and be careful." Harry called after her. Louisa stopped alongside the gate of their small front garden and stood on one leg, letting the machine rest against her hip. She took just a few seconds to turn around to acknowledge her brother's warning with a wave of her hand. Then, smiling gleefully to herself she pedalled furiously down the lane and round the corner towards the bluebell wood. She soon reached the dirt track that went through the wood. It was well worn by the miners who trod it several times a day on their way to work and on their way home again from the coal mine. The colliery pit head lay on the opposite edge of the wood in the neighbouring village of Gresford. Sometimes when Louisa cycled down the path she would pass some of the workers on their homeward journey, their eye lashes blackened with soot and their unwashed skin pale grey. She knew quite a few of the colliers, most of them were in their thirties, but several of the younger ones were only two years older than herself. They had left school at fourteen to work down the pit. Louisa shuddered. She would hate to have to go down a mining shaft, not even for a few minutes. The thought of working without natural light for a whole twelve hour shift appalled her. She admired those who did it, but she knew she could never work underground where even day time was like perpetual night. She gazed around her. There was no-one in sight at this hour, as the men from the early morning shift would have arrived home by now. They would have already passed their colleagues going the opposite direction on their own way down to the pit head to work the next shift.

The late afternoon sun glimmered through the trees, and the scent of the honeysuckle in the hedgerow wafted in the warm afternoon air. Louisa breathed in the delicate fragrance and sighed with pleasure. She loved the wild flowers and being in the woods. It made her feel free. Ever since Mr. Fern, her Father's employer had given her this old bicycle she had felt as if she had been given her independence. Her mother did not approve of her riding the bicycle. She told her it was unladylike. She often regaled her with comments such as "It's about time you behaved more ladylike, instead of cycling up and down the countryside with your skirt tucked up and your hair flying about like that. What will people think? You are fourteen now and as soon as a position comes up in service you will have to look more respectable! They won't take you on if you look like a scarecrow!"

Fortunately Louisa's two older brothers Harry and Arthur always defended her on these occasions. Their mother, a quietly spoken woman, though resolute nevertheless, always took more notice of the opinions of her sons, rather than those of Louisa. So on the occasions when they jumped to her defence, she would make an exasperated sigh and then turn away from her daughter with a vexed expression on her face. Then, for a little while at least, nothing else would be said and Louisa would continue to roam the countryside on her bicycle.

Louisa's father would say nothing and kept his own opinions to himself. William was a gentle and fair minded sort of man, and it was rare that he would disagree with his wife. Being a farm worker and loving to work outside in the fresh air with the shire horses, he shared his daughter's love of the freedom of being in the countryside. He tactfully stayed out of any potential quarrel with his wife and his daughter. He had been delighted when his employer Mr. Fern had given his headstrong daughter the bicycle, and felt he had to accept some of the consequences. For now though, whenever his wife became exasperated with their daughter's demeanour he wisely kept his own counsel. He knew that sooner or later, he would have to give his wife some support when they faced together the unpleasant task of sending Louisa away to work.

Louisa hated the idea of going into service. She didn't want to go away from home like some of her friends from school had done. Her friend Betty wrote to her now and again and Louisa knew she was very unhappy working in Kent. It was a long way away from Wrexham, but Betty was the oldest of six girls and her parents couldn't afford to keep her at home any longer. Louisa felt that as her two older brothers were working locally on Mr Fern's farm as well as her father, why should she have to work away from home? She accepted that she had to contribute to the household but she desperately didn't want to go as far away as Kent to work like poor Betty.

She dreamed of being a dressmaker. She was good at sewing and had a flair for designing clothes. She also thought of becoming a nurse. When she had broached the possibility of nursing to her mother she had been told that she was too young to work in a hospital. She had fobbed her off by telling her that she needed to be eighteen before she could enter a nursing college and in any case she needed a higher education to be admitted as a trainee. When Louisa had suggested she stay on at school to get a higher education certificate than the one she had, she was told she would be better off trying to get a job and to earn some money. The family couldn't afford for her to stay on at school any longer than necessary. Louisa was disappointed to get such a reaction from her mother. She had done well at school, was an avid reader and her teachers had encouraged her to be ambitious. She sighed. Surely there was something else she could do. She had heard that some women were now working in factories and others were learning to be secretaries, but her mother had been adamant that going into service was the best course. As regards dressmaking, her mother had said that there was no money in it, and she would be working long hours for little return.

The path through the woods narrowed and it was difficult to keep her balance on the bicycle, so she dismounted and leaned the bicycle against the kissing gate. She walked through the gate and strolled along the path to her favourite spot. Strands of honeysuckle had weaved themselves across the trees intermingling several times to create an archway of yellow and pink flowers. And as she looked through the loosely woven network of shiny green leaves above her head, splinters of the pale blue sky met her gaze. Standing underneath the bowers the heavy scent was intoxicating.

Rhubarb without Sugar – Pamela Cartlidge

1945
Chapter One

Louisa was on her way to Dodman's the shoe shop in Wrexham. Her two little girls accompanying her were as excited as their mother. However the pure excitement of buying new shoes was not the only emotional issue that occupied Louisa's thoughts. She was looking forward to the next day when her beloved brother Arthur was returning home from the war.

The minister of Labour and National Service – Ernest Bevin had been put in charge of demobilising the troops and now it was Arthur's turn to return home. The whole family were overjoyed that they would be reunited again soon and they had pooled their rations to make a welcome meal for him.

Louisa had been saving her coupons for months so that she could buy Christine and Susan new shoes. In any case Christine needed new shoes for school in September. Louisa reckoned that the occasion of her brother's return seemed an appropriate time to buy them. Both Christine and Susan would be able to wear their new shoes to Arthur's welcome home meal. Louisa was fortunate that she didn't have to use coupons for Susan's shoes as the Government had seen fit not to ration clothes for children under four. Of course she still had to pay for them.

The little girls pressed their faces in the High Street shop window and stared at the shoes on display. There wasn't a lot to choose from, yet this didn't diminish the children's excitement. Both girls liked the idea of having something new.

"I like those brown ones on the end mummy." Six year old Christine said. She pointed to the corner of the window display and Louisa was pleased that she was able to afford them. Susan at the age of two was bewildered when they walked into the shop. She looked up mischievously at the proprietor with her wide beguiling eyes and Mr. Dodman at once fell helplessly under her spell. Many people did. She was a wild child though very lovable.

Her sister Christine, though sharing Susan's inquisitiveness was more reserved around men she didn't know. It had taken her a long time to build up a relationship with her father who had returned from the war several months earlier. She had been nine months old when Fred had joined the Navy to fight for his country. He had missed a lot of her early years growing up. Each snatched short visit due to sick leave or survivor's leave had not given him the opportunity to bond with Christine. Fred had been heartbroken when she had shied away from him each time he returned home but understood that he had to be patient with his daughter.

Mr. Dodman was good-natured with the two children even when they started to run around the shop poking their prying little fingers at the boxes on the shelves. Both Christine and Susan were easily pleased and didn't need any encouragement to walk around the shop to try out their footwear.

Satisfied with her purchases, Louisa led her children to King Street to get the Chester bus home to Pandy. The bus was almost full. The two little girls squeezed together on one available seat whilst Louisa sat on the seat's edge. It was just a two mile journey to Pandy from Wrexham so Louisa didn't mind the slight discomfort. She smiled at her children who had engaged in chatter with their fellow woman passenger.

Louisa realised it was Mrs. Penson who had helped deliver both her children. She often wondered how many babies she had delivered over the years. As far as she was aware, Mrs. Penson was not a qualified midwife. However she was so experienced that many mothers trusted her to attend to them when giving birth. She was also cheaper than the midwife. Louisa caught her eye and they exchanged smiles.

Made in the USA
Middletown, DE
29 November 2021

53740528R00169